Advance Praise for
The Paradise Table

"Maryann Ridini Spencer creates a place, time, and mood that will make you want to come back for more. Sit back, relax, and enjoy a mystical island journey to *The Paradise Table*."

– James Michael Pratt
New York Times and *USA Today* bestselling author

"*The Paradise Table* is another plumeria-laced 'Kate Grace' mystery from talented writer Maryann Ridini Spencer. In this book that follows best-selling *Lady in the Window*, Spencer again magically weaves together the breathtaking beauty and spirituality of Kauai, miracles, and the power of faith and love into an intriguing quest for the truth. When violent dreams become reality in this peaceful island paradise, newlywed Kate unearths disturbing secrets that will change everyone's lives, causing her to embark on a sometimes heartbreaking and shocking path. *The Paradise Table* is not just another mystery—it is a heartwarming validation of self-trust, friendship, love, and healing."

– Kathy Strong
award-winning travel author
of recently released *Secret Southern California*,
columnist for *USA Today*/Gannett Newspapers,
and founder of *PSWishYouWereHereTravel.com*

"When friends band together to help one another, magic happens. *The Paradise Table* is a touching, beautiful book that explores the healing power of how 'doing unto others' and helping one another can transform lives in this often-arduous journey of life. Together, we can help soothe sorrows as well as celebrate in life's astonishing beauty."

– Alyce Morris Winston
founder and president, the Jeffrey Foundation
for children with special needs and their families

"Maryann Ridini Spencer follows up with her award-winning novel *Lady in the Window* with another enticing and empowering page-turner. *The Paradise Table,* with its touches of divine inspiration, demonstrates how out of heartbreak and loss, and with the love of ohana (friends and family), we can find hope, healing, and understanding."

– Marianne Pestana
show host of "Moments with Marianne"
and producer, "The Whitney Reynolds Show" (PBS-TV)

"As Kate Grace uses her intuition and heaven's synchronistic cues to help guide her earthly path, bridges of understanding are created that transform her life, as well as those of her ohana. *The Paradise Table* is a beautiful, visionary story about the human condition and how we knowingly, and unknowingly, impact the lives of those around us."

– Merry Aronson
president and CEO, Merry Media, and co-author of
The Public Relations Writer's Handbook, The Digital Age

"Maryann Ridini Spencer artfully portrays the strength and beauty of living authentically. She also shines light on the negative power held within secrets and reveals potential dangers of secret-keeping. *The Paradise Table* takes a reader on a mystical journey that demonstrates how there is more breadth to life than what the eye can see and more depth in the human heart than what anyone yet perceives."

– Charlene Costanzo
bestselling author of *The Twelve Gifts of Birth*

The Paradise Table

a Kate Grace Mystery

Other books by

Maryann Ridini Spencer

Lady in the Window
a Kate Grace Mystery

The Paradise Table

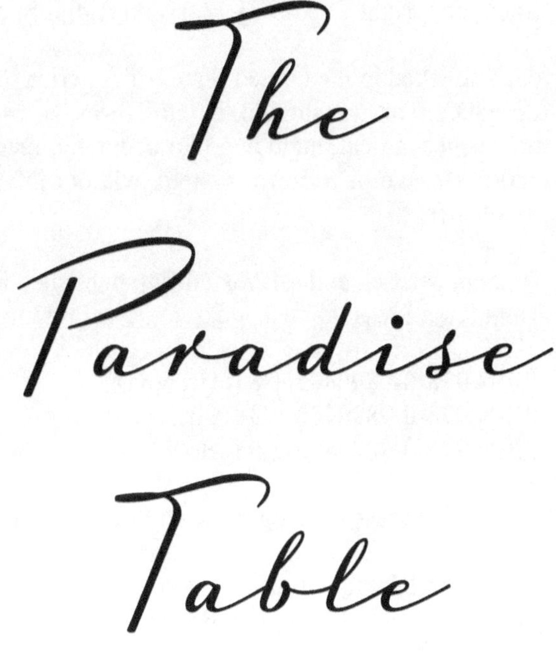

a Kate Grace Mystery

Maryann Ridini Spencer

Santa Rosa
PRESS
SantaRosaPress.net

First Edition, copyright © 2019 by Maryann Ridini Spencer

Hardcover, Trade paperback and e-Book edition published in 2019 by Santa Rosa Press, publisher@SantaRosaPress.net

ISBN 978-0-9890405-1-8 (Hardcover)
ISBN 978-0-9890405-6-3 (Paperback)
ISBN 978-0-9890405-7-0 (eBook)

Library of Congress Cataloging-in-Publication Data

Names: Spencer, Maryann Ridini, author.
Title: The Paradise Table: a novel/ Maryann Ridini Spencer.
Series: a Kate Grace Mystery
Description: Thousand Oaks, CA: Santa Rosa Press, 2019.
Identifiers: LCCN 2019943967 | ISBN 978-0-9890405-1-8
(Hardcover) | 978-0-9890405-6-3 (pbk.) | 978-0-9890405-7-0 (eBook)
Subjects: LCSH Friendship--Fiction. | Family--Fiction. | Hawaii—
    Fiction. | Love stories. | Mystery fiction. | BISAC FICTION /
    Mystery & Detective / General | FICTION / Mystery & Detective /
    Women Sleuths | FICTION / Romance / Christian Fiction/
    Contemporary
Classification: LCC PS3619.P4655 P38 2019 | DDC 813.6--dc23
Peacock feather graphic courtesy of Skeeze at pixabay.com
Flower images ©Kotkoa - Can Stock Photo Inc.
Edited by Trudi Roth, itsthetrustory.com and
    Jenny Margotta, editorjennymargotta@mail.com
Book Cover Graphic Design: Michelle Prebble, Michelle Prebble Designs

Printed and published in the United States of America

10 9 8 7 6 5 4 3 2 1

For my father and mother

And for my grandparents

THE PARADISE TABLE

Come! Gather 'round The Paradise Table,
A place of abundance, laughter, and love.
Revel in Nature's beauty; the sights and sounds of the flowers,
trees, and the singing birds above;
Partake of Nature's bounty, celebrating with all you hold dear,
Leave your worries and cares at the Garden's gate—
To Dissipate.
When you follow His path and do unto others,
Turning can't into *can* —
You'll be safely entwined in the loving hands of
The Great *I Am*.

– Maryann Ridini Spencer

Acknowledgments

Growing up, I have so many fond memories of cooking in the kitchen with my mother and grandmothers (Mary and Theresa) lovingly preparing a delicious meal to share with family and friends. On Sundays, we would visit my Grandmother Mary and Grandfather Leo Ridini for an early dinner then, hours later, head over to my Grandmother Theresa and Grandfather Leo Murphy's home for an evening meal (or just dessert). At mealtimes, accompanied by aunts, uncles, and cousins (and often family friends), we enjoyed sharing stories and many laughs, discussed the world's latest events and the various happenings in our lives, as well as our hopes and dreams for the future. It was and still is such a perfect way to connect—whether the occasion is an informal get-together or special celebration.

Research shows what I've come to know: gatherings with family and friends are vital to our health, healing and well-being, as well as our sense of belonging to a nurturing community. These types of gatherings also play a crucial role in living *Aloha*.

Aloha, the Hawaiian word used to greet a person "hello" or to bid a person "farewell," also means "with love and affection." It's also an attitude or way of living life. You've probably heard the terms *The Spirit of Aloha* or *The Way of Aloha?* These terms translate into a way of interacting with the natural world. Living "in the spirit" or "the way" of *Aloha* is living by a particular code of ethics which includes, but is not limited to, love, kindness, tolerance, compassion, respect, and honor of all humanity and living things. Living "the way" also includes the joyful sharing of oneself with others, caring for our community—"doing unto others"—and the act of being consciously committed to living sustainability. The list of ethics, also in line with what the Bible teaches, goes on, but clearly, *Aloha* means so much more than just "hello" or "goodbye."

Aloha is also why I decided to place the Kate Grace Mystery series in Hawaii. Ever since I first stepped foot on Hawaiian soil, I've had such an affinity, a "soul" connection, to the land and the community.

Hawaii, perhaps because it is so rich in beautiful vistas and glorious, peaceful nature, is where I truly see and feel God's grace and presence.

There are always many people who assist in the book publishing process. I'd like to extend a warm "mahalo" (thank you) and give a shout out to my dear parents, sister and brothers and their spouses; my nieces, nephews, grandmothers and grandfathers, aunts and uncles, cousins, Scott and Liam; all my dear friends; my editors, Trudi Roth and Jenny Margotta; Michelle Prebble for all her graphic design assistance; and to Danny Akaka, Jr., Hawaiian Cultural Practitioner and Director of Cultural Affairs at Mauna Lani Bay Hotel & Bungalows, for his continued assistance in helping me with Hawaiian translations. Filled with gratitude, I give thanks to our Creator for His love and guidance.

I would also like to thank Alyce Morris Winston, a wonderful friend, mentor, and founder of the non-profit organizations The Jeffrey Foundation and Special Child U.S.A. for children with special needs and their families. Alyce started the Jeffrey Foundation in 1972 when she couldn't find adequate daycare for her son Jeffrey, who had muscular dystrophy. With a desire to give her son a better life, and discovering many other parents in her position, Alyce began a series of grassroots programs. Today, the Jeffrey Foundation offers high-quality programming and support services to help both child and family successfully meet challenges posed by developmental disabilities, autism, multiple handicaps, Down's Syndrome, crippling accidents, poverty, abuse, abandonment, and neglect. A portion of the proceeds from *The Paradise Table* will go to assist the much-needed programs that the Foundation provides. Visit *thejeffreyfoundation.org*.

I also invite you to sit at my paradise table by visiting my award-winning *Simply Delicious Living* cooking and lifestyle blog, where I offer easy-to-make recipes, and creative inspirations for joyous living. My blog, as well as more information on my books, can be found by visiting *MaryannRidiniSpencer.com* or *AlohaWriter.com*.

Mahalo and with Aloha,

Maryann

Prologue

A violent burst of air bellows through the open window, making the sheer curtains framing it fly in a panic. The wind's loud howls rouse a peacefully sleeping young woman from her slumber. Rubbing her eyes, she attempts to make sense of the dark. It's then that she sees him: a tall, imposing male figure approaching her from the shadows.

She gasps, terrified, and attempts to run, only to be violently thrown back down on the bed by the ominous intruder.

A slow, deranged smile crawls across the perpetrator's face as he leers at her from behind a black eye-mask. The overwhelming, toxic, liquor-drenched scent of his breath nearly causes her to faint as he kisses and gropes.

"Stop, no, please!" She wrestles with her attacker, desperately trying to escape and frantically wondering how he could have possibly found entry into the house.

"Like to play rough, do you?" he sneers as he wins the upper hand. He pins the pretty woman's slender wrists to the bed and straddles her.

Unable to move, and knowing what's next, the young woman arches her back and lets out a blood-curdling cry.

"Help!" Kate screams into the darkness. The pretty, thirty-one-year-old bolts upright in her bed. Her wild eyes survey the darkened master suite, which is lit only by a single stream of bright moonlight that filters through the room's plantation-shuttered windows.

As she surveys her bedroom, a beautiful space understatedly decorated in soothing natural hues, she is brought back to reality.

It was only a dream.

She is safe in the comfort of the cottage that sits on Weke Road, her home for the past seven months, just steps from the shores of Kauai's otherworldly Hanalei Bay.

Unable to fall back to sleep, Kate gets out of bed and heads toward the kitchen to fix herself a cup of calming tea.

"Hey, girlfriend. What are you doing up in the middle of the night?"

Kate jumps, forgetting for a minute that her best friend and *New York View Magazine* co-worker, Cindy Maroni, arrived earlier that day from Manhattan with her husband, Vinnie. They wouldn't have missed Kate and her fiancé Kai's nuptials for the world. The fact that their friends will be taking their vows in the idyllic Garden Isle is just an added, most-welcome bonus.

"Sorry if I frightened you." Cindy winces and tightens the belt of her designer robe around her ample waist.

"I can't sleep, but why are you up?"

Cindy shrugs. "I think my body's still on New York time." "Vinnie's sound asleep, though, as usual."

"I'm hoping this chamomile tea will make me sleepy. Want a cup?"

Cindy nods and the ladies take their tea out onto the lanai for more conversation, being extra careful not wake up the house.

"Nervous?" Cindy asks as the two take a seat at a large, teak dining table illuminated by the starry sky.

"Not at all. Excited." Kate's face lights up for a second before darkening. "That's not why I can't sleep. I had an alarming dream."

"Tell me. I love when you share your dreams. I wish mine revealed things to me like yours sometimes do," Cindy says. She blows into her steaming cup as she waits for her friend's answer.

"This one was a nightmare. There was this woman. I didn't recognize her. She was being attacked in her bedroom at night by a masked intruder."

"Omigod – that's horrible!"

Kate nods. "I think he was about to rape her. I felt her fear. I wanted to stop it, but it was like I was in another dimension, looking in. I could see them, but they couldn't see me."

"Yikes. Not the kind of dream I'd want to have the night before my wedding."

"I know, right?"

"Did you see something on the news or read anything that might have triggered the dream?"

"Nothing that stands out. But it had such a real quality. Even though I didn't know the girl, she felt familiar," Kate answers, perplexed.

"Try not to dwell on it, okay? Only happy thoughts and dreams tonight. I bet you wish Kai were here." Cindy knows that Kai, an ER doctor with a soothing demeanor, would know how to calm Kate down instantly. In an obvious effort to change the subject, Cindy adds, "I think you and Kai are making a great choice choosing this cottage as your new home. It's utterly charming."

Kate smiles. "I love it here."

As the women gingerly sip their tea, enjoying the sounds of nature, Kate remembers that after Kai proposed, he asked her what part of the island she wanted to make her home. When she shared her desire to live right here, in the Weke Road cottage, Kai was on board, having so many wonderful family memories growing up in the charming cottage situated on Hanalei's picturesque bay. Kai's father Bradford had been toying with the idea of selling the family home, which became a vacation rental after the untimely death of his beloved Leilani, Kai's mother. However, when Bradford heard of Kate and Kai's desire, he gave his blessing, and a deal was made. In exchange for the Weke cottage, Kai's waterfront home in Princeville would now become the new rental.

"Looks like the tea is working its magic, my sleepy friend," notes Cindy when Kate audibly yawns. "I'm feeling a little tired myself. So let's get thee to bed. We've got memories to make tomorrow."

The Wedding

E Lei aku 'oe ku'u aloha.
Wear my love as a lei.

1

"You look radiant, Kate. I'm so happy for you." Catherine lovingly caresses her daughter's cheek.

Kate smiles at her sweet mother, a petite, elegant woman of sixty-eight, as they resume their walk along the pristine shores of Kauai's Anini Beach. The water, a vibrant aquamarine at the shoreline, dissolves into a deep cobalt blue as it moves toward the heart of the ocean. As Kate glances out to sea, she watches the sun's rays sparkle on the glistening azure waters; it's as if they are performing a celebratory dance in anticipation of the day's upcoming events. Even the waves of the gentle breeze that roll past and rustle through the lush green foliage seem to respond in unison to the love-filled electrically charged currents in the air on this picture-perfect day.

"You'll be by my side?" A slight tremble in Kate's voice betrays her nerves.

"With God's grace." Catherine reaches out her arms and brings Kate in for a heartfelt hug.

Kate relaxes into the warmth of their embrace. This close she can smell the sweet floral scent that her mother exudes—the subtle and intoxicating fragrance of plumeria, the fragrant flowers that are used to make Hawaiian leis.

"I love you, dear, to the …"

"… moon and beyond." Kate joins in unison with her mother and the pair chuckle at the perfect timing of their favorite expression of love.

"Come, let's continue our walk," Catherine says.

Thankful she can share this special time with her mother, Kate strains to savor every moment of this joyous communication—perhaps a little too hard. Suddenly, the blue of the ocean begins to fade. Instinctively, Kate reaches to grab her mother's hand, only to realize she is no longer by her side.

Kate's eyes bolt open. *I'm not on Anini Beach at all.* She takes a deep, cleansing breath to anchor herself.

Still feeling her mother's essence, Kate ponders her dream with a full heart, and as she does, warm energy enfolds her. She prays and gives thanks to God.

From her earliest memories, and especially since her mother's passing, Kate's daily prayers and connection to God have been paramount. God is her lifeline. She asks for His guidance when the path is not clear and, if it is His will, to let her know that her loved ones are near. While she sometimes finds herself saying "hello" or expressing a sentiment to her mom, it is God to whom she prays concerning what's on her mind and heart, and, whenever she has a particular "knowing" feeling or vivid dream, or receives what she interprets as a sign or synchronicity, she asks God to show her the way.

Although she was always a believer, ever since her mother's death, she's delved deeply into the meaning of life, and while so many things are much clearer to her now, others continue to remain a mystery, and that's okay. She gets great solace from reading the Bible, her daily conversations with the Lord, and in knowing that our spirit lives on past our physical form.

She has learned a lot from her studies, too. Before her mother's passing, she didn't always examine or question certain modern-day beliefs she had taken to heart. What she has since discovered, however, is that many of these beliefs and practices are in fact not God's word, and she has suffered the sting of how making her own rules to go along with some of today's standards has previously caused her trouble, especially with her ex-boyfriend Jason.

"Kate," a voice calls softly from the hallway. Carla, Kate's older sister, is knockings on the other side of the closed bedroom door.

"Come on in, Sis!"

"The delivery man just dropped these off," relays Carla as she sets a stunning array of tropical flowers on the dresser.

"They're gorgeous. I wonder who sent them." Kate embraces her sister, then plucks the tiny envelope protruding from the greeting holder, opens it, and silently reads the enclosed card: *"Wishing you and Kai every happiness. Sincerely, Jason."*

"Oooookay. Your face just went from enthusiastic to alien."

Kate hands Carla the card.

"That explains it. Jason is from another planet, and it certainly isn't Mars. More like planet 'Me.'"

Kate's mind darts back to a conversation she had a few months ago with Carla on FaceTime.

"I almost forgot to tell you, sis. Jason called," Carla confessed.

"You're kidding?"

"He told me he recently ran into some people from *New York View,* and when they mentioned that Mom had passed, he wanted to send flowers."

"Well, that's nice … I guess."

"How long has it been since you've heard from him?"

"Not since we broke up. Although, every so often, mutual friends fill me in on what's going on in his life. Remember that girl I told you about—you know, the one whose FaceTime call I intercepted the last time I saw Jason?"

"Oh, yeah. That fateful night when you met to find out if you were still on the same page about marriage."

"That's the one."

"His 'supposed' business associate that you said looked like a fashion model. What was her name? Haley, Hannah …?"

"Heather," snarled Kate.

"Ah, yes. Heather," Carla echoed back slowly.

"Well, it turns out that Jason *was* dating her."

"No way. While you were together?"

"I don't know exactly when it started, but I'm guessing yes. Because if that were the case, then it totally makes sense why Jason was so evasive about marriage and why Heather treated me like I was poison that night on the phone."

"Oh, Kate, I'm glad you finally spoke your mind to him and let him know in no uncertain terms that you were moving on if he wasn't coming through with a wedding date."

"Me too. It was an awful breakup, but I lived through it, and thankfully, I don't have any of that pain and angst anymore. You know, when I think about how I was back then, I realize now that, if I had been more in tune, I would have realized God was trying to tell me something about Jason. I've made a lot of mistakes, Sis."

"Don't beat yourself up; we all have to live and learn. Changing the subject for a sec before it slips my mind, which it's very likely to do because I have so much going on today, Jason was very persistent when we spoke about having flowers delivered to you. I hope you don't mind I gave him your address in Kauai."

"Oh, Carla, I don't know if that was such a good idea. But it's not like he's going to show up on my doorstep, wanting to get back together. That's definitely not his MO. At any rate, he's thousands of miles away in New York or somewhere, closing in on his next big real estate development deal."

However, about a week later, much to Kate's surprise and shock, Jason would show up on her doorstep, ironically interrupting another conversation between the two sisters.

"Carla, hold on a minute, will you? There's someone at the front door." Kate gasped as she looked through the peephole. Jason was standing there, holding a large bouquet of tropical blooms. "One second!" she screamed as she ran back to tell her sister.

"Sis, it's him."

"Him?"

"Jason! He's right outside my door, holding a bouquet."

"Seriously?"

"I'm dead serious."

"Remain calm," Carla advised. "Don't do anything crazy. And you better call me back the second you can."

"Will do, love you to the moon."

"And beyond." Kate blew her sister a kiss and clicked off FaceTime. Kate checked her appearance in the mirror. She smoothed a few misplaced hairs and tucked in her top. It was a force of habit left over from when Jason would call on her. Finally, she took in several deep breaths and opened the door.

"Hi, gorgeous." Jason's charm was in high gear.

Kate stepped onto the lanai and closed the door behind her. "What are you doing here?"

"These are for you," Jason said as he handed Kate the bouquet. "I'm so sorry to hear about your mother's passing. I would've come sooner, but I only found out last week."

"*Mahalo*," Kate blurted, nervously adding, "I guess."

The pair locked eyes for an awkward moment.

"This is totally weird, Jason. We broke up a year ago, and there's been no further contact, and now here you are on my doorstep, miles away from New York. That's not like you. I don't know what to say. I don't get it."

"As I said, when I heard about your mom, I called Carla, and she told me you were here. It just so happened I was headed for some meetings on Oahu, and since it's a quick hop to Kauai ..."

"Carla mentioned she gave you the address, but I certainly didn't think in a million years that you were going to show up and personally deliver the flowers. You have my cell. Why didn't you let me know you were coming?"

"I ... I guess I didn't think you'd take my call."

Kate shrugged, indicating that would have been true.

"I honestly can't blame you," Jason continued. "But I, uh, I've been thinking about you for months. I miss you, Kate."

"You didn't have to fly to Kauai to tell me that."

"I know I didn't have to," Jason interrupted as he reached for Kate. "I wanted to."

Kate shook her head in disbelief, stepping back to avoid Jason's grasp.

Undeterred, Jason put his hand on Kate's shoulder and gently squeezed it.

Kate winced. "Look, Jason, I appreciate the flowers and the gesture of you delivering them, so I guess thanks for that, but I'm not sure what you want from me." In fact, Kate had a pretty strong hunch what he wanted, but suddenly, she realized she wanted to hear Jason say it.

"Oh, babe, I'm here because I'd like to see you." Jason turned up the heat with a look that told her he wanted something more than lunch or dinner.

"You'd like to *see* me?" Shocked, Kate's eyes bulged. "Well, you're seeing me now, so get a good look, because I have to go."

"What I mean to say is I want to be with you," Jason blurted. He gave Kate one of his smoldering looks that used to melt her core.

"You're actually serious?"

"Never more serious about anything in my life."

"About dating again … or something more?" Kate continued to prod him.

"Let's get reacquainted and see where it takes us."

"Oh, that's right. You're not ready to settle down yet, so you want to pick up where we left off like nothing ever happened, like we were never apart?"

"Can we?"

"Seriously?" Kate threw the flowers onto the lanai table and shook her head. She was about to blow. Taking in the ridiculousness of the moment, however, she started to chuckle instead.

"What are you laughing about?" Jason's surprised expression clearly said this wasn't the Kate he remembered.

"YOU, Jason. You're one of a kind, you know?"

"Ahhh … does this mean things are a go between us?" replied Jason, clearly expecting Kate to invite him in.

"NO!"

"No?"

"NO!" Kate repeated with emphasis. "I loved you dearly for five years, Jason, but in between the time we broke up and today, I've changed, and I've grown up. *A lot!* And I see things more clearly now. Sure, we had good times, we did, but it turns out we were never really a great fit. I just didn't see it at the time, and well, I've moved on. I've met someone—his name is Kai—and he's everything to me you never were. I wish you the best, but now it's time for you to go. I have things to do, and a new life to lead."

Kate picked up the flowers from the table and shoved them into Jason's chest, causing most of the petals to fly. As she turned her back and retreated into the cottage, Jason was left standing speechless on the lanai, holding a handful of broken stalks to keep as a memento of his former girlfriend.

"Earth to Sis," Carla snaps her fingers in front of Kate's eyes.

"Oh, sorry, I just got lost in thought for a minute."

"I'll say."

"I was just thinking about the last time I saw Jason."

"Yeah, well, leaving him standing in the dust was too good an ending for that narcissist."

"Carla …" Kate's tone reveals that she doesn't want to trash Jason or entertain any further conversation on the matter. It's too negative, and she doesn't want to give that thinking any power.

"Just saying." Carla is obviously still mad at Jason for breaking her sister's heart.

Things actually might have turned out quite differently for Kate had Jason reached out to her before her mother's death … before she met Kai. After all, for five years Jason had been the love of her life. From the first night they met, she had been smitten. Jason was handsome, smart, Ivy-league educated, and from a good family. Plus, they had serious chemistry, and as a successful real estate developer, she knew he would be a dependable provider. Yet for all his good qualities, Jason could also be self-absorbed and downright selfish. The only time he had seemed to consider her was when Kate was in alignment with what he desired.

She realizes now that sometimes he told her whatever she needed to hear to get her to do what he wanted. Case in point: Jason had told her almost from the start that he wanted the same things she did—marriage and family—and he led Kate to believe they would become engaged within a year.

Kate's stomach begins to churn as she remembers how one year became two, then three, four, and five. Jason would come up with excuse after excuse to avoid any real, meaningful conversation about their future—until she finally had enough gumption to put her foot down and end their relationship.

But then, when Jason unexpectedly showed up on her doorstep, she had a fleeting moment where she softened toward him, imagining that he was at least somewhat genuine in his sentiments about her mom's passing. But after giving it some thought, Kate had to admit to herself that he had probably broken up with Heather, and that was why he was trying so hard to reconnect with her. Hearing about her mom just gave him an excuse.

After her breakup with Jason, Kate made some significant changes in how she went about courtship, sticking to what was more in line with her heart and her faith, and by the time Jason did re-enter her life, she and Kai had already committed to one another. The two men were as opposite as day and night.

"Are you okay?" asks Carla.

"I'm fine. If I only knew then what I know now." Kate sighs. "Jason and I were never really meant to be. I just didn't recognize the signs. I went about dating all wrong. When I met Kai, it was effortless. We were on the same page about everything, and there was so much synchronicity in the events that unfolded that led us to one another … and even to Kai's healing his relationship with his father."

Kate touches a locket that hangs around her neck on a long chain, a physical reminder of synchronicity, God's work in action. Kai's mother had worn the stunning marcasite piece all the time, and she had it on the day she died in a tragic boating accident in which Kai was at the helm of the vessel. During a morning beach run after a horrible, fearsome storm, Kate found the missing locket washed up on the shore.

The discovery proved to be a powerful portent for a miraculous reunion: Kai's father, Bradford, had placed the blame for his beloved wife's death on his son, and their relationship was nonexistent when Kate first entered the picture. Then, thanks to the hazardous road conditions caused by the storm, Bradford had a car accident. Hearing the news, Kai rushed to his father's side at the hospital, fearing that he'd lose him before they had the chance to mend fences. The linchpin was the locket, the discovery of which the men took as a sign that it was finally time to mend their relationship.

Before her mother passed away, Kate may have ignored the synchronicity of these events, but her daily prayers have since guided her to become more attuned. She is so grateful every time she receives this blessed awareness and divine guidance, which, as she reviews the past, was evident from her first trip to Kauai.

From the moment Kate first landed in town on assignment from *New York View Magazine* to interview Olivia Larkin, a well-known and respected TV talk-show personality, she felt a particular affinity for the Garden Isle. Kate and Olivia immediately connected when they discovered they shared the same family values, beliefs, and creative and independent spirits. The two then further bonded over the fact that they both completely resonated with "Living the Way of Aloha," which in part encompasses loving, respecting, and doing unto others— your family, neighbors, friends, work associates, community: your *ohana*, your family—as you would have them do unto you.

It was also the atmosphere or *mana* of the island that provided

Kate the peace, harmony, and space for her to connect to her creative-writing passion. And it was Olivia who led Kate to her soulmate, Kai.

"Well, you've got an amazing start to an awesome day," exclaims Carla as she gazes out the large picture window to a marvelous view.

"Who else is here?" asks Kate, snapping out of her reverie once more.

"At the moment it's just you and me and Cindy. All the guys are off doing manly things, and Cindy's in the kitchen, flipping pancakes."

Kate takes a deep breath and smells the delicious aromas of brewing Kona coffee and apple-cinnamon pancakes cooking on the griddle as they travel down the hall and into the bedroom. Her stomach lurches in hunger, and she quickly pulls on her short, silk floral robe and makes a beeline for the kitchen.

"Carla, I just may hold it against you if I can't fit into my dress later today." Cindy moans and reaches for another pancake, which she tops off with a dollop of yogurt and fresh fruit.

Carla laughs. "Don't blame me! Blame it on Kate. It's her pancake recipe."

"Duly noted." Cindy scowls playfully as she points an accusing finger at Kate. "Since it's your wedding day, I'll let it pass."

"Mahalo." Kate takes a plump blueberry from her plate and pops it into her mouth.

"You lucked out, sis," Carla observes, sipping her coffee as she stares out onto the horizon. "There's not a rain cloud in the sky."

The ladies, silent now, take in the gorgeous surroundings as another fresh breeze rolls of the nearby ocean and sweeps through the yard. The three friends continue to enjoy their leisurely breakfast on the cottage's backyard lanai.

"The plumeria trees have grown," notes Carla, admiring the tall beauties with their velvety white blossoms and vibrant yellow centers.

"You know Kai and his green thumb. He's always tending to them, and he's been teaching me, too." Kate's voice is filled with enthusiasm as she scans the bare round tables and chairs that dot the garden landscape and anticipates the magic the caterers and florists will work in a few short hours.

"Thank goodness," quips Cindy. "You've been known to kill an unsuspecting houseplant or two, although never with cruel intent."

Kate playfully picks up a blueberry from the bowl of fresh fruit on the table and flings it at Cindy. "I'll get back at you when you least expect it."

"Hey!" Cindy protests and immediately tosses one of her own berries.

"Decorum, please, ladies," Carla says with a laugh.

"Did you have any other strange dreams last night when you went back to bed?" Cindy changes the conversation, turns to Carla and adds, "I couldn't sleep last night and ran into Kate in the kitchen. We sat out here on the lanai and had a cup of tea."

Carla looks at Kate. "What was the dream about?"

"I dreamt a woman was being attacked."

"How awful."

Kate nods. "I'm trying to forget it. This morning, though, I had a wonderful dream that I was walking the shore along Anini Beach with Mom. When I woke up, I could feel her, as if she really visited me. The dream was so real."

"I love it when I get to hug and talk to Mom in my dreams," replies Carla.

"I know I joke around and act sarcastic, but I loved your mom, and I hope that sometimes she'll drop in on my dreams." Cindy speaks from the heart, touched by the conversation.

Carla chuckles. "You're a real softy inside, Cin."

"Shush, don't tell anyone or I just might have 'ta kill ya," Cindy grumbles in her best, tough, wise-guy voice. Then, shifting her tone, she adds, "I believe, like you both do, that under God's direction, our departed beloveds are around us at special times. I love it when I feel my Gram Russo around."

"What's that like?" asks Kate.

"Gram was a fantastic cook. When I think of her in my mind's eye, I see her wearing one of her signature housedresses and an apron. She was always cooking up something yummy in the kitchen—fresh pasta, yummy tomato sauces, you name it. Everything she made was Italian-inspired, with fresh herbs like oregano and basil that she grew in her garden. Oh, and lots of onions, olive oil, Italian cheeses, and *garlic*—I mean *lots* of garlic. She passed away when I was thirty-five, but to this day, when I'm missing her, sometimes I swear I can smell garlic. It gives me a warm feeling, like she's still around."

"I think of our Gram Mary whenever I eat chocolate," Kate says. "She was always carrying candy in her pockets."

"Or a peppermint sucker," Carla adds with a laugh. "She guarded her candy like it was fine jewelry, telling us it was more meaningful to her than getting a gift of diamonds."

"All we had to do was ask, though, and she'd share her bounty with us," Kate replies.

"And remember how Gram Anna Theresa always had clever expressions for everything?" reminisces Carla. "'You can't judge a book by its cover,' 'Curiosity killed the cat …'"

"'Where the tongue slips, it speaks the truth,'" Kate adds.

"My gram used to say, 'Lose an hour in the morning, and you'll be looking for it all day.'" Cindy laughs as she surveys the surroundings. "I love the way you chose to tie the knot, girlfriend. Right smack in the middle of the plumeria trees that you planted to honor Kai's mom and your mother, overlooking the ocean, followed by an intimate backyard garden reception. It's a fantasy come true."

Kate nods, smiling. "We were lucky we could get a special dispensation to marry in our garden."

"I can barely remember my wedding day," Cindy laments.

"You had an amazing wedding at your parents' country club, Cin," Kate reminds her.

"It was beautiful, but there were so many people—many of whom I didn't even know, and I might have done my wedding differently if I hadn't been so young. However, I'm definitely more *sophisticated* now."

Cindy shakes her shoulders for emphasis, and Kate and Carla laugh out loud.

"All I remember is stressing myself out about everything when I got married. The entire day was like a blur. If it weren't for the wedding video, I'd have no idea how it went. Although, I do remember *every detail* of my fantastic honeymoon."

"But of course, daaahling." The greeting, delivered in a lovely British lilt, comes from Elaine Harrison, an attractive woman in her mid-forties, as she steps onto the lanai. She is both Kate's real estate agent and a good friend. Today she is dressed in a stunning designer sundress. "What are honeymoons for if not to be absolutely luxurious, romantic, sexy, and fantastic?"

Elaine leans down and kisses Kate's cheek. "You look radiant, Kate," she says admiringly. "I brought some Earl Grey and scones, a wedding day tradition in my family."

Elaine holds out a large canvas bag heaped to the brim with goodies. In her other hand she holds a garment bag containing her bridesmaid's dress.

Carla intercepts both of Elaine's bags and motions for her to take a seat. "I'll go put the kettle on and hang your dress up."

"Looks like you've already had breakfast," Elaine says as she eyes the traces of leftover pancakes and fresh fruit on the table.

"I told Carla I wouldn't hold it against her if I can't fit into my dress this afternoon after everything I just ate," Cindy pipes up. "I promise not to hold anything against you either, Elaine, because I am definitely going to have one of your scones and a cup of tea."

"Well, celebrations like this don't happen every day, so let the calories mount!"

"Here, here!" Cindy raises her mug in a celebratory cheer.

An hour or so later, before the caterers and the rest of her friends arrive, Kate ducks out of the preparations to sneak in a quick beach run.

As she jogs along the shore, she inhales deep breaths of clean, crisp air and marvels at the voluminous white clouds that hang low and rest on the pristine blue horizon like big fluffy pillows. Tempted earlier to forgo her run, Kate is glad now that she stuck with her routine; exercise is her go-to stress reliever. Thanks to all the beneficial endorphins that working out rigorously creates, she always feels fantastic afterward.

On her turnabout back to the cottage, Kate sees a man walking toward her in the distance. As he draws nearer, she recognizes the thick gray hair and familiar gait. Kate waves as she calls out, "Dad!"

"Honey!" Glen picks up his pace.

Kate and her father embrace. "I thought you'd be at Bradford's with the rest of the men," Kate says.

"I wanted some alone time with my baby before everyone gathers. Carla told me you were taking your morning run. I hope you don't mind."

"Not at all, Poppy." Kate links arms with Glen and the pair walk along the water's edge. "I'm so glad the whole family could make it back to Kauai. It seems like only yesterday that we celebrated our engagement."

"Hon, none of us would miss your wedding for the world. Besides, traveling to Kauai for such a wonderful occasion, well, I wouldn't call that a burden." Glen pulls a small red velvet box from his pants pocket and hands it to Kate.

"What's this?"

"Something your mother would have wanted you to have on your special day." Glen winks. "It represents something old and something blue."

Kate opens the lid. Inside the box sits a delicate, oval, antique pendant, surrounded by tiny blue gems. The pendant hangs from a simple, sterling silver chain. "It's gorgeous. So dainty and elegant. I remember Mom wearing it."

"On the front of the pendant is your mother's BFF, the Virgin Mary." Glen points to the image of the Blessed Mother standing on top of a globe, with the head of a serpent beneath her feet. "This pendant is called a Miraculous Medal."

"'O Mary, conceived without sin, pray for us who have recourse to thee.'" Kate's voice is soft as she reads the words around the oval shape.

Glen turns the pendant over and points. "On the reverse side, the twelve stars surrounding the 'M' and the cross are for the twelve apostles who formed the first church. Below, you'll see two flaming hearts. The left heart, circled with thorns, represents Jesus. The right heart that is pierced by a sword symbolizes Mary and her sorrow for her son's death."

"I love the significance. What do the blue stones mean?" asks Kate, admiring the gems around the pendant's face.

"The color blue has been used since ancient times to represent heaven, and it's the color most associated with Mother Mary, so I guess that's why the stones are that color. You know, it's believed that those who wear the Miraculous Medal–especially around their necks–will receive great graces."

Kate hugs her father and kisses his cheeks. "I love it, Poppy, especially knowing it was Mom's. Mahalo."

Kate holds up her hair so that her father can fasten the necklace around her neck. "I'll cherish it always," she says, touching the medal.

Father and daughter walk for some time in silence, each in deep contemplation with their thoughts. Finally, Glen breaks the silence. "I miss her, Kate."

"I know, so do I."

During moments like this, Kate is not quite sure how to comfort her father. However, she does know that acknowledging their loss and not glossing over their pain feels healing.

"Dad, I hope you know that you can come to visit and stay with us any time you want. That's why we have the guesthouse, an *ohana* as we call it in Hawaii. We want family and friends to come and stay."

Glen nods with a smile, but his mind is elsewhere.

"We have plenty of room, so you can bring anyone you want," adds Kate, thinking of Peggy, the woman her father started dating a short time after her mother's death.

Whew, there I said it, she thinks. However, still raw over her mother's passing, as soon as the words exit her mouth, and although she would love for her father to come to visit, she realizes she's still grappling with whether or not she can truly handle the reality of her father bringing someone with him who's not her mother.

"I appreciate that, dear. I'll keep it in mind."

Kate smiles warmly at her father, searching his face for some understanding of what he might have on his mind.

"I'm navigating my way," adds Glen, sensing Kate's desire to know more.

Of course Kate has a million questions, but out of respect for her father—or possibly, her mother—she keeps them to herself and continues to listen, wondering what might be going on with Peggy.

Kate and her sister were shocked to discover that their father had started to date not even a year after their mother's death. Friends assured them it wasn't unusual for a widower who had a long and happy marriage to seek the company of a new woman to relieve the loneliness. However, it is Kate's belief that her father needs more time to heal, and now she lets him speak without prying.

"Being single is a process," concedes Glen. "At the end of the day, I'm just trying to find the joy in the time I'm blessed with."

"Dad, I love you so much, you know?"

It's okay that her father is evasive. If it were any other day, she might try dancing around the topic a bit to get him to open up. However, there's a lot on her mind today, so she's grateful the topic of Peggy is still on the back burner.

"I know." Glen smiles. "To the moon and beyond."

"To the moon and beyond." Kate hugs her father before they start back toward the cottage.

"It looks fabulous!" Kate's enthusiasm is obvious as she admires her hair, expertly done up into a modern French twist.

"Hold still, sis," Carla demands. She makes a few adjustments to the stunning white orchard *haku lei*, the traditional Hawaiian crown of flowers used for weddings, which sits on Kate's head. "One more tiny bobby pin should do the trick." She firmly tucks the hairpin in its proper place. "There. Perfect!"

"Let me snap a photo," exclaims Cindy, whipping out her smartphone.

The sophisticated hairstyle perfectly complements the elegant, classic V-neck of the gown. The sleeveless dress, made of chiffon and satin, showcases Kate's hourglass figure. A row of decorative, satin-covered buttons trails down the back to the end of the slightly sweeping train.

"You look so glamorous, just like a princess," insists Carla, just as someone knocks on the other side of the closed bedroom door.

"Are you decent?" Kate hears her friend Olivia call out.

"Come on in!" yells Kate, thrilled that her friend has arrived.

"Wow! Move over, Grace Kelly," squeals Olivia with delight upon entering the room. An attractive, vivacious African-American woman in her early forties with a commanding yet gracious presence, Olivia is dressed in an elegant, floor-length, designer gown and effortlessly looks every bit the well-known and respected international entertainment icon she is.

Carla beams. "I told her she looks like royalty."

"I think we all look fab!" adds Cindy with bravado as the women exchange alohas.

"Your makeup is Hollywood perfect, too," Olivia adds with a wink. "I can't wait to see the look on Kai's face when he sees you."

"Hair and makeup by Carla." Kate extends a sweeping open hand to her sister as if introducing her to a crowd of people on stage.

"Are you a professional?" Olivia asks Carla in earnest.

"Honey, we're all working girls in this joint," quips Cindy. "But speaking of hair and makeup, would you be so kind?" Cindy pokes her limp hair as she looks at Carla. "I need your help, big time."

"Sure, have a seat." Carla pats the top of the vanity chair.

Olivia opens a blue velvet case, revealing a delicate pair of antique Mother of Pearl and diamond drop earrings. "These are my grandmother's, to represent something borrowed."

"They're gorgeous, and I know how much these must mean to you. I promise to be very careful." Kate says as she embraces Olivia.

The other ladies move in closely to catch a view of the jewels as Kate puts them on.

"Hello, beautiful ladies," Elaine dramatically sings upon entering the room. She is followed by Sukey Tadashi, a stunning Japanese woman with a distinctly eclectic style and personality, and Kai's pretty sister, Malie Kapule, who is Kate's age. All the ladies are wearing elegant dresses in the same teal hue, their hair and makeup done to perfection.

"How's everything looking outside?" Kate asks Elaine.

"*Magnifique.* The caterer and decorator certainly know what they're doing." Elaine winks at Olivia.

"It better be magnifique," declares Olivia who, along with Malie, co-owns The Plumeria Café, a popular Hanalei fixture, and the obvious choice to cater the wedding.

"We're definitely pulling out all the stops for this one!" adds Malie.

Kate, emotional now, starts to dab at the corners of her eyes. "OMG, I think I'm going to ..."

"Oh, no! *DON'T!*" Carla begs. "Your makeup will run."

In an attempt to stop the waterworks, Cindy begins to perform a silly dance to distract Kate.

"You are a first-class goof-meister!" Kate blurts out, half crying, half laughing.

"Hey, at least I'm *first class*."

The room erupts.

"Hold up, do I spy one of my best friends, Mr. Dom Perignon?" Cindy asks, peeking into Malie's canvas tote.

Malie grins. "Yes, you do. We thought it might be nice for just us ladies to share a toast before the ceremony."

"Lovely touch, daaahling," trills Elaine as she heads toward the door. "I'll go tell the caterer to bring us some glasses and a bucket of ice."

With a firm grip, Elaine slowly pulls on the champagne cork, now buried in a cloth napkin to reduce any spillage. Minutes later, the loud "pop" of the champagne cork officially kicks-off the celebration.

"Expertly done!" praises Sukey.

"Yeah, she's a professional," affirms Cindy.

Elaine smiles and takes a small bow. "*Bien sûr*, ma chérie. In this and all matters of fine living."

"But of course." Cindy speaks with an affected French accent. She wiggles her shoulders and body, mimicking Elaine, which sends the ladies into roars of copious laughter.

"I'd like to make a toast to my baby sister." Carla says. She picks up one of the champagne-filled crystal flutes that line the bedroom dresser and holds it high. "I ran across a quote not too long ago that's similar to the one by Salman Rushdie about chocolate chip cookies. And because all women like chocolate …"

"Love, darling, not like. *Looove*," gushes Elaine with emphasis.

"Hey, that's my line," protests Cindy.

More laughter erupts.

"All I can say is that it's a sentiment that perfectly sums up how I feel about you, Kate." Now it's Carla's turn to tear up. She dabs the corners of her eyes, suddenly overcome with emotion.

"Oh, NO! DON'T!" Cindy echoes the same words Carla used just moments ago in response to Kate's near-emotional outburst. "Your makeup will run!"

"I'm okay." Carla composes herself and continues. "Seriously now—well, actually, not too seriously—in the cookies of life, sisters are the chocolate chips, and I lucked out. I've got the best, sweetest and most delicious sister ever! Mom would be so proud and happy. I believe she'll be here with us today."

Seconds later, a little bird alights on the window ledge, happily chirping.

"*Well, hellooo, Mom!*" Cindy calls.

"Hi, Mrs. Grace!"

"Great to see you!"

"Glad you could make it!" the ladies chime in, all following suit.

"You guys are crazy," Kate protests, but she joins in the fun with her own greeting. "Hi, Mommydoo!"

"Who you callin' crazy, girl?" Cindy dips a finger in her glass and splashes some champagne in Kate's direction.

Kate is about to return the favor when Carla intervenes. "Hey! No food or drink fights today! Remember the hair and makeup."

Cindy turns to Kate with a broad smirk. "Yeah, a little decorum, *PULEEZE* … chocolate chip."

Kai Stevens smiles adoringly at his bride as he watches her walk with her father toward him down the flower-lined path to the strings of the famous "Ke Kali Nei Au" Hawaiian wedding song. On either side of the walkway, some fifty-plus family and friends are gathered, seated in white wooden chairs.

Kai, 6'4", thirty-something, with dark hair, an impressive physique, and a chiseled mix of Hawaiian and European features, is movie-star handsome in his Tommy Bahama white shirt and pants. He wears a brightly colored red sash around his waist and a green maile lei with small white pīkake flowers around his neck. His lei is the perfect complement to Kate's lei of white pīkake and pink rosebuds.

Kai takes Kate's hand lovingly as they stand before Father Burke, the local parish priest. The vibrant colors of Hanalei Bay's mountains, lush greenery, and aquamarine ocean are magically illuminated by bright sunlight, making a stunning backdrop behind the altar.

The ceremony commences when Kai's friend, Haku, a Hawaiian culturist, blows a trumpet-like Hawaiian pū horn—made from a giant conch shell—to announce the official start of the wedding. Although Father Burke leads the ceremony, Haku is present to infuse the joyous occasion with customary Hawaiian touches and blessings.

"You are my soulmate, my life partner, my lover, and my friend," Kai says, beginning the vows he and Kate have written to express their love. "I give thanks to God that He has led us to one another, and I will be ever mindful of this wondrous blessing. It is with a joyous heart that I pledge to make you and our family a priority. I promise to love and care for you, to be honest, kind, patient, and true. I will always lend you an understanding ear and encourage your dreams. I promise to cherish you, in sickness and in health, through hard times and good, for the rest of my days."

"As I hold your hand now, so shall it forever be. You are my love, my partner, my soulmate, and I give thanks to the Creator for sending you to me," recites Kate. "Faithfully loving you is what I will always be. I will respect and honor you and all the things you hold dear, and I will cherish those moments when you are near. I look forward to our adventures and life's journey with special glee, never taking for granted how precious you are to me. No matter where life leads us, our hearts' light will shine, and I will stand by your side forever—with your hand in mine."

"Kai, do you take Kate for your lawful wife, to have and to hold from this day forward, until death do you part?" Father Burke intones.

"I do."

"Kate, do you take Kai for your lawful husband, to have and to hold from this day forward, until death do you part?"

"I do."

While Father Burke proceeds with the blessings, Kate notices that the wind's rustling sounds like a song. A gentle breeze caresses her shoulders. Tingles of energy dance on her skin, and when an overwhelming warm sensation permeates her heart, she thinks of her mother.

Kai winks at Kate, clearly aware of the wind's unique music.

Today is the happiest day of my life, thinks Kate.

Following Father Burke's lead, Kai places a diamond-crusted wedding band on Kate's ring finger. Kai had their wedding bands specially made to complement the custom design of Kate's engagement ring. Inside the wedding band is an intricate, circular and flowing design which represents "lani," or "heaven," and the continuous flow of life and love. It's the same design that's on Kai's mother's locket, which Kate found that fateful day on the beach. Today, Kate wears the locket on a pretty silver bracelet and her mother's Miraculous Medal around her neck.

"Kate, take this ring as a sign of my love and fidelity. In the name of the Father, and of the Son, and of the Holy Spirit."

Kate follows suit as she makes her sacred pledge and places Kai's wedding band on his ring finger.

"Kai and Kate, encircle one another with your love and as you move from this day forth as husband and wife," continues Father Burke as he pronounces them man and wife.

The crowd erupts with thunderous applause as they watch the happy couple seal their vows with a kiss.

Clouds dance about in the sky, turning shades of orange, pink and deep purple as a sublime ocean breeze meanders through the backyard-garden reception where the bride, groom, and their family and friends enjoy each other's company for the post-wedding ceremony festivities. Every detail—from the white lights that shimmer on garden trees to the Hawaiian tunes that harmoniously play on ukuleles in the melodic, fingerstyle, slack-key guitar genre of music that has come to be associated with the Islands—contribute to the evening's romantic and magical ambience.

With her characteristic boldness, Cindy grabs her husband, Vinnie, and makes a beeline for the first waiter to emerge from the kitchen with a silver platter full of delectable-looking appetizers.

"Care for some lomi-lomi with poi?" The waiter, dressed in a handsome blue and white floral shirt and crisp white pants, places his serving tray in front of Vinnie.

"What's lomi-lomi?"

"A mix of salmon, tomato and onion," replies the waiter, handing Vinnie and Cindy little serving cups of the salad from his tray. "Poi is a paste made from pounded taro root," he adds as he doles out some of the purple-colored mix over the top of the salad.

"Mmmm, very tasty," replies Cindy as she samples the appetizer.

"And how do you like it?" the waiter asks Vinnie.

Vinnie nods and smiles to be polite, but as soon as the waiter leaves, he complains to Cindy, "Seriously, Cin? Tastes like fancy wallpaper paste. Don't they have anything more like pizza or something?"

Cindy sighs and shakes her head. "You can take the man out of

New York, but you can't take the New York out of the man."

"Chardonnay or cab'?" A pretty waitress dressed in a floral sarong with a fresh white Hibiscus bloom in her hair offers Cindy a tray filled with wine glasses.

"Chardonnay for me," answers Cindy, taking a glass. "Mahalo."

"I'm going to the bar to get a *manly* drink." The emphasis Vinnie places on the statement leaves little doubt as to his opinion of white wine.

"Whatever you need, dear—as long as you bring me back some crab cakes and chicken wrapped in ti leaves."

As Cindy takes a sip of her wine, she glances over to the corner and notices Kate's father. He's looking a little forlorn. Concerned, Cindy heads straight for him. "How are you doing, Mr. Grace?"

"Fine, dear. Don't you look lovely," Glen greets her, managing a weak smile.

"Have you tried the mini quiches yet?

Glen chuckles. "I didn't think real men ate quiche," he replies, obviously trying to sound upbeat.

"Today, they do." Cindy grabs his arm. "Come, let's get a plate."

Immediately following the cocktail hour, and after the traditional bride and groom's first dance, Kate takes to the floor with her father, then her father-in-law, after which the bandleader invites all the wedding guests onto the dance floor.

"Today is perfect, *Mrs. Stevens*," Kai whispers admiringly into Kate's ear as the couple twirls around the dance floor while waiters set out dishes of fresh fruit served in bowls carved from pineapple shells at every place setting.

"I'm amazed that I'm able to take it all in." Kate's voice is soft as she gazes lovingly at Kai. "This morning Cindy told me she could barely even remember her wedding. I'm so glad we decided to do it like this."

"This macadamia nut-encrusted halibut is exquisite," comments Elaine during dinner as she scoops up a large bite of the moist fish with a bit of tangy peanut sauce and jasmine rice on her fork. "The grilled asparagus goes perfectly with it too," she adds.

"Cheers to the caterers!" calls out Trevor, Elaine's British husband, as he holds up his wine glass. "To The Plumeria Café!"

"I'll second that," chimes in Grant Anderson. Olivia's tall, dark, handsome boyfriend is a successful real estate developer and business entrepreneur.

Malie raises her glass with pride and clinks it with Olivia's. "Here, here."

During dinner, couples move on and off the wooden dance floor, which is strategically placed in the center of the garden and surrounded by round tables adorned with ivory linens, colorful tropical centerpieces, and sparkling dinnerware.

"You're delicious." Kai sensuously kisses Kate's neck while they dance to another slow, romantic tune sung by one of the band's featured soloists. "I love you, Mrs. Stevens."

"Hey, you two," chides Cindy playfully as she swirls past the happy couple on Vinnie's arm. "Why don't you get a room? Tee hee."

"By the looks of you two love birds tonight, I could say the same thing," Kate replies with a chuckle.

"Okay, ladies, ready?" Kate calls as she raises a stunning, tropical floral bouquet high in the air. A barrage of screams and hoots rises from the single women on the dance floor.

Seconds later, as Kate tosses the bounty high in the air, an enthusiastic crowd converges in the center. More screams ensue until a shocked Olivia emerges holding the bouquet.

"Way to go, Olivia!" yells Kate, happy for her friend.

Olivia's eyes meet Kate's—and Kate is surprised to see that she looks more shocked, and perhaps even disappointed, than anything else.

Kai pulls up a chair in the center of the floor as the bandleader ushers the other women off the dance floor and back to their seats.

"Here we go, *ku'u lei*," announces Kai, using the Hawaiian phrase to refer to a beloved as he pulls up a chair for Kate to sit on. "Garter throwing time."

Kate scrunches up her nose and makes a funny face that hints at her discomfort with the public display before taking her place on the chair.

With slow, expert precision, Kai dramatically removes the garter from Kate's semi-exposed leg while the band plays a saucy, horn-heavy burlesque.

"*Whit Whew!*" Bawdy whistles and taunts bellow from the crowd.

"Okay, men, let's see how you roll." Kai hoists the garter over the crowd of single guys hovering on the dance floor. He flings it into the horde and the men proceed to lunge, tackle, and pounce on each other for the silky item. When the scrimmage is over, Grant emerges the victor.

Olivia's shocked gasp is clearly heard over the commotion.

"Grant, you have to put the garter on Olivia!" shouts Kate, clapping gleefully.

"Baby, come on." Grant pats the top of the chair. "Take a seat on the throne here."

Olivia smiles painfully and takes her place.

"You okay?" whispers Grant in her ear.

Olivia shrugs and lets a little chuckle escape.

For those who don't know Olivia, all would appear normal. However, the nonchalant nature of the shrug and flat tone of the chuckle clues Kate in that something is off.

The crowd whistles, hoots and hollers as Grant gently lifts the skirt of Olivia's gown and slowly moves the garter up her leg. Once it's in place, he leans in and plants a big kiss right on her mouth.

"Grant and Olivia, when will we have the honor of coming to your wedding?" Elaine's husband, Trevor, playfully yells, riling up the crowd.

Kate once again catches Olivia's eye. She looks like the proverbial deer caught in headlights.

"Time to cut the wedding cake!" the bandleader shouts, shifting the focus and moving things along. The crowd applauds as the wedding cake, a stunning, four-tiered culinary marvel, is wheeled onto center stage. Delicate white orchids with light pink and purple centers cascade from the top of the ivory cake to the bottom.

Kai and Kate make the first cuts together and then proceed to tenderly feed each other pieces of the heavenly, red velvet confection.

"Ah, you guys are so well behaved!" screams Cindy. "I was kind of hoping for a food fight!"

Waves of laughter erupt from the crowd, but before things can get out of hand, the bandleader guides everyone to join in another dance with the bride and grown.

While guests make their way to the dance floor, waiters serve sliced wedding cake and offer coffee. Bountiful trays of sliced 'kulolo,' a traditional Hawaiian dessert made from mashed *kalo*, coconut milk and brown sugar are also placed on each table.

"The food is just sublime. Mahalo to you, Malie, and your staff for making tonight so extra special," gushes Kate, embracing Olivia when they meet in the ohana powder room.

"Our pleasure."

"I'm so happy it was you who caught the bouquet. You know what tradition says about that, don't you?"

"Oh, yeah …" Olivia rolls her eyes. "I'm the next to marry."

"*You never know*," singsongs Kate playfully. "You and Grant are crazy about one another. It might not be an accident that you …"

"It's just some silly wedding tradition, that's all," Olivia protests, trying to deflect a more profound meaning.

"I'm sorry." Kate touches Olivia's shoulder. "I didn't mean to offend you."

"I know." Olivia tries to act nonchalant. "This is your day, and we're here to celebrate. Let's you and me join the others outside and toast your marriage with some champagne."

Later that evening, as the two lovers stand in the glow of moonlight on the balcony of their honeymoon suite at a popular, upscale resort overlooking the Pacific, Kate smiles to herself, thinking about that fateful day when she first laid eyes on the man who is now officially her husband.

Flailing around in anger after a disturbing phone call with her then-boyfriend, Jason, Kate stubbed her toe on a lava rock close to the Hanalei Pier. Kai, amused by her dramatic and somewhat comical display, but also genuinely concerned, asked if she was okay. It wasn't until days later that their chance meeting turned into a formal introduction at an intimate barbeque Olivia held at her Princeville estate. Of course Kate recognized Kai the moment she saw him, but she prayed he wouldn't recognize her. At least she had been lucky enough to be wearing a big floppy hat and sunglasses during the embarrassing toe-stubbing incident.

Little did she realize Kai knew her secret—a fact that he later confessed. He was such a gentleman, not wanting to make her feel ashamed or otherwise put her on the spot during their "proper" introduction. Kai was so considerate of her feelings. He was the very opposite of Jason. From the moment of that confession, the dam broke, and Kate shared a rush of emotions with Kai, from her fears and concerns about not wanting to be led astray to her desires for the future. She was taken with Kai's straightforward demeanor and honesty and thrilled to learn that he was at that time in his life where he was also ready for a committed relationship. She was also grateful they shared the same values and beliefs. Being with him was so natural and effortless; in a matter of one month, they knew they were meant for one another, and Kai didn't waste any time proposing.

As if reading her mind, Kai confesses, "From the first moment I met you, it's all been more than I could have dreamed of." His arms tighten around Kate's waist as they stand in silence for a time, watching the beauty of the stars and moon illuminating the quiet ocean.

"Something a little strange happened today," Kate says softly, breaking the silence.

"I saw that look on your face during the ceremony. Maybe it was our moms looking down on us?"

"When you winked at me, I knew you knew what I was thinking. But that's not what I mean."

"What then?"

"Olivia had a strange reaction when I suggested that maybe it was a sign that she caught the bouquet and Grant the garter."

"Really? How so?"

"When I mentioned they might be next in line, I could tell by her tone and the way her energy shifted that something about that idea bothered her. She called the tradition 'silly,' then quickly changed the subject. When I first met her, she didn't seem to mind talking about the idea of marriage—she even mentioned that although she wasn't in a rush, it could be a possibility someday."

"Well, sweetheart, maybe getting up on stage, so to speak, and catching the bouquet did strike a chord somehow. It's hard to say. She and Grant appear to be very happy, but maybe there are some things they're working on that she or they need to come to grips with."

"She's a dear friend. I hope she knows she can talk to me and that I'm there for her like she's been there for me."

"I'm sure she does. There might be another opportunity where you can ask her, or maybe it'll just come up. Since you know it's a soft spot, tread lightly, that's all."

"That's good advice, Dr. Stevens." Kate smiles, touched by Kai's genuine concern and valuable insight.

"Glad I can be of service," Kai says suggestively, his voice low and husky as his hot breath grazes her face. He sensuously plants another row of kisses on the back of Kate's neck.

When Kate turns her head ever so slightly to catch Kai's lips, their embrace grows tighter and more passionate.

Kate moans with a shiver of delight when they finally break for air. "More of that, please."

"As I said, glad I can be of service," whispers Kai. He gently pulls Kate toward the master suite's generous king-sized bed.

"All that is known is that the thirty-year-old woman, whose name is being withheld, is doing well and is expected to be released from the hospital shortly," announces a reporter on television during the local news the next morning.

"What was that on the TV just now?" Kate asks Carla as she enters the cottage's kitchen. In true Grace-family style, the entire clan has convened, along with a small group of friends, for a post-wedding brunch buffet.

"I wasn't paying that much attention," replies Carla. "Something about an attack on a woman during a home invasion in Hanalei, but she's going to be okay."

"Auntie Kate, what's for brunch?" Carla's son, Lucas, bursts into the kitchen and diverts attention away from the disturbing news.

"We're going to have eggs, potatoes, smoked salmon, bagels ... lots of yummy things," replies Kate.

"Lucas, be a dear will you, and take this fruit salad out to the lanai buffet table," Carla instructs.

Gathered at several long tables situated in the garden are Kate's father, her brother, Derek, and his wife, Julie, Carla's husband, Frank, and their respective children, as well as a handful of Kai's relatives, including his father, Bradford, sister, Malie, and Malie's husband, Aukai. Also present are a few of Kate's colleagues from the two publications for which she is a contributing editor—the Island publication *Simply Aloha Living* magazine and *New York View Magazine*. Most of the East Coast contingent is heading back to New York later in the day, but Cindy and Vinnie are continuing their vacation, staying at the cottage while Kate and Kai honeymoon on the Big Island's Kohala Coast.

"This meal is fit for a king," praises Glen, definitely enjoying the breakfast feast.

"And OMG, Kate!" Cindy moans as she munches on a slice of Kate's lemon coconut bread. "This is orgasmic!"

"You mean it gives you as much pleasure as I do?" Vinnie's retort is playful as he plants a big wet one on his wife's cheek.

Cindy gives Vinnie one of her raised-eyebrow looks and is about to say something when Carla intervenes.

"Be careful, children in the mix," blurts Carla, motioning that her ten-year-old son, Lucas, is standing close by and all ears.

"Ah, come on, Mom, what do you think I am … a kid? I know about the birds and the bees."

Lucas' retort causes all the adults to laugh out loud.

"Do I think you are a kid? Yes, I do. You're my little boo!" Carla is unable to resist her son's cute glare and gives him a big squeeze.

"*Mom!*" Lucas cries out in a voice several octaves lower, as if being lethally attacked. He rolls his eyes, feigning upset, but it's obvious he's enjoying his mother's attention.

Carla plants a series of kisses on his check. "To me you'll always be my baby."

"Come here," Kate calls to Lucas, wanting in on the love fest. "Give your auntie a hug." When Lucas dutifully complies, Kate adds, "Why don't you get your suit on and join your cousins for a final swim at the beach before you have to head for the airport?"

"Cool!" Lucas shouts, and he runs into the cottage to change.

"Sissypoo, I wish we could stay longer." Carla sighs as she and Kate embrace at Lihue Airport's boarding gate.

As a teacher, while Carla has months off in the summer, her vacation days are limited during the school year.

"Just come back and visit soon. The ohana will be waiting."

"Auntie Kate, don't cry!" declares Lucas when he sees Kate's forlorn expression. "Dad said we're coming back during spring break. That's not too far away at all!"

"*Really?*" Kate's mood immediately lightens.

"Sorry I didn't mention it to you and Kai first. It was a spur of the moment response to Lucas' *unrelenting prodding*," Frank admits with a wink at Lucas.

"You're welcome anytime." Kai embraces Frank, then Glen.

"Got all your *accoutrements?*" Frank asks Carla in a French accent.

"Oui, mon amour. Got 'em all." Carla grabs her shoulder tote in one hand and suitcase handle with the other.

"Bye, sweetheart." Glen kisses Kate on the cheek.

"I love you, Poppy."

"To the moon and beyond." Glen waves as he walks toward the gate.

"Call or text me when you get in," Kate yells.

The moment is bittersweet as Kai and Kate wave to their ohana entering the airport boarding area.

"Hey, sweetie, we'll see them soon," Kai tells Kate as he places a comforting arm around her shoulders for solace. "We'll FaceTime with them tomorrow, 'K?"

"Yup."

"Besides, we'll be off on our honeymoon adventure soon." He smiles and plants a big kiss on her lips.

"Thanks, doc."

Kai's medicine works like a charm.

The pristine waters of Anini Beach are light aqua along the shoreline and dissolve into a deep, vibrant, cobalt blue farther out to sea. The quiet, secluded beach, dotted with patches of grass, hosts a plethora of shady trees and is Kate's go-to place to write, think, and enjoy nature's astounding beauty. Energized by Anini's tranquil beauty, Kate closes her eyes and breathes deeply. From the otherwise-still day, a balmy breeze suddenly crops up, caressing her bare shoulders.

"Aloha, sweetheart."

Kate opens her eyes when she hears her mother call to her. "Aloha, Mom."

"How's my girl?"

"Wonderful. Especially now that you're here."

Catherine wears a long, flowing dress. It's the same texture and shade of teal the bridesmaids wore at Kate's wedding. "Let's walk." Catherine places an arm around her daughter's shoulder. "You were such a beautiful bride."

Without any further conversation, Kate knows God granted her prayer: that her mother be present at the wedding two days prior. With that thought, Kate also becomes aware that she is dreaming. Trying to remain calm, she breathes in deeply, catching the scent of sweet plumeria. She places her arms around Catherine and revels in the vivid warmth of their embrace. As she experiences the overwhelming currents of love washing over her, she tries hard to soak up every detail, willing herself not to wake.

"Oh, no," Kate sighs when her eyes fling open. She knows that with dreams like these, if she tries too hard to hold on, she inevitably wakes up. She looks at Kai, who is still sound asleep. *How lucky am I?* Kate gives thanks to the Creator for his blessings. *Mahalo for my loving family and friends, and Kai.*

Watching Kai sleep, Kate feels the need to be closer to him, so she gently wraps her arms around his waist and places her head on his back in a comforting, spoon position. Never tiring of the absolute bliss she finds in the heat and energy he exudes, she allows herself to drift to the sound of her husband's rhythmic breathing.

Seconds later, Kate, enveloped in Kai's warmth, finally falls into a peaceful, contented slumber.

The Paradise Garden

Awake, north wind, and come, south wind!
Blow on my garden, that its fragrance may spread everywhere. Let
my beloved come into his garden and taste its choice fruits.

– Song of Solomon 4:16

2

———

"Kai, look!" Kate points excitedly to a fabulous view outside the cabin window as their plane nears the Big Island and Hawaii's Kona International Airport. "I can't wait till we're on the ground!" She is giddy with excitement on their first adventure as husband and wife.

I have got to be the luckiest woman in the world. I have to journal my thoughts to remember every detail of this trip.

Dressed in a long, flowing, floral A-line cotton skirt and a sleeveless, white scoop-neck top, Kate revels in the warm welcome of the sun's heat on her bare skin as they disembark the plane via a mobile staircase that leads to the tarmac.

The sweet scent of orchids and plumeria leis greet them once inside the terminal. Almost immediately as they enter the welcoming space, an elderly Polynesian woman holds up an armful of blooms for purchase.

"Two leis, please," Kai says, pulling some cash out of his wallet. "One for my wife, and one for me. Mahalo."

"Mahalo. *Aloha e komo mai,*" the woman utters with a smile as she places the leis around their necks.

"What did she say?" Kate whispers to Kai as they head toward baggage claim.

"It was an affectionate way to say, 'Come in, welcome to the island.'"

After picking up their luggage and rental car, a white Mustang convertible, Kai and Kate drive down the plush, tree-lined, expertly manicured airport exit toward the freeway. Once on the open road, the lush landscape makes an abrupt change.

"I feel like I'm on the moon or something!" Kate marvels at the dark-colored lava rock bordering Highway 19.

The dark, jagged rocks set against the blue and white sky and

39

cobalt-colored ocean to the left are the only colors visible except for an occasional bit of greenery or a small patch of flowers bursting through the ebony earth.

"It does look like another planet, doesn't it?" Kai agrees with a laugh. "I never thought of it that way before. When we get closer to Waikoloa Village though, the view does a one-hundred-eighty-degree turn into a lush, flowering landscape and there'll be definite signs of civilization."

Entering through the plantation-style hutted front gates of Waikoloa Village, Kate's mouth drops in awe at the surrounding beauty. The twists and turns of the road to their destination make a welcome aloha. Flowering beauties, from scarlet Hawaiian Royal Poinciana, with their umbrellas of abundant blooms, to plumerias, both white and fuchsia varieties with deep yellow centers, stand majestic. Rainbow Shower trees with cascading blossoms in shades of pink, white and yellow, as well as other flowering stunners, intermix with tall palms, and red Ti plants greet them with their petals that wave in the wind.

"The colors and shapes are awesome," Kate enthuses. "So vibrant and alive! I'm going to have to take some photos."

"They'll be plenty of time for that once we settle in," Kai assures her.

Moments later, the newlyweds follow the long driveway up to an impressive, lava-rock-gated entrance surrounded by flowering beauties. An exquisite-looking, plantation-style townhome complex that serves as private residences as well as a resort is visible in the distance.

Immediately hit by a strong wave of cool breezes as they enter through the complex's massive entryway into the open-air lobby, Kate is struck by the beautiful, natural-colored stone floors, soaring ceilings, and strategically placed seating areas surrounded by walls decorated in stunning island art. In the distance, the lushly planted and appointed grounds and pools frame a stunning view of the Pacific.

"Aloha!"

Kate hears a high-pitched squeal, then notices it's one of the multi-colored parrots housed in a bronze cage. "Aloha," she mimics in response, chuckling as the bird dances about the cage. Seconds later, she joins Kai at the check-in counter.

Their two-story suite is a sophisticated, L-shaped space consisting of a living room, dining area, and kitchen. It thrills Kate and Kai that this luxurious suite will be their home for the next two weeks. The décor features creamy white, beige, and sage-green hues mixed with tropical designer fabrics and dark koa-wood furniture to create a casually elegant, distinct island-style ambience.

Through the sheers on the patio doors, which lead out to the private lanai, Kate spies the expansive ocean beyond. "This place is amazing!" she squeals with delight, running around to assess every detail of the well-appointed space.

Kai nods with satisfaction. "My friend Akemi came through."

Kate climbs an attractive, wrought-iron and wooden stairway which leads upstairs to the master bedroom. The king-sized room has the same comfortable, welcoming feel as downstairs. A generous bed with an attractive, dark wood headboard sits to the left, and an impressive, matching dark wood dresser, complete with large-screen TV, sits on the right. A wall of windows leading out to the bedroom lanai displays the same breathtaking view of the lagoon, ocean, and lush green foliage.

Inside the master bath, adorned with stones of varying shades of cream and beige with wood accents, sits an oversized tub.

"Kai, they have a sunken tub!" Kate yells to her husband, who is still downstairs, knowing he'll appreciate this luxury.

Moments later, as Kate unpacks, she feels the warmth of Kai's hand on her back. "Well done, my sweet," she says, turning to him and smiling broadly. Seeing the love in Kai's eyes shining back at her, Kate's knees turn weak.

Kai leans in and kisses her lips. One delicious kiss leads into another, igniting a blaze so intense that the world around them simply melts away, and the task of unpacking is long forgotten.

Hours later, showered and changed into fresh, crisp, casual beach clothes, the lovers, walking hand in hand, stroll through the local King and Queen's shops that showcase various collectables, a plethora of beach and casual wear, and art galleries displaying magnificent Asian and Polynesian artwork.

A jaunt around a nearby ocean walkway finds them at a favorite local resort that is decorated to perfection and exhibits such items as large decorative vases, intricate wood carvings, stunning embroidered robes, and paintings depicting eras gone by to giant marble statues, beautiful jewelry, and antique swords. The pair take their time as they peruse all the treasures along the museum-style stone walkway that leads around the grounds and connects the resort's many buildings and archways. A tram breezes silently overhead every so often, delivering resort guests to their various destinations. Just beyond the tram sits a canal with motorboats, another mode of guest transport. Views of the glorious blue Pacific and expertly manicured grounds are visible from every angle.

"Hungry?" Kai chuckles when he hears Kate's stomach growl.

"Well, we did work up an appetite, didn't we?" Kate's smile is both sweet and sexy.

"Be careful, or I just might devour you for lunch too." Kai teases, giving Kate a playful peck on the neck.

"Oh, goodie!" giggles Kate as they choose an outdoor table at the resort's grill for a quick bite.

"I wonder what Cindy and Vinnie are up to at the cottage?" Kai muses before he sips his fruit smoothie.

"Let's FaceTime them and find out." Kate sets down her iced tea and places the call.

"Why, alooooha, Mrs. Stevens. So, how's it going, girlfriend?" asks Cindy playfully. From her expression, it is clear that she's hoping to hear some juicy honeymoon details.

"Cin," Kate admonishes, clearly putting an end to that particular line of conversation.

Cindy bats her eyes. "Okay, I'll get a full report later."

"Incorrigible as usual."

Cindy smiles proudly.

"How many times do I have to tell you, I don't kiss and tell."

"Oh, I see … Kai's there."

"Aloha!" Kai pops his head next to Kate on the FaceTime screen and they all laugh.

"Hey, where's my man Vinnie?" asks Kai.

"Vinnie!" Cindy calls, looking around.

"What?" Vinnie yells off-screen.

"It's the love birds!"

"Hey, guys!" Vinnie greets them, appearing on the FaceTime screen seconds later, a little out of breath.

"How's it going?" asks Kai. "You seem a little out of breath."

"I was just exercising."

Cindy raises her eyebrows and looks at her husband. "Seriously?"

"Yeah, I was exercising," repeats Vinnie, looking at his wife sternly.

"Oh, okay, exercising—if you call running around the yard once, then stopping to take a bite of donut, and then doing another slow lap before you take another bite exercise, then okay …"

"I only took one bite of donut," Vinnie protests.

"Yeah, but you're not going to leave it at just one bite, now are you? You intend to finish that donut off, am I right?"

"So what if I finish the donut? I am exercising, so I can eat the donut."

"Hello. Hello. Earth to Cindy and Vinnie. We're still here," Kai reminds them with a chuckle.

"Oh, yeah, sorry," Vinnie replies.

"What are you two going to do today?" asks Kate.

"You mean after Vinnie finishes 'exercising'?"

"Yes." Kate bites her cheek to keep from laughing at Cindy's deadpan delivery.

"We're going to take a drive around the island and take in some of the sights you were telling us about, like Anini Beach and the Kilohana Plantation."

"Well, have a great time and text photos. We'll speak to you later. Love you," replies Kate.

"Love you too, dollface," says Cindy, followed by a round of kisses and alohas before exiting FaceTime.

"They're a trip. Salt-of-the-earth friends with big hearts and hours of guaranteed entertainment," Kai acknowledges as they finish lunch.

Opting to spend the rest of their first afternoon swimming at their resort where three glorious pools are connected by meandering winding pathways, the toughest decision of the day will be which to choose. In the end, the obvious choice for the newlyweds is an adults-only pool in a peaceful, secluded setting.

After retrieving their pool wristbands and towels, Kate places her large straw bag, wide-brimmed beach hat, and towel on a small table by a chaise that sits under an umbrella. She slips out of her cute, flowing beach dress to reveal a sexy, hot pink and white-polka-dot bikini.

Kai lets out a loud wolf whistle and flashes her a lustful smile of appreciation as he peels off his T-shirt; he's already wearing his floral-patterned swim trunks.

He's effortlessly gorgeous and with a killer bod to boot. Maybe I'm prejudiced, but I think not. Kate watches a woman sunning poolside give Kai the once over as he walks to the pool's edge, plunges in and begins to swim laps.

Sorry, sweetheart, the boy is mine. The scene reminds Kate of the classic Brandy and Monica pop song, "The Boy Is Mine," and she mentally chuckles.

Still wearing her sunglasses as she hums the popular tune, she removes a hair clip from her oversized bag and pins her hair up. "Ahhh," she sighs as she slowly descends the pool's stairway and sinks below the surface into the sublime, refreshing water.

After luxuriating in the sun, swimming, reading, and enjoying passion-fruit teas poolside for several carefree hours, Kate and Kai head back to their suite just after six o'clock to shower and change for a romantic dinner at one of the local hot spots.

Greeting them as they enter their suite is a massive, colorful display of tropical blooms in a large, impressive vase placed on the entryway table. Kate immediately makes a beeline for the flowers and removes a small envelope from the cardholder.

"I wonder who sent them?" asks Kai as he places bottles of water and snacks purchased at the resort's poolside market on the kitchen counter.

"Thinking of you and Kai and wishing you a most beautiful honeymoon," reads Kate, smiling. "Sending you our love and lots of good *mana*. Hugs and Kisses, Olivia and Grant. "

"Typical of them."

"I'm going to take a photo and text it to Olivia with a big *mahalo*," says Kate as she whips out her cell and snaps a few shots of the stunning display.

"You look sensational tonight, Mrs. Stevens." Kai strokes Kate's bare arm affectionately.

The lovers are gazing out at a stunning water view from their choice table at a romantic beachside restaurant just north of Waikoloa Village.

The open-air, upscale restaurant, dotted with elegant wooden tables and tropical greenery, sits right on the beach, with unobstructed panoramic views of the ocean and mountains. To make the evening extra special, Kate has opted to wear a classy, scoop-necked white and red floral-patterned halter dress. Her hair, pulled up at the sides, hangs in carefree curls around her shoulders. The day of loving and relaxing poolside has made her skin and eyes glow.

"You look rather handsome tonight yourself," Kate replies. She bites her lower lip in a sultry fashion as she grabs and strokes Kai's free hand.

Her smoldering look and loving gesture invite Kai to plant a passionate kiss on her lips. As soon as they part, a waitress greets them and takes their drink order.

As Kate observes the sky turn brilliant shades of blood orange, yellow, and purple, she digs into her shoulder bag to retrieve her digital camera and places it around her neck. "Do you mind, hon? I've just got to capture the sunset."

"Go ahead. I'll order our appetizers."

As Kate makes her way onto the sandy beach, she slips out of her sandals to make the walk more comfortable. It isn't long before the overwhelming beauty in the sky makes her skin start to tingle, and she gets lost in her photo taking, snapping images of the kaleidoscope show of colors in the sky as the gentle sounds of the tide sweeping into shore serenade her.

Even though she hears muffled restaurant laughter in the distance, and the clang of glass now and then, all that matters to her at this moment is capturing God's brilliant artistry unfolding before her. It's this keen focus that makes her feel as if she is almost one with the sky, water, and trees. Moments later, her mother's smiling face pops into her mind's eye.

Aloha, Mommydoo.

As Kate stands still, she feels such peace and warmth in her being. She sighs deeply, and after some time she notices a massive cloud begin to take shape in the sky. It's a vast and glorious angel with a long body sheathed in a flowing skirt and wearing an ethereal crown. A pair of wings stretch to either side of the angel, who prays with her arms by her side and her hands clasped over her heart.

Kate wipes the tears that now freely flow from her eyes. Once again, she picks up her camera and begins to snap a quick succession of photos. When she is finally satisfied that she has captured the angel image, she continues to watch in awe as the heavenly form moves toward another destination in the sky. A title for the photo immediately pops to mind.

Angel Wings.

As darkness descends over the ocean blanket, Kate makes her way back to her beloved. The restaurant tables, now illuminated by white candlelight, flicker and shimmer like stars in the night sky. She silently acknowledges the beautiful sight and is warmed by Kai's welcoming smile.

"Did you see it?" she asks Kai, beaming.

"How could I not? It was stunning."

Kate takes her seat at the table as the waitress serves them their farmer's market salads made with local baby lettuces, heirloom tomatoes, shaved sweet onions, dried cranberries, and macadamia nuts.

"Let's say a little prayer for our marriage, this beautiful evening, and for our angel in the sky," whispers Kate softly as she takes Kai's hands to express their gratitude to the Creator.

The sublime evening, full of great conversation in such a stellar setting, is made even more divine when their delicious fresh fish dinners, served with roasted vegetables and jasmine rice, arrive.

"I love you so much, Kate," Kai softly whispers before he tenderly pulls Kate close for a kiss.

For a moment Kate is lost in the sweet taste of Kai's lips and the feel of his muscular arms enfolding her, but she suddenly becomes aware of the sun's warm rays streaming down around them. In the next instant of this heavenly dream, Kate is magically alone in a different setting. Rays of golden light streaming down from above peek through the vibrant garden pathway lined with bright red- and green-tipped haleconia, spikey hot-pink lehua flowers, and majestic birds of paradise with their feathered hats and multi-colored beaks, which intermix in the green with other blossoms like glorious gems.

Kate focuses on a lush plumeria and feels that familiar warmth envelope her. Instantly, her mother appears at her side, and they greet one another with a loving smile.

As they begin their stroll down the dirt road, Kate is thrilled to see her relatives in spirit, as they were alive on earth. In this tender dream state, it all seems natural, and her heart jumps for happiness when she bids aloha to grandmothers, Mary and Anna Theresa, her grandfathers, both named Leo, as well as Kai's late mother, Leilani, in the distance. They embrace her when they finally meet in the natural clearing.

Kate is awed with the beauty of the rustic setting. In the center of the peaceful landscape sits a wooden table, exquisitely set with silver cutlery and pretty white plates that rest on ivory muslin placemats. Baby pink roses sit atop cloth napkins and, down the center of the table, several large wicker baskets display expert arrays of more roses, white orchids, and beautiful greenery. The tops of each of the chairs that surround the table are also decorated with muslin and adorned with pink and white roses strung together with greens that flow down the backs of the chairs. Music created from the chirping of tropical birds and the soothing flow of water as it moves across the rocks in the brook's streambed contribute to the garden's tranquility.

While stunning, Kate intuits that this garden is also a unique, healing place—a site of warmth, love, and connectedness.

Kai suddenly appears at her side, and they all sit at the table, which is laden with platters of fresh fruit—strawberries, pineapple, papaya, banana, passion fruit, and other recently harvested organic produce. An overwhelming feeling of joy enters Kate's heart, but just as she allows herself to sink deeper into the moment, she awakes.

The first thing she sees when she opens her eyes in the moonlit bedroom is her sleeping hubby. She watches him for a time, loving the fact that he is close and delighting in the warmth his body exudes. She can't help but caress his back, which causes Kai to react slightly. Careful not to wake him, Kate lays her head back down on her pillow and begins to review her dream, and as she does, she drifts back into a sound sleep.

"Where are we now?" asks Kate on the second day of their honeymoon adventure. She and Kai, having just passed the famous beach resorts of Mauna Lani, Mauna Kea, and the Samuel M. Spencer Beach Park, continue their drive north around the Big Island on Highway 19.

"Hawi."

The picturesque small town, situated on the Big Island's north tip, also known as the North Kohala district, is a tourist haven. Once a hub of the now-defunct sugar industry, the main street through town is dotted with charming shops, art galleries, and restaurants situated in colorful, plantation-style buildings.

"Look, Kai." Kate points to a quaint yellow shop. The sign over the door reads "Homemade Fudge."

"I get the hint," chuckles Kai.

"What'll it be folks?" asks a kind-looking Polynesian woman behind the counter of the shop, which offers a myriad of specialty hot drinks from lattes to cappuccinos—all made with 100% Kona coffee— as well as a selection of shave ice, ice cream, baked goods, and candy.

"A few pieces of the coconut and mac nut fudge, mahalo," Kai says, as he points to the delectable treats inside the glass counter.

"And a few of the red raspberry fudge too," Kate adds.

"Anything else?" asks the woman as she proceeds to place several pieces of creamy chocolate wedges into a box.

Kate, examining a bag of Kona coffee interspersed between other locally crafted gift items on the shop's shelves, holds it up to Kai, who nods, agreeing to the purchase as he hands the shop clerk a few cold bottles of water and his credit card.

"Wouldn't this be great for a honeymoon photo?" enthuses Kate, holding up a hand-painted wooden frame painted to look like a tropical garden.

Kai winks at the clerk. "Add that to our order, too, please." For the next half hour or so, Kate and Kai peruse the colorful shops along Akoni Pule Highway. Now and then they step inside one of the boutiques to look at a piece of art, handmade trinket, or jewelry that has caught their attention.

"He was born not far from here," Kai explains. The landmark Kapaau statue, the majestic figure of King Kamehameha, Kai comments on is cast in bronze and stands eight and a half feet tall.

The statue, positioned in front of the North Kohala Civic Center, showcases the great king in his royal garb, wearing a helmet of rare feathers and a gilded cloak. The spear the king holds in his left hand represents the kingdom's willingness to defend itself against hostile nations, while his right hand extends in aloha. Around his neck sits a bounty of colorful leis.

"I read that he was a superb warrior and leader," Kate says, staring at the impressive sculpture.

"In eighteen ten, after years of conflict, he united the Islands into one nation. Oh, and you'd like this little fact—Hawaiian legend prophesized that light in the sky with feathers like a bird would signal the birth of a great king. Historians believe Kamehameha was born in seventeen fifty-eight, the year Halley's Comet passed over Hawaii."

"Yeah, you're right. I like it." Kate smiles and her eyes twinkle as she readies her camera for yet another round of photos.

"Come on, hon," Kai gently protests. "We've got to get on the move. There's a lot more we want to do today."

Minutes later, back in the car, they drive past lush lands on their right and the sparkling Pacific Ocean on their left until they arrive at their next destination, the Waipio Valley Lookout.

"This hike will take you down eight hundred feet into the 'Valley of the Kings,'" announces a young, fit Hawaiian tour guide to a group of tourists that includes Kai and Kate. "Be sure to grab a few photos of Waipio Valley before we start down—this is the perfect vantage point to get some amazing shots."

Kate is only too happy to comply.

The valley is a stunning sight to behold. The land dramatically curves to meet the ocean, at the end of which sits the Waimanu Gap, a tall, massive landmass at an elevation of 2,089 feet.

"Pace yourself, folks, and watch your step," instructs the guide as the group starts down into the valley. "This road descends eight hundred vertical feet in six-tenths of a mile. I can guarantee you this is one hike you'll remember."

Waterfall views, tropical lushness, and welcoming nature sounds bid them an enchanting, memorable aloha as the group begins the steep decline.

"This is unbelievably gorgeous, Kai," Kate whispers, careful not to disrupt the quiet magic as she reaches into Kai's backpack for bottled water.

"Grab me a piece or two of that red raspberry fudge, okay?" Kai asks.

"Great idea. A perfect time for chocolate."

"Is there ever not a time for chocolate?"

Kate chuckles. "See. That's just one of the reasons why I knew you were the man for me."

"Oh yeah?" Kai playfully grabs Kate and tickles her.

"Kai, I can't get at the chocolate if you do that," Kate protests, wrestling with the backpack.

"Okay, but I'm going to get you later."

"Promise?"

"Oh, yeah," chuckles Kai.

"Well, I have to say you are even more irresistible than chocolate, and that's a serious compliment," says Kate, standing on her tippy toes, lips puckered.

"Follow me, folks," they hear the tour guide shout in the distance.

After their Waipio Valley tour, Kai and Kate's next stop is Akaka Falls State Park for another short hike. The lush rainforest teems with bamboo groves, draping greens, wild orchids, and a host of other native foliage. They follow the paved footpath to view the 100-foot Kahuna Falls, and then Akaka Falls, a majestic, cascading waterfall that plummets 442 feet into a deep gorge.

"Would you mind taking a photo of my husband and me with the falls behind us?" Kate asks a fellow tourist, who gladly complies and snaps a series of photos with Kate's camera.

Kate reciprocates the kind gesture by snapping a few pictures of the tourist with her boyfriend. Moments later, it's just her and Kai, alone on the path.

"I love you so much and give thanks for you every day," Kai declares.

"I love you, too, and do the same." Kate returns the sentiment, moved at Kai's sweet, unexpected outpouring.

"Let's always make the time to walk in nature," Kai adds, pulling Kate close. "To feed our souls and to appreciate nature's joy and wonder."

No further words are needed as the two lovers, holding each other tightly, breathe in the beauty of the falls. They both vow to remember this precious moment forever—the warmth of their embrace affirming their love, the glorious sounds of streaming water, and the cool breeze as it filters through the trees.

"I'm completely famished," Kate says as she scans both sides of the highway for a café or a rest stop. "Look, up there!" She points to a homey-looking place in a welcoming spot not far from Onomea Bay and close to their next destination, the Hawaii Tropical Botanical Garden. Kai nods in agreement, and the pair make their way to the charming outdoor café.

"We'll take two turkey sandwiches on whole wheat, a large bag of the taro-and-sweet potato chips, and two pears, mahalo."

"Something to drink?" the woman behind the counter asks Kai.

"An iced tea for my wife and a pineapple coconut smoothie for me." Kai pulls a wad of bills out of his wallet.

"I'll get us a table," Kate offers and runs her hand affectionately down Kai's back before exiting the café.

Other couples and a few families are eating their lunches at the wooden picnic tables situated on the attractive lanai. Kate selects a small table for two in the corner next to some green foliage. "Look at the pineapples growing in the bushes!" Kate motions as Kai takes a seat across from her. "I never knew they grew like that."

Characteristically, Kate pulls out her camera to snap a few shots. "What are these dainty flowers?" she asks, pointing to a gathering of lovely, white, fragrant blooms. "They look like the blossoms in my wedding lei."

"They're the same," replies Kai. "The flower is called pīkake."

" Pīkake. I like the sound of that word."

"It's a jasmine variety brought to the Islands in the eighteen hundreds. Hawaii's Princess Victoria Ka'iulani loved the blossoms as much as she adored the peacocks that used to roam through the plants. So she named the flower 'pīkake,' after the Hawaiian word for peacock."

Kate takes another whiff of the flowers. "They smell wonderful."

"Wait till you see the Botanical Garden. You're going to love it. They have some of the most exotic flora species you'll ever see."

"Speaking of gardens, I had the most beautiful dream last night," whispers Kate as she takes a sip of her tea. "I was in a lush setting where I was walking down a dirt path toward a clearing ..." Kate stops mid-sentence, fondly remembering.

"Just you?"

"Just me."

"Where was I?"

"I'll get to that in a minute. The sights, smells, and sounds were stunning," recalls Kate. "My mother and grandparents were there, and I saw your mother, too. It was then that I realized you were standing next to me. We all sat down around a gorgeous table laden with all types of fresh tropical fruits and vegetables in the most beautiful, serene setting. There was a feeling of overwhelming love, and it felt as if they were acknowledging our marriage and celebrating with us."

Kai sets his smoothie down on the table and moves his chair closer to Kate. "What a beautiful dream," he says, stroking her back tenderly.

"When I woke up, I felt that the dream and the setting had a special meaning somehow."

"How so?"

"I'm not quite sure. I keep replaying it in my mind."

"Pray on it, and ask God if he has a message for you. If he does, I know you'll receive it."

"The Hawaii Tropical Botanical Garden is a museum of living plants in a forty-acre valley with a collection over two thousand species representing more than one hundred and twenty-five families and seven hundred and fifty genera," Kate says, reading the garden's website description on her smartphone.

"Sweetheart, we'll get there soon enough. You're missing the beauty of the Hamakua Coast. This is one of the most scenic drives ever," insists Kai as they drive down lush Highway 19.

"You're right. I'll put away the electronics." Kate places her phone in her handbag on the car seat. "Let's just enjoy the experience."

"You're like a kid in a candy shop."

"Woo-hoo! Gimme some of that candy!" yells Kate at the top of her lungs, playfully stretching out her arms as if to gather the good vibes.

After passing through the archway of the impressive botanical garden entrance, Kate and Kai meander down the 500-foot long elevated boardwalk into a narrow ravine bordered by the most fantastic foliage Kate has ever seen. Towering, majestic bamboos stand beside colorful ginger plants with their yellow, rust and red hues. There are also elegant orchids in shades of purples, pinks and whites and exotic red heliconia with their lobster-claw leaves. It seems that every curve of the path brings them in contact with a bubbling brook, peeks of the ocean, awe-inspiring waterfalls, or families of the most exotic plants as far as the eye can see.

"Caw, caw," sound a pair of blue, red and gold macaws as Kate and Kai pass them on their stroll down the Orchid Garden path.

"Caw, caw," Kate returns the cry.

Kai marvels at the birds while Kate snaps a few shots. "I read that macaws can live for over a hundred years," she says.

The walk leads them to Lily Lake, which is surrounded by a bevy of lotus, ti plants, and other native species and abundant with water pools where multi-colored koi make their home.

After they pass through a forest of giant coconut palms, monkeypod trees, and over sixty different species of Indonesian ginger, Amazon lilies, Philippine orchids, and a beautiful array of bromeliads, they find themselves overlooking Onomea Bay.

Kai points and asks, "See those twin rocks over there at the head?"

Kate nods.

"Legend has it that one day the village chief of Kahali'i spotted boats he didn't recognize heading for their village. Fearing attack, two young lovers willing to sacrifice themselves for the good of the community agreed to stand guard over the shoreline. The following day, when the villagers went to the shore, there was no sign of the pair, only two new gigantic rock formations positioned side by side, jutting out into the bay's entrance. The rocks were positioned just so, causing such treacherous currents that no boat could pass. The villagers believe that the rocks were the young lovers, forever willing to stand guard and keep the village safe from future attacks."

"That's a horribly sad story." Kate frowns, disturbed by this tragic lover's tale.

"It's bittersweet," Kai admits. "However, the lovers stand together always, honored for protecting their family and friends. Don't worry, I promise you that we're not going to turn to stone, at least not today."

"Not funny!" Kate bats Kai playfully with the garden map.

On their ride back to the resort, Kate thumbs through her new tabletop book, purchased in the garden gift shop. "I'm so in love with the exotic plants we saw today, Kai. It would be great to have beauties like them in our little slice of paradise."

"You think so? Can I share something with you?"

Kate is all ears.

"You know how much I like to putter in the garden and grow avocados and all types of citrus?"

Kate nods.

"I've been thinking about something I'd like to do in our yard now. I want to plant a huge garden—flowers—like you just suggested— vegetables, herbs… Maybe we could even sell the produce at the local farmers' market."

"I'd love that," gushes Kate, excited at the prospect.

"Who knows. Maybe we could even supply The Plumeria Café."

"Yeah, we know a few folks there." Kate grins. "Will farming like that be too demanding, with your work at the hospital and all?"

"I can make it manageable … and if necessary, hire helpers. I've always wanted to grow my food. My culinary skills are, however …"

"Yeah, I know," Kate agrees and laughs out loud.

"Now that I have you, though, and the fact that you're such an *amazing* cook …"

Kate beams, enjoying the praise.

"I just started to think why not? If we grow food for ourselves, it really won't take that much more of an effort to do it on a small scale for farmers' markets and such, and I'd get so much pleasure out of it."

"It sounds like a great idea. You enjoy taking care of people and helping them with their health, and I write about eating fresh and natural and the benefits of farm to table. Gardening would be a nice adjunct to my writing and the organic produce to our meals."

The pair sits in silence for a couple of minutes, their minds swirling with ideas.

"Kai, do you think there might be some space in the garden for a gathering area?"

"You're thinking about the dream you had last night, aren't you?"

"It would be a wonderful entertainment space."

"I don't see why not. So you're in?"

"Nothing ventured, nothing gained," enthuses Kate before she leans over and plants a big kiss on Kai's lips.

The next day, visiting a local farmers' market in the heart of Kailua-

Kona, Kate and Kai, along with many locals and tourists, peruse scores of vendor booths that sit side by side in the eclectic outdoor space. The pair is bowled over by the bounty of locally grown produce, as well as the vast selection of arts and crafts, jewelry, and other local wares.

At one point, Kate holds up a bag of fresh mixed lettuces. "We could grow all types of organic greens and veggies, maybe even heirloom tomatoes and cucumbers."

"And fruits, too, like mango, pineapple ..." Kai trails off in thought.

Kate pays for the lettuce and puts it in the large cloth satchel slung over her shoulder that is already laden with other produce. Tonight, they've planned for a quiet, romantic dinner on their lanai.

"Certain vegetables grow well here. Others have to be planted a certain way because of the nematodes," Kai explains.

"Nematodes?" asks Kate, loading some mangos and avocados into her canvas tote.

"They're a kind of roundworm that can infiltrate the soil and destroy a harvest. So that's something we'll need to investigate."

"I'm sure there's a lot to learn, but I'm game."

"Here, try this." Kai picks up a juicy pineapple sample and pops it into Kate's mouth.

"Mmmm. It's sweet."

"It's Kona Sugarloaf, grown right here on the Big Island. They grow white pineapple on Kauai, too."

Kate picks up a brochure promoting a dinner benefiting Island farmers. "They're having a 'Taste of the Big Island' event tomorrow night. Want to go?"

"Sure. It's for a good cause, and I'd love to talk with some of the growers."

A series of long tables with white tablecloths, tropical floral arrangements, and flickering candles decorate the sizeable grassy yard of a macadamia-nut-and-coffee farm at the farmers' benefit the next evening. The picturesque dinner setup, which faces a stunning vista of the Pacific Ocean, is also home to one of the evening's hosts.

"The menu looks divine," Kate comments to Kai. "Fresh fruit

served in pineapple shell cups, organic wild green salad with heirloom tomatoes, pears, and candied macadamia nuts, followed by grilled opah with a mango and avocado salsa. The sides look amazing too: seasonal veggies and coconut rice. And for dessert, papaya coconut cream cake. Yummy!"

"Makes my mouth water just hearing you read the menu."

"Aloha!" Susan and Brent Thomas, a middle-aged couple, greet Kate and Kai as they sit down opposite them at one of the long tables.

As the couples get acquainted, servers distribute the fruit appetizers.

"These dinners are a real treat, and for a good cause—supporting our community of growers," Brent mentions, dipping into his fruit cup.

"Food grown in harmony with nature," Kai says, taking a line off the brochure. "I like the entire concept."

"It's much healthier and better for our environment to grow produce without using pesticides," comments Kate.

As the couples enjoy their first course, live slack-key guitar music starts to play.

"They always have great entertainment at these dinners," Susan comments, joining the conversation. "Sometimes it's Hawaiian slack-key guitar like tonight; other times, they host classical concerts, pop artists … it varies."

A few minutes later Kai and Kate clink wine glasses with each other and their new friends as the main course arrives. *Huli pau!*" says Kai.

"Cheers," Brent echoes.

"Ahh!" Kate takes a sip of her wine, a local varietal, leans back in her chair, and smiles with pleasure. She looks all around, admiring the gorgeous hues that have begun to appear in the darkening sky. "Another delicious dinner and picture-perfect sunset. I don't think I'll ever tire of spending evenings like this."

The next morning, rising early to the pleasant sounds of Hawaii creeper birds harmonizing outside their suite's open window, Kate slips out of bed as quietly as possible so as not to wake Kai. Their romantic honeymoon, the idyllic location, the excellent fresh food, and spending free, quality time together are a perfect recipe for happiness and contentment. For Kate, the energizing combination allows her to forgo her usual seven or eight hours of sleep.

She finds early mornings, while the rest of the world is either asleep or just rising, is a splendid time to write, as her mind is clear and open. The very thought of sitting down to a cup of Kona coffee on the lanai and pecking away on her laptop while the morning breezes dance through her hair serves as inspiration she can't ignore.

Kate is especially motivated to start writing since taking time off from her religiously scheduled two to three hours a day of allotted writing time due to all the wedding festivities. Now, as she sits down to work on her manuscript, with the painstakingly crafted, scene-by-scene breakdown next to the computer, the words flow as her fingers fly across the keyboard. A lover of mystery novels, Kate has finally decided to put herself on schedule to write one. And even though she knows what will happen from scene to scene, little ideas pop into her head as she writes, fueling the drama and intrigue of the story. Her book involves a family mystery, which takes place at a manor house in the English countryside. It's the in-between daily excursions and conversations with the characters in her novel that take her to places that are truly a surprise. She loves how conversations crop up unexpectedly. Before she knows it, two and a half hours swiftly fly by.

Just as she decides she's got to do something about her rumbling stomach, Kai, still sleepy-eyed, appears at the lanai's screen door. "Hey, pumpkin, what are you writing?" he asks incredulously before planting a quick kiss on her lips as he bends down to greet her.

"Working on my novel."

"On our honeymoon?"

"I take advantage when inspiration hits. I'm satisfied for today, however." Kate saves her work and powers down her computer. "Hungry?"

"Starving. Let's go grab a bite."

For their honeymoon days that follow, it's more of the wonderful same—swimming, snorkeling, lounging poolside, staying up late, sleeping in, taking in more of the historic sites, and alternating between dining out at local hot spots and grilling up homemade feasts.

"We'll come back," Kai promises. He squeezes Kate's hand when he notices how sad she looks gazing out the plane's window, watching the Big Island's coastline get smaller and smaller.

"It was a wonderful time. But the best part is I get to spend the rest of my life with you."

"Ditto," Kai says as he plants a big kiss on Kate's lips.

The Circle of Love
Nā Pīkake

Together we can do great things.

– Mother Teresa

3

"Aloha, girlfriend!" Cindy yells out to Kate. "You're gorgeous and glowing." When she reaches Kate, she gathers her into a big hug.

"Aloha, Cin," Kai says, kissing Cindy on the cheek.

"Speakin' of lookin' good." Cindy playfully gives a wolf whistle as she gives Kai, looking tan and buff, the once-over.

"Hey, I look good too, don't I?" brags Vinnie, showing off his physique. "I lost ten pounds!"

Cindy looks at Vinnie as if he's lost his marbles.

"I weighed myself this morning," says Vinnie defensively.

"Oh, well, I guess the donut diet is working its magic!" chirps Cindy.

"Let the barbs begin!" Kai laughs out loud. "Come, you two, our luggage awaits."

"I'm so glad you've been enjoying the cottage, Cin," Kate tells her friend as she unpacks her swollen suitcase that is lying on the master bedroom's king-size bed.

Cindy sits on an elegant upholstered bench nearby, watching. "It's better than I even dared dream," she replies.

"See, I told you," Kate says as she turns to hang some of her clothes in the closet.

"Vinnie is taken with it here too. He's already thinking about when we can make it back out again."

"Just say the word. *Mi casa es su casa.* Say, I'm a little thirsty. Want to join me in an iced tea or something?"

"Honey, it's five o' clock, and technically, we're both still on vacation. How about a drink-drink?" Cindy suggests, following Kate

63

into the kitchen.

"I like that logic. Chardonnay?"

"Now that's my girl."

As usual, the next morning Kate wakes before the rest of the house so she can write for a few hours. However, twenty minutes into her attempt, Kai wakes up for an early day in the ER, and she helps him gather his things for a quick dash out the door before returning to her desk.

Even though she's still on "official" vacation from her "day job" writing for *Simply Aloha Living* and *New York View Magazine*, she is determined to return to the promise she made to herself. Taking some time off for a wedding is one thing, but now that she's back home, and with a few hours to kill before Cindy and Vinnie rise, it's back to her daily routine. She pours herself a cup of coffee, grabs her computer from the kitchen counter, and heads out to the lanai table, intending to enjoy the sublime garden view as she writes.

Usually, if no one else is home or if she's working inside in her home office, Kate might play some soft music to transport her into the scenes of her book. This morning, however, which is still fresh and wet from the early rain, and with the sun just peeking out from behind the grayish clouds, she has a different kind of background "music" to enjoy: birds singing in the trees, trilling sweetly against the gentle rush of recycled water flowing through the garden's fountain.

Still, after reading over her work, Kate realizes that something feels off—she's strangely disconnected from the pages. She can't seem to access the necessary energy and mood that the writing requires. Trusting her instincts, she saves her manuscript and powers down the computer.

Maybe walking in nature will do the trick.

With that, Kate heads toward the beach to explore nature's beautiful gifts.

"How long have you been up?" asks Cindy several hours later when she sees Kate sitting at the cottage's lanai table.

"Got up at six o'clock, when Kai left."

"I'm impressed. How's the novel coming?"

Kate winces. "*Weeell.* I'm trying to keep to my twenty-pages-a-week commitment, but something isn't jelling this morning. I need to channel the right vibe."

"Maybe that vibe should be to just enjoy our last day of vacation together and truly vacate?"

"That's something my mother would say," Kate says with a chuckle. When she writes, especially, on mornings like this, thoughts of her mother drift through her mind. To make herself feel better and more peaceful, she'll talk to God and maybe go for a walk in the garden, taking her cup of ice tea, to share what's on her mind.

Suddenly, a cute little hummingbird buzzes around Kate and stops and stares right into her eyes. Kate is mesmerized.

Cindy's mouth drops open. "OMG!" she shrills. "That was amazing."

"Yup. Aloha, Mom," Kate says playfully. "I love it when this type of synchronistic event happens out of the blue."

"What do you mean?"

"Sometimes, when I think of Mom, something unusual happens." Kate begins to ponder the many examples. "You know that she loved to entertain and to bake, right?"

"Oh, yeah. I was definitely the beneficiary of many of her culinary goodies."

"Well, here's a funny example that happened while Kai and I were honeymooning. One morning I felt like making some of her banana bread. Mom had the most fantastic recipe."

"You wanted to bake on your honeymoon?"

"Yes. We had a great kitchen and lots of organic ingredients, so why not?"

"I can think of plenty of reasons why not, but go on."

"Besides, eating out every meal is tiring," continues Kate.

"A real tragedy," Cindy proclaims sarcastically.

"Cin," chuckles Kate. "Anyhow, I didn't have the recipe on my computer, because I keep those types of things in a zip drive at home. I even started to dial home to talk to Mom, and then I remembered … Shortly afterward, I started making a fruit salad."

"Geez, when I get up, I can barely manage to put a piece of bread in the toaster, and you're zooming around like Rachael Ray."

Kate laughs out loud then continues. "Anyway, I hear my cell phone ping and the screen lights up. When I pick up the phone on the kitchen counter, it's a text."

"And?"

"It's a recipe for banana bread."

"What?"

"You heard me."

"From where? From whom?"

"My sis, Carla."

"Are you kidding me?"

"No."

"Why? Had you asked her for the recipe?"

"No," chuckles Kate, shaking her head. "Carla just happened to be making banana bread that morning as well. She sent me the recipe, saying that she was thinking of Mom and me and didn't know if I had the recipe."

"Wow."

"Yeah, I know. I'm always totally amazed when things like that happen. It's such a treat."

"Okay, what else?"

"So many things ..." Kate trails off, remembering.

"Give me one more example, and then I'm going to faint if I don't have a cup of coffee."

"Come on, let's get you a cup. I can talk, walk, and pour coffee at the same time."

"Wonders never cease."

"Okay, here's one that pops into mind," adds Kate on their way into the kitchen. "After my mom passed, when Carla and I were running some errands, we began to reminisce, talking about how much we loved cooking with Mom, her energy, and the fact that as she got older she was just so sweet that you wanted to hug and kiss her all the time. Sometimes, we even used to call her 'Sweet Momma' or 'Mommydoo.' Well, around lunchtime, we began to look for a place to stop and have a bite. We couldn't seem to find anything. Then my sister spotted something that looked like a cute restaurant. Neither of us saw the name of the place until we pulled into the parking lot, and when we both read the restaurant sign, well ..." Kate pauses dramatically.

"So, okay … I'm on pins and needles. What was the name?"

"*Sweet Mama's … Good Kitchen*," Kate says. "Now that's synchronicity." Kate pauses. "Doesn't that describe my Mom to a T?"

"Ooooooh," croons Cindy with delight. "I love it!"

"And the image on the restaurant logo was this cute brunette lady with a short bob, you know, like a woman you'd see straight out of the nineteen fifties or sixties, wearing a pretty dress and a huge smile and holding a mixing bowl and spoon. I'm not kidding, that's just what she looked like back in the day. The restaurant was the type of place that serves delicious home-style cooking with an ambience that makes you feel like you're eating in someone's kitchen."

"Now that's really cool."

"When things like that happen, I just praise God."

Kate and Cindy pause for a moment.

"You know, since you're writing a mystery novel, maybe you should add some of these synchronistic elements that you experience," Cindy suggests. "Ever think of that?"

"Mmmm," hums Kate sing-song, nodding. "Not a bad idea."

"Come on, girlfriend, it's my last day. Let's you and me grab some breakfast and build more memories. Some retail therapy—that's what we need!"

"I'll take the framed print of the Hanalei Pier." Cindy points to the photo Kate took of the historic pier against a multi-colored sky.

The photo, surrounded by several other eye-grabbing images taken by Kate, hangs on the wall of The Princeville Art Gallery owned by Sukey and her husband, Kamal.

"Cindy, you don't have to buy one of my photos," whispers Kate under her breath.

"I love it, I want it, and as synchronicity would have it …" Cindy whips out a credit card from her wallet. "Vinnie gave me his American Express."

"Well, it's a great choice. It's by one of our local multi-talented artists." Sukey winks at Kate as she processes the order. "So what do you think of our beautiful home?"

Cindy nods. "This place has totally got it going on!"

"Cindy and Vinnie are headed back to New York tomorrow," interjects Kate. "However, I think she's still got a bit more shopping to do before she leaves."

"Oh, you got that right, girl! The day is young, and this card is gonna be smokin' by the time I'm finished." Cindy laughs out loud as she fans the plastic card through the air.

"Seriously, Cin?" whines Vinnie as he views the massive inventory of his wife's latest purchases. "We'll need to get an extra suitcase to pack all this stuff."

"Oh, sweetie, it isn't that much," she protests, but, busted, she winces when Vinnie's not looking.

"Come with me, handsome. I'll fix you a cocktail before dinner," coos Kate to sooth Vinnie's angst and to aid Cindy's rescue. She puts her arm around Vinnie's shoulder. "What can I get you?"

"What was that blue drink we had the other night? The one with pineapple juice?" Vinnie asks. He is still pouting but the offer of a drink is soothing him a little.

"Oh, a Blue Hawaiian. Sure, I'll make you one of those."

Cindy rolls her eyes playfully as Kate turns and winks at her.

"Kate, I love that little angel bench you picked up today at the art fair," Cindy acknowledges, looking in the direction of the plumeria trees where the pretty new garden addition sits.

"The bench does look inviting," Kate agrees. "Kai, what do you think?"

"I told you I like it, hon. It works," Kai yells as he and Vinnie tend to the fish on the grill. "Now we just have to figure out the garden design."

"It's so cool you'll be able to pick produce and flowers from your own garden—and just a few steps from your back door," Cindy comments as she lights the white votive candles in clear glass holders left over from the wedding reception.

"I told Kai I want to figure a way to make a few different entertainment spaces in the garden, too." Kate sets the table with beach-themed dinnerware: white plates decorated with rims of starfish and shells that she places on bamboo placemats.

"Well, this dining area is already fab. I'm sure whatever you guys add to it will make it even more so." Cindy places a spray of freshly cut tropical flowers on the table.

As the sun continues to descend on the horizon, Kai flicks on a light switch. Immediately, strings of white lights illuminate the tropical outdoor living space, creating a warm, romantic glow.

"Look!" shouts Vinnie as he peers out to Hanalei Bay. "The sky is changing colors again."

Strands of peach, yellow, pin, and purple hues change shape as they illuminate the sky. Finally, the sun slowly maneuvers between the clouds and descends on the horizon over the azure, still waters of the bay.

"I've got to get a shot of this," says Kate, excited, as she finishes tossing a large green salad with a lilikoi passion fruit vinaigrette and quickly picks up her camera.

"Kate, with all the photos you have of various sunsets, you'll have to put together a coffee-table book," Cindy chides as she pops an olive into her mouth from the crudité platter resting on the table.

"It's always a different show." Kate is all smiles as she snaps away on her digital camera. "Hey, let me take a shot of you and Vinnie against that backdrop."

"Now, Kai and Kate, it's your turn," says Vinnie as he relinquishes Kate of her camera to frame the perfect shot of his friends against the colorful horizon.

"Gorgeous!" exclaims Kate as she looks in the viewfinder at Vinnie's work.

"Okay, guys!" shouts Kai, holding a platter of the grilled Ono. "*E `ai kākou*! Let's eat!"

"Love you," Cindy says. Her eyes are moist as she hugs Kate the next day at Lihue Airport.

"We had a fantastic time. We wish you lots of love and happiness. Tell Kai again when he comes home from work," Vinnie adds and chokes back tears.

"Oh, don't cry, big guy." Kate reaches out and hugs Vinnie tightly.

"Vin, don't you dare start!" commands Cindy as she places her arms around both her husband and Kate. "We better stop or people will think we're weirdoes—which we are, of course." Cindy's self-deprecating humor instantly brightens everyone's mood. "What are those?" she inquires when Vinnie holds up some keys dangling on a chain.

"A set of keys for the ohana. Kate had Kai make them for us to surprise you."

"Mahalo!" sings Cindy as she squeezes Kate. "I'll FaceTime you when we get home, and we'll figure out a future visit on our calendars." She grabs Vinnie's arm and the pair head to the security clearance line. They wave to Kate and then disappear from view.

Knowing that she needs some ohana support today, Kate selects some melodic Hawaiian instrumentals from her phone's music library to stream on her car's Bluetooth and heads toward Hanalei where she's made plans to lunch with a few of her friends at The Plumeria Café.

4

Patrons fill the homey plantation-style café and sip on their lattes and other designer drinks while mingling around wooden tables positioned near rustic hutches decorated with sea art, tropical coffee mugs, bags of the café's signature coffee, and other gift items.

Kate waves to Malie, who's dressed in her typical work outfit—jeans, T-shirt and a thigh-length baker's apron in light beige. "Aloha, and welcome to The Plumeria Café," is silk-screened in the center of the apron in beautiful calligraphy interlaced with images of white plumeria blooms.

"Am I the first to arrive?" asks Kate, unable to see any of the gang inside. She kisses her sister-in-law Malie on the cheek.

"Everyone's out on the lanai. Go ahead. I'll be out in two seconds."

Jessie, a shy, sweet, attractive, fit woman somewhere in her mid-sixties, sets down a large glass pitcher of iced tea at the center of the table where Elaine, Olivia, Sukey, and Kate sit.

"Ladies, I'd like you to meet the café's newest addition, Jessie Andrews," Malie says and puts her arm around Jessie.

"How are you enjoying your new ohana?" Elaine inquires after a round of introductions. "I helped Jessie secure her rental, a guest ohana on a large Hanalei estate," she tells the others.

"The *ohana*?" Jessie is puzzled for a moment. "Oh, the *guesthouse*. I have to keep up with my Hawaiian words now that I'm a local."

"It can be confusing, especially when so many Hawaiian words have more than one meaning," Sukey tells her. "Take ohana for instance. Generally, it means "family," and that includes extended family who aren't necessarily related by blood. But it can also mean a guesthouse, one that's separate from the main house—like the one you're renting."

"Where are you from originally?" Kate inquires.

"I, um, I moved here from Michigan a few weeks ago," Jessie answers shyly. When she sees the surprise in everyone's eyes, she quickly responds, "I know, it's a long way away."

"Jessie needed a change of pace and scenery, right?" offers Elaine.

"My husband and I used to love to visit the Hawaiian Islands, especially in the winter to get away from the snow and the cold. We always felt it was our special place, so, I ... when he ..." Jessie stalls and nervously coughs, clearing her throat. "He passed away not too long ago."

Almost in unison the group begins to offer their condolences.

"Thank you. Uh, mahalo. When my husband passed, well, I just felt that I needed a little something special in my life, so I moved here."

Olivia nods. "We hear you, sister."

"Have you had a chance to look at the menu yet?" Jessie politely changes the subject with pen and pad in hand. "Kate?"

"The garden salad with grilled salmon for me, with the citrus dressing on the side, mahalo."

"Make that two," Olivia adds.

"The Nicoise salad with the seared tuna *pour moi*," blurts Elaine dramatically as Jessie proceeds to take the rest of the orders.

"Hey, ladies, how about an appetizer of fresh chopped veggies with a trio of hummus?" suggests Malie. "The hummus recipes come courtesy of Kate and are exclusive to the café."

Jessie takes note of the group's enthusiastic responses and heads back into the restaurant to place the orders.

"She seems lovely," comments Kate.

"She's a gem ... always on time, courteous, and willing to go the extra mile. I think we lucked out with her," Malie tells the group.

"I'm so glad you called us gals to get together, Kate," Elaine announces mid-lunch. "It's great when we party with our men, but sometimes, we need to talk to friends about women things. Know what I mean? Shopping, fashion, world events, romance ... men, manicures, pedicures, aging, anti-aging ... *men* ... not all necessarily in that order."

"It is fun, isn't?" Malie agrees, chuckling.

"I'm glad the show's on hiatus so I could join you all," Olivia adds with a smile. "In fact, now that I have some free time, I almost don't know what to do with myself."

"I doubt you'll let much dust settle under your feet," quips Elaine.

"You're right. Olivia's already planning …" Malie pipes up. "Oops, care to share Olivia?"

"I'm working with my company to launch a new lifestyle magazine."

"Do you have a name for your magazine?" asks Sukey amidst all the excitement at Olivia's news.

"*Olivia!*" Olivia announces, throwing her arms up in the air in the traditional "ta-dah" gesture.

"Well, I think we know someone at this table who'll be quite an asset to your editorial staff." Sukey looks in Kate's direction.

"I've already thought of that," Olivia says. "And she's on board."

Kate smiles broadly.

"Us ladies getting together like this reminds me of when I was a kid. I used to go with my Italian Grandma Mary to her 'club night,' as she would call it," remembers Kate. "She and her women friends met once a month for a few hours to eat and play bridge or some board game. They talked about all kinds of things. Although whenever they shared things they didn't want me to hear, it was always in Italian."

"Why don't we all form a 'club' of sorts?" offers Olivia. "That way we'll make sure we get together at least once a month—and don't worry, Kate, we won't speak in Italian."

"Only Hawaiian!" Malie laughs, with the other ladies joining in.

"Fabulous idea, daaahling," trills Elaine.

"So, when we get together, should we meet for lunch? Dinner? Here? Where do you think?" asks Sukey.

"Lunch or dinner once a month works for me," comments Kate.

All the ladies nod in agreement.

"Maybe for some of our get-togethers, we could do a spa day or go shopping," adds Sukey.

"Yeah, mix it up," agrees Olivia.

"Okay, so if we're a 'group,' are we going to have a particular name we call ourselves?" Sukey, as always, is the businesswoman and planner.

"Name ourselves?" Malie thinks out loud. "Now that could be

fun!"

"We don't have to decide right now," comments Kate after a few moments of silence. "Let's just set a date for our next 'official' get-together, and we can come up with some ideas between now and then."

"Olivia, what happens when you're done with your hiatus and have to tape in New York?" asks Sukey, taking a sip of her drink.

"I might miss a few get-togethers. However, another FYI—we're planning to film the show here a lot next season. And since I have an in with the producer..." Olivia winks.

"Works for me," Sukey says with a smile. "How about the third Wednesday of every month? Does that work for everyone?"

All of the ladies pull out their phones to check their calendars—and agree. It's set.

The next morning as Kate jogs down Weke Road toward the pier, she notices a gray mist grappling with the sun over who dominates the morning sky. Only slight rays of light have been allowed to peek through the thick blanket of haze, which comfortably covers the quiet town. Earthy scents from the early morning rain permeate Kate's senses.

I love this time of day.

A gentle breeze rolls by and sweeps through Kate's hair. Suddenly, a pair of sea birds fly past Kate and land just a tad in front of her. They proceed to watch intently as she draws closer to the pier.

"Aloha." Kate greets the birds as if she were welcoming members of her ohana.

She makes a left around a grouping of trees and soaks in the vast expanse of the Hanalei Pier, which juts out into the water some 340 feet. At the pier's end is a roofed structure where locals and visitors often snap photos or take in nature's magnificence. At this early hour, however, Kate is alone in the morning's stillness.

The site of the exquisite pier and the majestic, lush mountains that surround the bay never cease to thrill her. She pulls her smartphone out of her waist pack to snap a few more memorable scenes to add to her collection then jogs for another hour before heading home. Today, it will be the usual routine—shower and dress, then breakfast at her computer, where she'll work on her novel for two or so hours before tending to the tasks required by her magazine jobs.

At about six o'clock that evening, satisfied with what she's accomplished for the day, Kate heads to the kitchen to prepare a simple dinner. She clicks the TV remote and sets the volume to low and then proceeds to gather the ingredients she'll need.

First, she places several peeled and sliced garlic cloves on an aluminum-foil-covered cookie sheet. She drizzles some extra virgin olive oil over the garlic and places a lovely piece of fresh wild salmon on top. Rows of sliced lemons in the shape of half-moons decorate the center of the fish, followed by sprigs of fresh dill all over the top.

Opening a bottle of chardonnay, Kate pours a half cup or so around the edges of the salmon, then proceeds to fold the large piece of exposed tin foil into a hut over the fish, carefully crimping the sides of the foil down on either side of the salmon with her fingers. She leaves a small opening at the front end of the tray for heat to circulate while dinner bakes in a preheated oven set to 400 F.

During the twenty-five or so minutes it will take the fish to bake, she prepares a spinach salad with diced Roma tomatoes, red onion, diced sweet apples, cranberries, and candied walnuts. Next, she makes her citrus vinaigrette in the Cuisinart and warms up some leftover Broccolini, cauliflower, taro, and sweet potatoes.

To some this feast might seem complicated after a long day's work. However, in reality the preparation is quite simple, and Kate finds cooking an excellent way to relax after a long day in front of the computer. She also knows that when Kai gets home, they'll both be able to connect over a delicious, healthy dinner—the thought of which puts a broad smile on her face.

With the salmon in the oven and everything else as ready as it can be, she glances at the clock: 6:30. *Kai should be home any minute.*

With a few minutes to spare, Kate heads to the master bath to freshen up.

"The salmon melted in my mouth," Kai compliments Kate and squeezes her hand on their now-customary after-dinner walk toward the Hanalei Pier. "As your dad would say …"

"Fit for a king!" Kate finishes Kai's sentence.

The two lovers set a leisurely pace on their jaunt down Weke Road. As always Kate is wearing her camera around her neck in anticipation of the evening's light show.

She and Kai swing their clasped hands as they walk down the long pier that juts out into the bay, and upon reaching the end, Kai stops, turns to Kate, and kisses her lips with exquisite tenderness.

"What?" Kai asks when they finally come up for air and he sees Kate wearing a huge grin.

"I was thinking about our first official date—when you took me boating and snorkeling, wearing the sexy board shorts you have on now … and nothing else."

"Oh, okay. I see where your mind's going," Kai answers with a mischievous grin.

Kate squeals like a schoolgirl as Kai playfully pokes her in the ribs and starts to tickle her. When she finally breaks free, she runs back down the pier toward the beach, beckoning him to run after her.

"Oh, so that's how it's going to be?"

"Hah!" Kate screams and laughs as Kai chases after her on the sandy beach.

"Please stop … or you'll be sorry," Kate cries, but Kai gently tackles her to the ground and continues to tickle her. And despite her protests, he doesn't let up. "My dinner might end up all over you," she threatens with a laugh.

Kai heeds the warning, and shaking with laughter, he releases Kate and helps her stand.

"I love you sooo much!" Kate tells him with a grin.

"I love you too."

The lovers embrace again, and when they part, Kate notices that the sky has begun to turn. "Kai, look!" she exclaims. She grabs the camera case, which is lying next to them in the sand, and whips out her camera.

As Kate photographs the multicolored sky from various angles, clouds begin to form in what appears to be the shape of a flying angel. "Kai!"

"I know. I see it!"

"That's two cloud angels in a little over two weeks!"

"Somehow that doesn't surprise me." Kai smiles, enamored with the sky ... and with his wife.

"Olivia, it's me," Kate speaks into the intercom located at the driveway entrance to Olivia's gated estate. It is the first official lady's night.

"Buzzin' ya up now, doll."

Kate drives through the two, large, custom-built, elegant, black wrought-iron gates poised between a set of massive lava-rock columns and proceeds up the windy paved road which leads to Olivia's front door. She never tires of the lush surroundings, always finding something new to appreciate; today, it's the abundant and colorful yellow kahili ginger with its red stamen that seem to stand at attention among the imposing, prolific greenery.

"Hello, Ruby!" Kate greets the towering Royal Poinciana tree with an umbrella of crimson blossoms as she parks near Olivia's front door.

"You said you were just going to bring a salad!" Olivia playfully chides as she helps Kate retrieve two large bags from the car's trunk.

"Guilty as charged," Kate admits. "But it's just a few healthy eats."

"You shouldn't have, but of course I'm glad you did." Olivia relieves Kate's arms of one of the overflowing bags.

The two women enter the impressive foyer where the lush tropical foliage from the outside carries through onto the walls of the home's sizeable, circular entryway. Rich koa wood lines the vaulted, beamed ceilings, and dark wood floors complement the white-paneled entryway that is decorated with exquisite hand-painted murals depicting island people in tropical settings. The sounds of trickling water emanating from two stunning, floor-to-ceiling fountains that grace either side of the foyer enhance the serene ambience.

The L-shaped kitchen and great room exude a welcome, warm, beachy vibe, and an impressive, all-glass, retractable wall offers a million-dollar view of the ocean framed by the estate's expertly manicured and maintained grounds.

"Aloha!" Elaine, Sukey, and Malie greet Kate. They are sitting on overstuffed sofas amidst an eclectic, casually elegant blend of hand-painted tables, chairs, and hutches in calming hues.

Kate and Olivia deposit the shopping bags on the massive center island in Olivia's gourmet kitchen. The island, surrounded by a series of high-back wicker chairs, is laden with a variety of appetizers, salads, a large pitcher of iced tea, and bottles of chilled wine in silver ice buckets.

"Daaahling, grab something to drink and join us," commands Elaine as Olivia motions to Kate that she'll take care of things in the kitchen.

Just as Kate is about to take a seat, Jessie enters from the hallway.

"I thought Jessie would be a great addition to our group," Malie tells Kate as they all sit on the sofas and chairs surrounding a koa-wood coffee table.

"Being invited tonight means a lot to me," confesses Jessie.

"Olivia was gracious enough to introduce me to the group when I first arrived too," Kate says with a smile. "They're a great bunch."

"Olivia, stop fussing in there. Sit!" Malie yells out.

"Okay, okay, I'm coming!" Olivia quickly finishes laying out Kate's dishes on the kitchen counter and joins her friends.

"For our first 'official' club night, ladies, I want to share some names I've been pondering for our group," begins Elaine.

"I jotted down some names too," Kate says, jumping up to retrieve her purse from the kitchen counter.

"Me too," adds Malie, pulling out her smartphone.

"Me three," Olivia joins in as she fetches her list from the kitchen desk. "Elaine, why don't you start."

"Okay. 'The Golden Goddesses' is one name I came up with."

"Not bad, but isn't the term 'goddess' a little overused these days?" asks Sukey.

"I don't know, I kind of like being thought of as a goddess," Elaine replies with a shrug. "But okay, here's another. It's the name of a song from one of my favorite musicals, 'Company.' What do you think of 'The Ladies Who Lunch?'"

Malie shakes her head disapprovingly. "I think that song mocks women who sit around doing nothing."

"Geez, you ladies are a tough crowd," whines Elaine.

"What about the ladybugs or soul sisters?" reads Olivia from her list.

"Cute," comments Elaine.

"They're fun names," Kate agrees. "But what about choosing a Hawaiian name?"

"Duh," Olivia admonishes herself. "You're right … a Hawaiian name. Does anyone have a Hawaiian word on their list?"

"What about a flower of some kind, like a gardenia—*kiele* in Hawaiian," offers Sukey.

"I was also thinking along the lines of a flower," adds Kate. "What about *pīkake*—the fragrant flower used to make leis?"

"Pee-kaw-kay," Jessie repeats, sounding it out. "What does it mean?"

"It's a climbing jasmine," Malie replies. "In Hawaiian it also means peacock. Pīkake leis are usually worn on special events to represent eternal love and aloha."

"On our honeymoon Kai mentioned pīkake was a favorite flower of Hawaii's Princess Ka'iulani, and that she gave the flower that name because of the peacocks that roamed in the jasmine bushes. She loved them both."

"I like the sound of that word … and the sentiment it evokes," Sukey says with a nod. "How about it, ladies?"

"Works for me!" Olivia concurs. "What say y'all—do we agree on pīkake?"

"Pīkake!" the other ladies shout as they pronounce the happy, energetic-sounding word.

"The word *nā* in Hawaiian is for the plural meaning, so we could call ourselves *Nā Pīkake*," explains Malie.

"Anyone object or have any other ideas?" inquires Olivia.

The ladies shake their heads.

"I nominate we use the term Nā Pīkake for our group," says Elaine.

"I second that," says Kate, raising her hand.

The other ladies follow suit.

"We could even make ourselves a logo … maybe a pretty grouping of pīkake buds or a pīkake lei with a nice treatment of the name next to it. Want me to work on coming up with some designs for our next meeting?" inquires Kate.

"Sure." "Great." "Go for it," the ladies respond.

"Now for our first item of business. I have a serious problem," laments Elaine dramatically. "My hairdresser is moving to Maui. I don't know how I'll survive. Can anyone *puleeze* make a recommendation?"

The ladies, who all have recommendations, burst out in laughter as they dive in on the potluck buffet.

"I'm fading." Elaine yawns as the clock approaches midnight. "I hate to be a party pooper, but I have quite the busy day tomorrow with a new open house, and I just know that Trevor's anxiously waiting up for me."

"He is?" asks Sukey.

"*Not!* He's probably sound asleep with the telly still playing."

"So, ladies, it's agreed. Another get together a month from today, at my place?" Malie's announcement is greeted with enthusiastic responses as the ladies bid each other goodnight.

"Mahalo for taking me home," Jessie tells Kate on their drive back to Hanalei.

"We live right near each other, so no problem at all."

"Your friends are a great group."

"Told you. You haven't seen anything yet. It was tame tonight."

"I appreciate everyone bringing me into the fold."

"I was in your shoes not too long ago," remembers Kate. "On my first trip to Kauai, I was on assignment to interview Olivia for *New York View Magazine*. Right after that interview, my life changed. I broke up with a man I thought I was going to marry, and several months after that my mother passed away."

"I'm sorry."

"I met up with Olivia in New York just after that article was published. When she saw how badly I needed a timeout, she offered me an opportunity to stay at the cottage where Kai and I live now. My husband grew up in that house, but after Kai's mother died, his father,

Bradford, decided to make it a rental. Olivia had gifted some friends a vacation there. However, when they had to cancel, she offered it to me as a place to relax and regroup, and it was just what I needed. I fell in love with the cottage at first sight, and since Kai feels the same way about it as I do, we chose to make it our home after we married."

"How did you meet your husband?"

"At one of Olivia's parties. But we didn't start dating until my second trip. I stayed at the cottage then, too. One thing led to another, and that was it."

"It was meant to be."

Kate nods. "That's exactly right."

"I love how God works," Jessie says before becoming a little preoccupied. "When I met you at the café, I mentioned that my husband passed not too long ago."

"Yes, I'm sorry for your loss, as well. I hope I'm not overstepping, but was your husband sick?"

"No." Jessie shakes her head. "He was in wonderful health. It was a car accident. A truck ran a red light and broadsided him." Jessie gulps at the memory. "I'm told he died instantly."

Moved, Kate reaches over and squeezes Jessie' hand, a gesture Jessie appreciates. "It's tough to lose the ones we love," Kate says with a sigh.

"It's hard when you're not prepared—if you ever can be when your world gets rocked. You know, after my husband passed, my friends told me not to do anything drastic in my life—like sell our house, change jobs, that sort of thing. So for the first ten months, I didn't change a thing. Then one morning I woke up, and I can't explain it, but I had an overwhelming desire to change *everything*. Since Peter was in my heart, I knew I was free to move should I choose. We had no children, and both our parents had passed. Peter's brother and a sister live in Maine, and my sister and her husband live in Florida, but neither place felt completely right for me. So as I began to think more and more about where I wanted to go, I remembered where, other than home, we were the most happy. Hawaii." Jessie smiles at the memory. "In truth it could have been any one of the islands. But our last few vacations were on Kauai, so I came here."

"That makes perfect sense. Were you always a waitress?"

"Oh, no." Jessie laughs out loud. "I was an accountant. My husband and I both were. We had our own company, and luckily, we did extremely well." When Kate shoots Jessie a questioning look, Jessie continues. "I know what you're probably thinking. Why am I working at The Plumeria Café as a waitress?"

Kate nods.

"I don't have to work. I just wanted to try something out of my comfort zone. I thought it might be a good way to get out there and meet people, if even just for a while."

"You're something, you know that," Kate says sincerely, impressed by Jessie. "Very brave."

"Mahalo. Take a right turn at the next block." Jessie points the way.

"You're a hop, skip and jump away from where we live on Weke Road."

"Take another turn right here."

Kate drives slowly down a sweet cul-de-sac.

"I live in the ohana behind this main house right here." Jessie points to a charming, plantation-style home surrounded by tall palms that are illuminated by the car's headlights. When the car stops, she gets out and starts toward the long drive. "Aloha," she calls over her shoulder.

"See you soon," Kate promises and waits until Jessie disappears from view before pulling away. On her drive home she can't stop thinking about her new friend's story; she can empathize with that type of pain.

Jessie puts up a good front, but I can see a deep sadness in her eyes. I'm sure she's doing whatever she can to stay emotionally above water. I hope she gets to a place where she can find peace.

Kate says a prayer asking God to send Jessie some solace as she undresses for bed. Slipping under the covers next to Kai minutes later, she wraps her arms tightly around his waist.

"Hey, babe," moans Kai, half asleep as he turns toward Kate.

"Hi, pumpkin." Kate plants a quick kiss on Kai's lips before he settles back into slumber. With the moonlight streaming through the semi-open shutters, Kate watches him sleep peacefully, and as she does, she thinks of Jessie and her loss, which only calls her to recognize what a gift life is.

Thank you, God, for Kai. Please bless us so that we may have a long, happy, fruitful, loving life.

The Storm

God moves in a mysterious way,
His wonders to perform.
He plants his footsteps in the sea,
and rides upon the storm.

–William Cowper,
18th Century English poet and hymnodist

5

A menacing blast of wind pierces an open window, causing a pair of sheer curtains decorating them to fly about in a frenzy.

The disruptive, howling jolts awake a peacefully sleeping African-American teenage girl. As she gets up and attempts to close the window, a dark figure steps out of the shadows and violently pushes her back down on the bed.

The girl's mouth drops open in shock, but no sound is released.

The imposing perpetrator, dressed all in black, with gloves on his hands and a black ski mask covering his face, swiftly moves to straddle her. "You're going to do what I say," he growls in a harsh whisper. Placing one large hand around the girl's neck and pointing a razor-sharp knife directly at her throat with the other, he adds, "Or else you'll die. *Understand?*"

The terrified teen nods her head in agreement.

Satisfied that she's complying, the intruder puts down the knife and pulls a roll of duct tape out of his jacket pocket. He rips off a swatch and roughly slaps it over the girl's mouth, muffling her cries.

"Shut up!" the attacker snarls. He smacks her across the face as she begins to moan behind the tape. Next, he ties her hands to opposite bedposts.

Knife back in hand, the man violently rips at her clothes with his blade as the girl continues to shake and whimper in fear. "Quiet!" he orders, giving her another hard slap.

Her protests now silent, the only noise in the room is an ominous jangle as the man unclasps his belt buckle.

Kate bolts awake from her dream with a loud yelp, waking Kai.

"What is it?"

"I had another dream about an attack on a young girl. It was terrifyingly real."

"Not the same dream you had the night before our wedding?"

"No." Kate shakes her head.

"Do you know who the girl is?"

"I have no idea … but this time the girl was younger, a teenager. The man who was attacking her wasn't the same either. This guy was massive and wearing a ski mask over his head, so I couldn't see his face. It was like before. I could see what was going on, but they couldn't see me and I couldn't do anything to stop it."

"Come here," says Kai as he envelops Kate with his arms. He glances over at the digital clock on the nightstand. It's 6:10 a.m.

"I don't think I can get back to sleep," gulps Kate, her mouth dry.

"I have to get up soon. Want to have a coffee with me before I leave for work?"

Kate nods and Kai kisses her forehead.

An hour or so later, with Kai off to work, Kate takes her usual morning jog along the beach and pier. As she does, her thoughts drift back to her disturbing dream and she desperately tries to extrapolate some meaning from it.

The room.

In her dream the room was dim and shadowy, which made it all the more ominous.

The night table lamp. The bed's headboard and the room's coloring. Where have I seen them before?

A few seconds later, Kate stops in her tracks.

Olivia's bedroom? No. It can't be. Besides, it was a teenage girl.

Stop it, Kate! Stop thinking about that horrible dream. Shake it off and get on with your morning run on this stellar day.

Kate heeds her internal pep talk and makes a conscious effort to breathe in the sweetness, light, and beauty of her surroundings. After several minutes of this, she is keenly aware of feeling infinitely better. Glad to be free of the oppressive thoughts, she heads home, where she intends to reward herself with a healthy breakfast and a cup of cinnamon chai tea.

Showered and changed into a comfortable, knee-length jersey skirt and tank top, Kate flops down on the great room couch with her tea and a fruit-and-yogurt parfait. She clicks the television remote to the local news, capturing a story in progress.

"Police are looking for a suspect in the attack of a local woman early this morning in Hanalei. At present, all that is known is that the man is described as white, tall, approximately one hundred and fifty pounds, with long, stringy, dirty-blonde hair. He's thought to be in his late twenties or early thirties. He was wearing jeans and a white T-shirt at the time of the attack. The woman, whose name is being withheld, sustained only a few bruises."

Another attack? Kate clicks off the TV when the news story ends. *I wonder if they're related?* She shakes her head in disgust, remembering the home invasion she heard about the day after her wedding, and then turning her thoughts to her recent nightmares.

Okay, enough. Time to get to work.

As soon as she enters her home office, she is greeted by a large, open, creative space. The tall ceilings are supported by wooden beams and the large window opens to an expansive view of the ocean and garden. The room, filled with natural light, is warm and inviting. Floor-to-ceiling, white, wooden bookshelves, filled with great reads, sentimental memorabilia, and a variety of photos depicting happy times with family and friends, line the walls of her little corner of the world. Kate's expertly framed nature photography hangs on the walls. Colorful, tropical, nature-inspired, hand-painted, multi-drawer cabinets and hutches are filled with more books, papers, and work-related items.

Walking between the slipcovered sofa and wooden coffee table, Kate heads toward the French doors, which lead to a small lanai surrounded by lush foliage. She opens the screened doors wide to allow the crisp morning air to fill the room and then heads over to her white antique desk. Its position takes full advantage of the picturesque view out the window. Kate sits on her comfortable, mesh office chair, places her tea to one side of her computer, and powers up her laptop. She notices the time: eight o'clock. Her first order of business for the day is her novel. She'll write without interruption for a minimum of two hours, after which she'll work on her magazine assignments. If all goes according to plan, she'll head over to The Plumeria Café to meet Olivia for lunch at one o'clock. They'll brainstorm ideas for her new magazine then she'll head back to her home office to complete the rest of her agenda, calling it quits around 6:30—leaving plenty of time to whip up dinner for Kai before he gets home.

She lights an aromatic candle scented with ylang-ylang and myrrh and plays a track of nature sounds while she works. Taking heed of Cindy's comment to incorporate examples of synchronicity into her plot, she rearranges her outline until she is pleased with the direction. With a renewed sense of purpose, she begins to write, only lifting her head from the computer when the preset alarm on her cell phone rings, indicating it's time to head to the café.

"In addition to writing feature stories for my magazine, *Olivia!*, I think I might want you to write a food and recipes section entitled ..." Olivia stops as she gazes, wide-eyed, around the cozy eatery.

"The Plumeria Café?" intuits Kate.

"Touché! I'd love for you to contribute some of your culinary confections to that section, just like you do for the actual café," Olivia continues.

"What fun!"

"It's a deal then?"

"It's a deal!" confirms Kate.

After the energizing lunch break, Kate, back at her desk, picks up her work where she left off.

"Aloha," Kate answers her cell when it chimes several hours later.

"It's me, hon," answers Kai. "One of the other docs on call is sick, so I have to pick up the slack tonight. I won't be home until really late.

Probably after midnight. 'K?"

"Okay, sweetie." Kate is used to fluctuations in her husband's schedule by now.

"Don't wait up. But I might wake you up when I get home," Kai says in a low, sensual voice. "I'm missing you so much today. I'd love to hold you in my arms and kiss you right now."

Kate is delighted at his words. "I love you," she whispers.

"Me too. To the moon and beyond."

Kai blows a kiss into the phone, which Kate reciprocates. "Aloha. I'll see you tonight," she says, ending the call.

An hour or so later, after wrapping up her work, Kate's internal clock cues her that it's time for dinner. She heads toward the kitchen and peruses the shelves of the fridge for inspiration, finally settling on leftover lentil soup, a large green salad and a chunk of her yummy cornbread, which she enjoys out on the lanai.

To fill her evening after dinner, she heads to the beach by the Hanalei Pier. Drinking in the multi-colored sunset, she chooses to take a few minutes for an impromptu tête-à-tête with God. When she finally returns to the cottage, she decides to forgo watching television, opting to spend the night with a good book.

A lover of fiction, Kate searches the cottage's great-room shelves for some recent purchases and settles on *The White Queen*, a historical novel by best-selling author Philippa Gregory. Pulling the book free from where it is sandwiched tightly between another book and an *object d'art* bookend, Kate reads the back cover. It tells her that Elizabeth Woodville, the main character, is a commoner who ascends to British royalty in the fifteenth century. She is forced to fight for the survival of her family and becomes embroiled in a still-unsolved mystery involving her two sons, known as the "Princes in the Tower."

"Perfect!" Kate declares, heading toward the master bedroom. When Kai works late like this, she loves to sprawl out in the comfort of their bed to either watch television or read until the wee hours.

6

A ferocious wind bellows through the master bedroom's open window, causing the sheer curtains framing them to fly in a panic.

Moments later, a peacefully sleeping Kate is jolted awake by the howl of the wind. As she slips out from under the covers to close the window, a tall, dark figure steps out of the shadows and pushes her violently back down on the bed.

"Stop! NO!" cries Kate as the perpetrator, a disheveled man with long, stringy hair and wild eyes, swiftly moves to straddle her.

"You sure are pretty," the man croaks with a deranged smile as he tries to kiss and grope his prey. "Wanna have some fun?" he asks, pressing his face into hers. His noxious, liquor-drenched breath almost causes her to faint.

"Wait! Stop!" cries Kate in distress as she wrestles with her attacker.

How did he get into the house?

As she continues her fight, eerily acknowledging the scene is unfolding like her dreams, she spies a large slit roughly cut down the middle of the open French doors' mesh screen.

"We're going to play hard to get, are we?" The man slurs his words as his grasp around Kate's arms tightens.

"Ow! Please stop, you're hurting me," implores Kate.

Get to the door! Kate hears her mother's voice command inside her head as she struggles with her attacker.

Instinctively, without even understanding why she utters the words she does, Kate boldly announces, "Wait! It's cold. If we're going to get undressed, let me close the door."

"Okay," mumbles her attacker, taken aback by Kate's sudden change in demeanor.

Kate calmly walks to the French doors, acting as if she's going to pull them shut, only to suddenly hurl herself through the tear in the mesh.

"Help! Help!" Her blood-curdling screams pierce the dark, still night as she tumbles onto the ground. Powered by adrenalin, she leaps to her feet and runs away as fast as she can.

Glancing over her shoulder, Kate sees her attacker push through the screen door and scurry off in the opposite direction, clearly aiming to put some distance between himself and his hysterical victim whose cries have begun to wake up the neighborhood.

"Is there anything else you can tell me about him?" asks Alana, the forty-something uniformed officer who questions Kate a short while later. Alana, sister to Aukai, Malie's husband, is especially doting on Kate.

"No, I can't think of anything."

"Kate!" Kai calls out as he runs through the front door and makes a beeline for his wife.

"Oh, Kai."

"I'm so sorry," moans Kai, holding Kate tightly.

"I've checked all the doors and windows several times, and we're locked up like Ft. Knox." Kai's face shows his concern.

"Honey, come to bed and hold me," Kate whispers.

Kai dims the attractive, hibiscus night lamp near the bedside to low, then switches off the overhead lights. The lamp's illumination enfolds the room in a warm, comforting, gold-orange glow. Then Kai envelops Kate with his arms as she nestles into his chest. He strokes her hair tenderly.

After silently saying a prayer and thanking God for His protection, Kate can't help but rerun the attack in her mind until she makes a forceful, conscious choice to put the negative thoughts aside. She kisses Kai several times on the chest, cheeks, and lips in gratitude. "Oh, honey, I'm okay," comforts Kate. Her loving, tender action prompts Kai to choke back a wave of unexpected tears. He is overwhelmed by thoughts of what might have been. "I should have been home tonight."

"You had to take that extra shift. We didn't know this would happen."

"But it did," whispers Kai. He continues to stroke her hair, and after he clears his throat of emotion, he admits, "I thank God you're okay. I don't know what I'd do if you weren't."

Kate turns on her side and eases back onto Kai's chest. Spent from the emotionally charged evening, it doesn't take her long to drift into a sound sleep. For Kai, however, it will be a sleepless night as he keeps a watchful eye and continues to process what has transpired.

"It looks much worse than it feels." Kate manages a weak smile as she greets Olivia and Malie at her cottage door the following afternoon. There's a small bandage over Kate's left brow, and the marks on her sleeveless arms are various shades of yellow and purple.

"We're glad you were up for some lunch," Malie says by way of greeting as she hands Kate a wicker basket filled with goodies from The Plumeria Café. "Is Kai home?"

"Still sleeping," answers Kate as they all walk toward the kitchen. "He fell asleep when I got up this morning. Can I get you two anything to drink?"

"Here, let me take that," commands Malie, relieving Kate of the basket. "Why don't you and Olivia go out onto the lanai? I'll bring us out something to eat and iced teas."

"Are you really okay?" Olivia asks Kate as they make their way through the glass slider.

"I was scared and shaken, but I'm okay now," Kate assures her friend. "This neighborhood is normally very safe." The welcome serenity of the tall greenery on their property, and the host of flowering plants with inviting colors and textures provides a calming atmosphere.

"I know you told your brother and sister. What about your dad?"

"I decided not to tell him," reveals Kate. "It would worry him too much, and my dad's got a lot on his plate right now. He's still grieving for my mom, and I don't want to cause him any stress when he's so far away."

Olivia nods understandingly, and as she does, Kate catches her eye. Mixed with compassion, she also sees something else: fear.

"Are you alright?" asks Kate.

"Yeah, I'm fine," says Olivia, none too reassuringly. "Just trying to process," she continues, hugging her mid-section.

Kate isn't buying Olivia's answer. She knows Olivia well enough not to press the issue but makes a mental note of the response.

Breaking the tension, Malie arrives with a plateful of wrap sandwiches and three, green iced teas.

During lunch, the conversation turns to more pleasant happenings, but even so, Olivia's energy is different. Although Kate well knows how empathetic Olivia is, she can't help but wonder just what's on her friend's mind.

"Well, ladies, I'm going to have to head back to the café," says Malie a few hours later. She gives Kate a goodbye hug. "I'll call you later?"

"Sure," Kate agrees. "I'll walk you to the front door."

"Olivia, I'm not sure what your plans are," Kate says when she returns to the lanai. "I was thinking of just being a couch potato for the rest of the afternoon. You can join me if you'd like."

"Love it," replies Olivia.

Pleased that Olivia has elected to stay, Kate enjoys her company throughout the afternoon. Still, she can't help but intuit that Olivia is the one who needs comforting.

But over what?

The Secret

*Secrets, silent, stony sit in the dark palaces of both our hearts:
secrets weary of their tyranny: tyrants willing to be dethroned.*

— James Joyce

7

A young girl whimpers as Kate struggles to see through the dark, hazy mist. Suddenly, the murky veil dissipates to reveal the same, pretty black teen Kate witnessed previously in a dream. This time she's distraught and alone in her room, with no evidence of the transgressor. She cries as she cradles herself, rubbing her arms as her tears flow unrelentingly.

Kate stirs abruptly from her slumber.

"Honey?" Kai, still half asleep, sits up sensing something is amiss.

When Kate turns around to face him, their arms naturally envelop one another. "Remember the dream I told you? About the attack on the teenage girl?"

"You had it again?"

"Not exactly the same. She was alone this time. She was so lost, not knowing which way to turn. I felt her fear."

Feeling Kate trembling against him, Kai holds her tighter. "Maybe this dream has something to do with what happened to you, do you think?"

Kate shrugs and looks at the night table clock. "I'm sorry I woke you, honey. It's the middle of the night."

"It's okay, sweetie. I want you to be able to talk to me anytime you need," Kai assures her, stroking her hair.

"Thanks, but let's try and get some sleep now." Kate closes her eyes and sinks into the safety of Kai's loving arms.

Several weeks later, Kate finds she's feeling better and less on edge. Things appear to be getting back on track, except for the fact that Kai has become a little overbearing and controlling when it comes to what

Kate does and where she goes. When she mentions it to him, he tells her it's because he's worried about her safety.

"It's only a short walk to The Plumeria Café, Kai. I'm okay. I like the exercise. Besides, you know how much I love to walk to town. I can't live in constant fear everywhere I turn."

"I know. But if I'm driving to work, why not let me take you?"

"Kai, please. Stop." Kate can feel her frustration level rise.

"Okay, but you'll have your phone on you, right?"

"Yes."

"And the can of mace I bought for you?"

"Yes."

"And the whistle?"

"Kai! Please! Honey … honestly, I'm good."

"Okay, I'm going to leave now. But call me when you get to the café?"

Kate bites her lip before answering, "I'll text you." She sighs in deep relief when Kai finally drives off to work.

Walking down Weke Road toward the café, Kate contemplates the last few weeks. Initially, she had some PTSD and was frightened of being alone in the house for an extended period. Instead, she'd opt to stay at Olivia's or Malie's or have one of Nā Pīkake come to be with her when Kai worked a night shift. In the last few days, she has finally gotten past that anxious feeling—especially since Kai had a new security system installed. Knowing that she'll hear a chime when someone enters or leaves the house is enormously helpful, as is keeping the system activated when she's home alone. There's great comfort in knowing that the police will be notified of any unwanted intrusion.

"Kate!" Malie calls from behind the counter when she sees her sister-in-law enter the crowded café. "What'll it be? Passion fruit iced tea?"

"How about that new combo?"

"Sure, black and pineapple. I'll have one of those too. Pick a table out on the lanai, and I'll meet you there in five."

"What about Olivia?"

"Oh, she asked for a raincheck. She had some business work crop up."

"Okay," answers Kate, feeling a little sad that Olivia didn't reach out to her directly.

A few minutes later Malie brings their teas to the table, along with two lemon-blueberry muffins.

"So, how goes it, sis? Is Kai behaving?"

"Oh, I almost forgot! Just a sec." Kate reaches for her cell and sends Kai a text that she's with Malie at the café.

"So he still has you checking in wherever you go?"

"Well, he's worried."

"I can tell. And actually, I wouldn't be surprised if the incident you went through is also triggering Kai's behavior because of what happened with our mom."

"You think? How so?"

"You know the story. Taking her out on the boat that day against Dad's wishes. And then, when the weather changed, Mom fell and hit her head."

"Sure, but that was a horrible accident."

"Oh, I know. But Kai still blames himself for not heeding the weather report that day. I bet some of those feelings are resurfacing again, and he's feeling responsible for not being there for you that night."

"That wasn't his fault either."

"We all know that consciously, but sometimes, even when we know something, we have reactions that don't necessarily make logical sense. Loving communication of our true feelings, and giving ourselves permission to grieve and heal, that's the key."

"It always is," agrees Kate.

"Hey, I like that design." Kai points to Kate's illustrator's pad as they sit out on the lanai several nights later. Kate is working on logo ideas for Nā Pīkake.

"Mahalo. I think simple is best, especially when it comes to printing. What are you working on?"

"Look." Kai shows her his own sketches.

"What's this?" Kate points to a line extending from the front sides of the cottage around to the back of the house.

"A lava-rock wall and gate. What do you think? We could make the wall blend into the landscape and plant beautiful greenery around it.”

"For privacy?"

"And protection."

"I like that idea," agrees Kate. She puts down her pad and places her arms around her husband. "What's this square image here?" she asks, pointing to another area of the landscape.

"Since we're changing our landscape and doing some construction, I thought it might be a good time to plan for the expansion of our existing ohana."

"Seriously?"

"Sure, with all our family and friends coming to visit and stay, I figure we could use some more space. Maybe we can even make a separate garden area and entrance around the ohana. This way, everyone will have privacy."

"Are you thinking of adding another room?"

"We have space, so I figure why not add another master suite with bath. While we're at it, I'd also like to expand the lanai, kitchen, and maybe even add an outdoor shower."

"*Outside?*"

"Yeah, plenty of people have them. It would be private, but essentially, you're taking a shower *au naturel*."

"That sounds like fun."

"Oh, yeah, it could be a lot of fun," Kai purrs suggestively, looking at Kate and causing her heart to flutter.

"I was thinking, in addition to using the ohana for family, when they're not visiting, if and when we're comfortable with it, we could list it on Airbnb. That way, over time, it would even pay for itself."

"Say …" Kate has a lightbulb moment. "Maybe we could make the kitchen-area design one that would be conducive for me to give private cooking classes to small groups. I've always wanted to do that. We could also use the area as an extra entertaining space."

"Well, pull together some inspiration photos to show the contractor."

"I love it!" Kate claps gleefully. "I'll Google some images to print and go through some of my home and garden magazines."

"What is it about women and decorating?"

Later that evening, Kate stays up as long as she can keep her eyes open. Before she nods off, though, she forces herself to go back outside to see if she can coax Kai to come to bed. Since the incident, their lovemaking has inexplicably ground to a halt—and Kate is determined to get their intimacy back on track. Kai's flirtatious comment about showering in nature earlier that evening makes her think tonight might be the night. "Coming to bed?" she asks, planting a kiss on the back of her husband's neck.

"In a few minutes, hon. I just want to finish up a few things on this design."

"Okay, but don't be too long." Kate kisses the back of his neck and cheek again, hopeful for a romantic rendezvous.

Once back in bed, Kate waits patiently for as long as possible. However, the late hour finally takes its toll and, unwillingly, she succumbs to a deep slumber.

8

A few days later, the Nā Pīkake ladies gather at Malie's lovely plantation-style Hanalei home for their second "official" meeting. As the women get caught up on everyone's news, and discuss future Nā Pīkake events, they take turns fussing over Kate and ask how she's doing. Only Olivia sits apart from the group, engrossed in reading something on her smartphone.

Am I imagining it, or is Olivia purposely keeping her distance? Her friend's uncharacteristically distracted behavior stumps Kate.

"Dig in, everyone!" instructs Malie. The ladies fill their dishes and take seats at the long, wooden, lanai table.

"We've got a lot of ideas for our first event, but let's hone in on one and lock it in," directs Sukey as she dives into her chicken salad.

"On our honeymoon Kai and I enjoyed a charming farm-to-table event at a private residence and farm," Kate starts. "First, there was a delicious dinner held in a pretty garden, and it was followed by a concert to benefit local farmers. Maybe we could do something similar—host a social event to benefit our community in some way." She pauses to take a bite of the Indian curry-vegetable-rice dish Sukey has prepared for the potluck.

"That sounds lovely," Elaine agrees, taking a bite of Kate's salmon topped with pesto.

"Maybe we can use our group as kind of good Samaritans to assist all types of people and families in distress—whether it be physically, emotionally, financially or spiritually. Nā Pīkake could spread aloha to make the world a better and brighter place," adds Kate.

"I love it." Olivia has finally joined the conversation and agrees with the rest of the women.

"We can help heal in deeds and with education," offers Elaine. "There are all types of community events we could hold."

"Events with music and culture," comments Sukey.

"And fantastic food," adds Malie. "Let's make our first focus be on crime victims. What happened recently to Kate gives it special meaning."

On a mission, the ladies begin to plot the details of their first event.

For the next week or so, other than doing some legwork to follow up on the brainstorming session of Nā Pīkake, Kate's days return to the status quo. To break up the hours spent in front of her computer, working on her novel and magazine work, she takes brief nature walks and delves into cooking therapy by creating delicious dishes with fresh, organic ingredients that she photographs for her recipe blog, *thewriterspantry.com*.

Kate's blog features her favorite recipes and breathtaking photography, as well as her behind-the-scenes stories and musings which allow her to extend a wide variety of home, garden, and lifestyle content to those magazine readers who enjoy her print articles. Thanks to her bylines in *New York View Magazine* and *Simply Aloha Living*, Kate now has thousands of followers. A source of pride for Kate, her blog is the perfect creative outlet, serving her passions for writing, cooking, photography, and graphic design. While it's mainly a labor of love that energizes her, it has also inadvertently given her a career a boost as well. Her editors love the extra value *thewriterspantry.com* delivers to their magazines, and their advertisers love the additional exposure and networking the popular blog provides.

Every so often Kate stops in at The Plumeria Café for a latte and scintillating conversation. She's thankful that, for the most part, life has gone back to "normal." Even she and Kai seem to be getting back on track and have planned a romantic date-night dinner out for the following evening, one that Kate anticipates will finally reignite their passion.

"Aloha, Olivia. What are you up to?" Kate asks, phoning her friend late morning.

"Oh, this and that." Olivia is evasive. "I'm in lots of meetings about the magazine and brainstorming ideas for the television show."

"Think maybe we could sneak in a lunch or dinner this week or next?"

"I'm swamped. But sure, I'll check my schedule and get back to you. Got to run now to get ready for a conference call in five."

"Okay, aloha."

Gee, was that a brush off or what? I wonder if I did or said something that offended her. Should I call her back to talk to her about my feelings or wait until an opportune moment opens up?

Kate, dejected and wondering why Olivia has been keeping her at arm's length for the last several weeks, frets for a few more minutes but then decides to let it go for the time being. She has to trust that whatever's eating Olivia will be revealed when her friend is ready.

"Aloha, Chef Keoni!" Kate calls out the following morning as she enters the farmers market in the heart of Hanalei. She makes a beeline for the nearest organic produce stall with her friend and *New York View Magazine* colleague, photographer Ken Yoshida. Ken is close in age to Kate and also a New York transplant.

The chef, a large, jovial-looking man, places one of his leafy purchases in a canvas tote that hangs from his shoulder.

"Meet one of the local farmers, Danny Akamu." Chef Keoni introduces Kate and Ken to Danny and his pretty wife and son, who are also operating the booth.

"Chef, do you mind if I take a few candids of you talking to Kate and Danny and his family?" asks Ken, his camera poised for action.

The men oblige, and after the chef has bought two more tote bags full of local produce at Danny's stand, he and Kate move about the market while Ken, snapping photos, makes himself as unobtrusive as possible.

"Taste this," Chef Keoni instructs Kate, handing her a little paper cup overflowing with a crunchy Thai peanut salad.

"Delicious!" enthuses Kate, munching on the tasty mix.

The two continue their pleasant walk in the eclectic market that also features exotic flowers, arts and crafts, freshly baked bread and pastries, locally produced and bottled jams and hummus, and other enticing items.

"My friend Tommy over here makes the best fruit smoothies,"

Chef Keoni informs Kate with a smile. "Can I treat you and your photographer to one?"

Kate reads the smoothie menu board displayed between a host of fresh fruit and a giant blender and orders a mango-banana-coconut drink while Ken opts to take a raincheck until he's completed the day's assignment.

With their smoothies in hand, Chef Keoni leads Kate over to a seating area to conduct a more formal interview away from the hustle and bustle of the market. In addition to talking about seasonal fruits and vegetables, Chef Keoni shares his favorite tips and dishes that use that day's fresh picks, while Kate makes notes on her computer.

A half hour later, as Kate concludes the interview, Chef Keoni promises to email Kate some recipes, and a date is set for Ken to photograph a few of the chef's creations to accompany the article.

Free now to explore and capture some of the market's spectacular offerings for her blog, Kate begins snapping photos, and using her smartphone, conducts several informal interviews with some of the local farmers, all the while gathering business cards and ideas for future stories. A few hours later, satisfied with what she's accomplished, she heads back toward her car.

Suddenly, Kate hears a woman scream, "Let go of my arm!" Kate looks through the crowd of people, but there doesn't seem to be anyone in distress. Then she hears another cry, this time even more forceful.

"I said, let go of my arm!"

Kate catches sight of a forty-something woman slapping a tall, lanky man hard in the face with her handbag. Taken aback, the man immediately releases the woman's arm and flees into the crowd. With her adrenaline spiking, Kate quickly takes a few photos of the man speeding off in an old white van, then she runs to the victim's aid.

The woman, who introduces herself as Emily Johnson, is, more than anything else, angry that the perpetrator got away.

"It was him. I know it. I wish I'd been able to get a clearer photo of him. Or even the license plate of his van," moans Kate.

In Malie's office at The Plumeria Café, Malie studies Kate's smartphone photo. "Yeah, you really can't see his face at all," Malie says with a shake of her head. "Regardless of whether or not he's the same guy that attacked you, you witnessed an attempted assault. We should tell Alana. Let's go."

The Hanalei Police Department's building, a modern, beige structure with a green roof, blends in seamlessly with the local plantation architecture of the area.

After checking in at the front desk, Malie and Kate take a seat in the reception area, and minutes later, Alana bids them a warm aloha before leading them to a nearby conference room. "So, this guy got into a white van?" Alana repeats as she examines the photo. "Did you happen to catch the year and make?"

"It was a Dodge. Not sure of the year though, sorry. It was old and beat up, as you can see."

"Anything else you can think of?"

Kate shakes her head while Alana jots down some final notes.

"Mahalo for letting me know. I'm glad you're okay, and thank you for getting this woman Emily's number. I'll give her a ring." She pauses then adds, "Say, will we see you and Kai at Malie and Aukai's barbecue Friday night?"

"You bet," Kate promises, and the ladies say their alohas.

9

"I'm fine," Kate reassures Kai. The two are sipping chilled chardonnay as they dine on sushi at a secluded table at a local romantic spot in Hanalei. Malie had suggested that Kate share the news about witnessing the incident at the farmer's market with Kai face-to-face so that he could see Kate is okay, and Kate is determined that nothing is going to derail her from having her date night with Kai.

"Luckily, the lady wasn't hurt, and Alana's on the case," Kate continues. "As for me, I've had several weeks now to process what happened to me, not to mention being surrounded by awesome family and friends. I feel healed and thankful that I escaped with only some bruises."

"I know," sighs Kai.

"Honey, this is kind of hard to say, but since the attack, I've noticed that you've, um, well, you've been finding all types of activities to do late into the night, and I feel like you're avoiding me."

"Oh, Kate," answers Kai, a little surprised. He grabs her hand. "I'm sorry. I've just been so caught up."

"I know, making the house safe and secure."

"I was trying to be careful, courteous. I wasn't sure if, well, I don't know. I was feeling responsible somehow, guilty."

"It wasn't your fault," Kate reassures him.

"I also wanted to give you time. It was a scary thing that happened to you. I guess I've also been processing, and I wasn't sure if you were feeling like being … too close."

"Seriously? I thought I've been pretty obvious," pronounces Kate dramatically. The pair burst into laughter.

"Oh, yeah?" Kai looks at her with a devastating, alluring smile. "Why didn't you tell me?"

"Kai, I … I," stammers Kate, excitement coursing through her veins. "I'm sorry I kept my feelings from you. That I allowed myself to get to a place where I was about to burst."

"And I'm sorry for being oblivious and lost in my angst. I guess we're neither one of us a mind reader. Well, maybe you are," jokes Kai. "Just know you can tell me anything."

"And you do the same," urges Kate.

Kai grabs her hand and kisses it. "I love you so much."

"To the moon and beyond." Kate continues their favorite family expression. The lovers lean in for a passionate kiss.

"Dessert?" the waiter offers with a smile, handing them menus when they finally break for air.

"Just the check, mahalo," Kai responds and winks at Kate when the waiter leaves.

Praise, God, thinks Kate. She has her husband back.

10

"Ahhh," sighs Kate, finding the constant pounding of hammers, the whir of electric drills, and grate of power saws that resonate from the backyard extremely annoying as well as distracting. Typically, on a beautiful day like this, her "desk" is the wooden table located just outside the French doors of her office. However, during the recent construction of the new ohana, she's been confined to her inside space.

The sacrifice will be worth the wait. Kate turns up the volume on her speaker and the soothing sounds of a rain forest replace the harsh sounds of construction. However, just as soon Kate gathers her thoughts to write, her cell phone chimes.

"Hi, hon. I hope you're not busy. I just wanted to hear your voice."

"Dad, are you okay?" replies Kate. "You don't sound it."

"I miss *her*."

"I know. I miss Mom too." Kate feels his pain. "What have you been up to?"

"Not much."

"Mom would want you to be doing things—activities you enjoy—she wouldn't want you to sit around the house. What about that local theatre you said you were going to join … you know, the one where they have lectures, movies, and live events?

"I joined."

"And are you going?"

"Yeah …"

"Didn't you say they have a little coffee shop where folks hang out before and after shows?"

"Yeah, but Peggy's out of town, and I hate going by myself."

Oh, so he is *seeing Peggy.*

"Where did she go?" asks Kate, hoping to get her father to open up.

"To visit friends in New Jersey."

"For how long?"

"Honey, I don't know. I'm not her travel agent."

Kate tries not to take his frustration personally. His angst is about Peggy—or perhaps more precisely, her absence.

"Okay, well, maybe you can invite one of your men friends from the church group, or do your best strike up a conversation with someone interesting."

There's a long silence on the other end of the phone and another pronounced sigh from Glen.

"Earth to Dad."

"I know. I'm trying."

Really? Every idea I offer, he flat out rejects.

"What about reading. You always enjoyed a good book."

"I don't feel like reading."

"Then what about participating in some of the activities at your country club?"

"Like what?"

"Cards, bridge, chess. You and Mom used to golf, too. Why not start playing again?"

Glen moans and grumbles.

"Daddy," whines Kate, a bit frustrated at her father's lack of motivation.

"I know, I know, I'm just a stick in the mud lately."

"What are you going to do tonight?" Kate asks in an upbeat tone. She's hopeful this last attempt will help lift her father's spirits.

"Your sister invited me over for dinner, and then I'll just come home and watch a movie on Netflix, I guess."

"That sounds great, Dad. You'll be around family, and I know Sis always cooks up something yummy. It'll be fun."

"Yeah, we'll have a good time. Look, honey, thank you for the pep talk. I have to get to my eye doctor's appointment, but I'll call you tomorrow, okay?"

"Okay, Poppy, love you."

"Love you too, dear."

It must be so hard and lonely for him, losing the love of his life after fifty happy years. I hope he gives himself time to heal and doesn't rush into anything he might regret—with Peggy or with someone else—just to ward off the loneliness.

A few days previously, Carla had revealed to Kate that there had been several widows and divorcées hitting on their father, passing him notes at church, corralling him into buying them cocktails at the country club, striking up conversations in the grocery aisles.

Attractive, fit, sophisticated, intelligent, financially secure, even in his advanced years—Dad's hot stuff. Kate chuckles at the image of her father as a "hot" bachelor.

She knows that while her father is enjoying the attention, he's not a player; her father is a one-woman man. Sometimes, this type of consideration only underscores the fact that her mother is not by his side and that, in turn, makes him sad and depressed. Kate does nothing but worry when she thinks of her father in the dating world—especially in this modern technological age of instant gratification, not to mention how dating sites tend to misrepresent a person's true essence and intentions.

I had to live through the dating scene, but thankfully, I found Kai. Dad is a grown man, but life was so different when he met Mom, and not all women out there have the heart and values that Mom did.

The thought of her father dating still doesn't seem right to her. It's a jarring concept and a little too perplexing for her to grasp at the moment while she's still trying to heal her own heart.

Kai had mentioned to Kate that after long, happy marriages, some men wind up getting back into relationships almost immediately after their spouses die, even getting married within relatively short amounts of time. While she can understand the abstract concept of her father dating, the reality of his ever getting "close" to someone else, or even, *yikes*, married again, is way too much for her to process.

Maybe, with a little more time, Dad will find peace in the many blessings he has, as well as contentment in his memories, so that keeping Mom alive in his heart will give him solace and foster hope that they will see one another again someday.

BANG! BAM! ZZZZ! The orchestra of saws and hammers continue to play outside so loudly that the racket permeates through the walls and closed windows for ongoing days in a row.

Okay, here we go again. I'll have to write later today when the racket ceases.

Instinctively, Kate heads to the kitchen to put her creative talents to use in another way. As she thumbs through her digital recipe archive on her laptop, she smiles at a tantalizing image of an apple galette staring back at her on the computer screen.

Baked apple and cinnamon in a whole-wheat crust is comfort food any time of year.

Kate preheats the oven to 400° F and removes a large cookie sheet from underneath the kitchen's center island. First, she cuts a piece of parchment paper to fit on the bottom of the pan. Next, she assembles the ingredients on the counter: an organic pastry crust from the local natural foods market, red mountain apples locally harvested, pungent, ground ginger, cinnamon, dried cranberries, freshly squeezed lemon juice, macadamia nuts, and some shredded sweet coconut.

She gets lost in the task of peeling and slicing the sweet apples, which she places in a large bowl, adding in the spices, juice and shredded coconut. Measuring out half a cup of the macadamia nuts, she pours them into a plastic bag.

"Take that!" Kate playfully smashes the nuts with a wooden mallet. "And that!"

When she's satisfied the macadamias are a perfect size, she mixes them in with the apples and tosses in some dried cranberries to add natural sweetness. Next, she unrolls the pastry shell onto the parchment-lined cookie sheet and places a hearty spoonful of the fruit mix into the center of the dough.

"*Et voila!*" Kate comments as she folds the edges of the exposed dough over the center of the fruit to make a free-formed rustic tart. Her cell phone rings as she pops her creation into the oven.

"It's me, Olivia. Malie just told me you recently witnessed an attack? Are you okay?" she blurts out.

"Yeah, we went to the police department and filed a report." Kate is glad to hear her friend's voice. After their last conversation, they hadn't been in touch, which has upset Kate. Still, she had held fast to her theory that when Olivia is ready to talk, she will reach out.

"Are you driving?" Kate asks, hearing a lot of background noise on the call.

"I had to do some business on the mainland and flew back to Kauai last night. I just left The Plumeria Café. Are you sure you're fine?"

"It was shocking and scary, but, yeah, I'm okay. You sound a little shaken up though," probes Kate.

"What can I say? Hearing about another attack upsets me."

"Do you have any plans for the rest of the afternoon?"

"Nothing much."

"Want to come over and do nothing much together?"

"I'm turning the car around right now and heading your way."

Kate is thrilled that Olivia seems back to her old self.

11

"Ahhh, garden therapy," enthuses Oliva as, several hours later, she plants the last of the colorful bromeliads in Kate's backyard. The yard is quiet now that the construction work has stopped for the day. "Getting your hands in the dirt is good for the soul."

"The kitchen or the garden are my go-to places when I'm feeling overwhelmed and needing a good distraction." Kate pats down some earth around the base of a hibiscus bush with vibrant red blooms.

"For the new magazine, in addition to highlighting recipes from The Plumeria Café, we should also include a farm-to-table section. Would you want to take something else like that on?" Olivia asks.

"You mean articles on sustainable gardening?"

"That, and home entertaining and décor. Maybe talk to other local chefs and feature farmer profiles. We can bullet out some ideas."

"I love it! Right up my alley. You know me well, my friend." Kate smiles, excited by the possibilities. "Say, speaking of healthy eats, I've worked up an appetite. How about you?"

"Ditto."

"I call this my 'Leftover Lazy Salad,'" says Kate, munching on some crispy greens tossed with roasted vegetables and a citrus vinaigrette.

"I love that name. It's a great way to reduce food waste, too." Olivia takes a forkful of salad and smiles. "Today is just what the doctor ordered."

In the serenity of the moment, Kate intuits that it's the right time to talk to Olivia. "I know how much what happened to me bothered you," she starts, looking directly into Olivia's eyes and reaching out to take her hand.

114

That is all Kate has to do. The damn breaks. Olivia's tears flow freely.

"Olivia ..." Kate didn't expect this reaction. "It's going to be okay. I'm fine. Lucikly, no one was hurt in this latest mishap."

"I know, I know." Olivia wipes tears from her eyes.

"What is it then?"

Olivia looks tentatively at Kate. It's obvious from her expression that she's debating what to do next.

Kate decides to break the ice by sharing her recent troubling dreams in an attempt to relate to Olivia that she understands the depth of her friend's unsettled feelings. "You know, the other night I had a strange dream. I've had a few dreams that have the same teenage girl in them. In the first dream, I witnessed the young girl's assault by a masked man. In the second, it was the same young girl, only a different day. This time, she was crying and confused and didn't know which way to turn. I honestly felt her sadness, her angst."

Olivia becomes eerily still. She locks eyes with Kate.

BAM! The meaning of Kate's dreams is now suddenly crystal clear, and the message hits her like a ton of bricks.

Olivia has been the victim of a violent attack. That's why what happened to me and the other recent incidents are having such an impact on her.

"I can feel your pain, even though I don't know exactly where it stems from," Kate continues tentatively, concerned that she may be overstepping.

"Your dream ..." Olivia begins.

Kate takes Olivia's hesitancy to mean she is still pondering if she should come clean. She hopes Olivia knows she can trust her. And their connection is undeniable.

Olivia's pause is brief. "Your dream was uncanny, but considering it's you, I'm not surprised," she gulps, reaching for her glass of iced tea and taking a sip. "I have something I'd like to share with you. I'm not quite sure how to start, but I'd like it not to go beyond this table. Can you promise me that?"

"Yes," Kate answers without hesitation. "On my life."

"I was attacked by a man I didn't know when I was a teen."

"Olivia!" Kate feels a stab of pain to her heart upon hearing her suspicions confirmed.

"It was a truly awful, traumatic experience," remembers Olivia.

Kate reaches out and touches Olivia's shoulder. "I'm here to support you."

"It was after my parents divorced and my mother had passed. I was living with my grandparents in what we thought was a very safe neighborhood. It was summer, and when we went to bed, we kept the windows open to let in the cool night air. The next thing I knew, in the middle of the night, a man wearing gloves and a mask and covered from head toe with dark clothing was on top of me."

Kate's hand instinctively flies up to her mouth to quiet her loud gasp.

"He muffled my cries by putting duct tape across my mouth, and then he tied me to the bed and raped me," admits Olivia, her eyes filling with tears at the memory.

Kate leans over and wraps her arms around Olivia, which causes Olivia to break down completely for several minutes, sobbing uncontrollably. "That's right. Let it out. It's okay." Kate maintains a tight embrace to reassure her friend of her loving presence.

Finally, Olivia's sobs subside. She wipes her tear-stained face, sniffles, and takes a deep breath.

"Olivia, there are no words …"

"Thanks for just listening and being here for me now. I appreciate it."

"Can I get you anything? More iced tea?"

"Please," says Olivia as she stares out at the calm ocean and clear sky slowly turning to dusk. A sudden, warm breeze springs up, and she rubs her arms, feeling the comfort.

Moments later, Kate sets a tall glass of tea down in front of Olivia and another on the table for herself.

"It feels good to get that secret off my chest," confesses Olivia. Her mouth dry, she takes a sip of tea. "I think it triggered me to relive my experience when you were attacked. Everything came flooding back. I didn't want to face it at first, but now I can't seem to put the lid back on it."

"I think you're very courageous," empathizes Kate. "I feel honored that you felt safe enough to share this with me. I knew something was up. I kept the faith that you'd tell me when you were ready."

"I'm sorry if I've seemed distant to you," Olivia apologizes. "I was processing so much. I don't even really know why I acted as I did. Forgive me?"

"Of course, and I understand, but I was wondering if I had done anything wrong."

"You? You did nothing wrong. I'm sorry for what happened to you … and for my keeping my distance."

"I know. Don't worry. It's okay now," answers Kate. After a few moments, Kate asks, "Olivia, did they ever prosecute the man?"

"They never found him. It was my fault."

"No! Why would you say that?"

"Because I kept it a secret. When I finally had the nerve to tell someone, the man was long gone."

"Olivia, don't blame yourself."

"I was young and innocent. I hadn't even kissed a boy yet. I didn't want to tell my grandparents about the attack, because I felt so ashamed, like it was my fault somehow."

"There's no shame. You were the *victim*."

"I know, but at the time, I didn't know what to do. I was in shock and denial; that is, until I couldn't be in denial any longer."

Kate's eyes widen. She senses she is about to hear something foreboding.

"Several months after the attack, I realized I was pregnant."

"Oh my God, Olivia."

That is the angst I gleaned from the young girl in my dreams. She was frightened, not knowing where to turn.

"I got one of those over-the-counter pregnancy tests and nearly died when it came out positive. I did two more tests, just hoping and praying that it wasn't true, but it was. Afterward, I *had* to tell my nana." Olivia takes a napkin from the holder at the center of the table and wipes her eyes.

"I'm so very sorry," Kate whispers, reaching out to hold Olivia's hand.

"Nana was so worried for me. I realized then that I should have told her right away. She and Pops came to my support immediately. They were upset that I had kept the attack from them, and rightly so, but they also understood. We filed a report with the police, but it was too late. The man was never found or heard from again."

Kate looks at Olivia with questioning eyes.

"I know what you're thinking … *the baby*."

"What happened?"

"Well, there was a push for me to abort, not by Nana and Pops, but by my doctor. Even the counselor my grandparents had me speak to thought I should consider the option—especially because of my age and the circumstances. I thought about it, oh, I did. To have it all be over and done with … But somehow, I just couldn't. Even though the little being inside me was the result of something horrific, it was still part of me, and for some reason its soul found its way to life. Do you know the poet Kahlil Gibran?"

Kate nods.

"He's been a favorite of mine for years," continues Olivia. "He wrote, 'Your children are not your children. They are the sons and daughters of life's longing for itself. They come through you but not from you, and though they are with you yet they belong not to you …'"

Olivia and Kate both begin to cry.

"The Bible is clear. Jeremiah, chapter one, verse five reads, 'Before I formed you in the womb, I knew you, and before you were born I consecrated you,' and in Exodus, twenty-one, verses twenty-two through twenty-five, the Bible speaks about harm against a fetus, 'if there is harm, then you shall pay, life for life,'" Olivia recites as she wipes more tears from her eyes. "I could go on quoting. I believe children are a divine gift, and even though the pregnancy was happening to me the way it was, as unfathomable as it was, I couldn't choose to end it."

"Oh, Olivia." Kate wipes a tear from her cheek. "What happened to the child?"

"It was a little girl. I seriously thought about raising her. Nana and Pops said they would help, but I was terrified—overwhelmed, really—and the more I thought about it, and the closer I got to giving birth, the more I felt the baby deserved to have a home with a mother and father. At thirteen I was just a child myself. So we put her up for adoption. At the time, I felt it was best."

Kate moves her chair closer to Olivia and puts her arm around her friend's shoulder. The two women sit in silence for a long while, looking out to the ocean, welcoming its calming influence.

12

"I know I sound like a broken record, but I feel like such a weight has been lifted, Kate. I can't thank you enough."

"Thank you for trusting me."

"Besides my grandparents, only a handful of people know."

"Grant?"

Olivia shakes her head and looks as if she's about to cry again.

"I'm sure he would understand," consoles Kate.

"I'm sure he would, but as I said, it's been a part of my life that I've locked up and thrown away the key ... until now."

"Did you ever think that keeping a traumatized part of yourself so secret might affect you in different ways? Especially with someone you deeply love? Just my two cents, but I can see where this might cause a space between you two where there shouldn't be."

"I know. I talk to men and women on my show about these types of things all the time, and yet here I am."

"Don't be too harsh on yourself, but maybe, if you let Grant in, he can also help you heal. I'm sure it can only grow the love between you."

Olivia sighs. "Let me ponder that one for a while."

"Whaddaya makin'?" Kai calls from the living room on a lazy Saturday morning a few weeks later. He's sprawled out on the sofa, watching TV and doodling on his writing tablet.

"I'm trying out a new applesauce muffin recipe for breakfast that replaces a cup of sugar with applesauce, lemon extract, and coconut cream concentrate," announces Kate proudly as she licks the spatula after scooping the last bit of sweet, creamy batter into the cast-iron loaf pan.

She pops the muffins in the oven, and then heads over to Kai, picks up his legs, and plops down next to him.

"So, what do you think?" Kai shows Kate the updated sketch he's made of their new garden landscape now that most of the remodeling is complete.

Kate mulls over the plans with keen interest. "How about adding an arbor or pergola, so if it rains while we're entertaining, we can still sit comfortably outside?"

"Like a gazebo, you mean? Something with a solid roof?"

"Yes, near the outdoor kitchen and grill."

"Okay," agrees Kai and points. "And here's where you can host events, your private cooking classes, and such."

"I'm picturing something like the garden in my dreams—lots of different seating areas and paths where people can walk and sit amongst the flowers and a bountiful table where the love of ohana can surround us."

"I'm with you." Kai nods. "Here's a fire pit, and over here is a little seating area with a recycled, lava-rock waterfall. It will be our botanical garden."

"YES!" Kate claps her hands. "Why not, right?"

"Why not? How about letting me get some estimates first?"

As Kai watches Kate's eyes sparkle with ideas, he gets a warm glow in his eyes. Brushing his hands through her hair now, he can't resist her lips. His arms soften around her, and the two lovers slip into a passionate embrace.

When Kate's cell rings, she tells Kai, "Hold that thought."

"I finally told Grant," Olivia blurts out. "He was amazing. You were right. Now I don't understand why it took me so long. I feel at peace, and I think it brought us closer, too."

"I'm so proud of you."

"What are you doing this afternoon? Can we get together to talk?"

The ladies make a plan to meet early in the afternoon after Kai leaves for the hospital.

"Who was that?" asks Kai as Kate ends her call.

"Olivia."

"Why are you saying you're proud of her?"

Kate thinks about her promise to Olivia to not tell anyone about the attack. She realizes that now she's the one who has to keep a secret.

From the world, yes, she can keep one, but from Kai? Now that Grant knows, maybe Olivia will give her the okay to let Kai in.

I'll ask Olivia.

"Oh, she just did something that she's been wanting to do, is all," answers Kate as she walks toward the kitchen. "Want some ginger tea?"

"Sure, and maybe one of those applesauce muffins?"

"Comin' up."

Later that afternoon, the sun's golden rays burst through the small gaps in the thin blanket of gray mist that hangs over Hanalei Bay as Kate and Olivia walk out toward the end of the pier.

"After Grant and I spoke, he suggested that since I'm a public figure, I should probably tell my story—it can help a lot of other victims," Olivia begins.

"It would be courageous of you, and I bet it would impact countless people by sharing what happened to you," agrees Kate.

"However, I'm thinking, if I tell my story, it should be me that does the telling. What do you think about me breaking my story as a cover feature to coincide with the launch of the new magazine?"

"Are you ready for that?"

"Probably as ready as I'll ever be. At some point, I might even want to invite victims of similar crimes on my TV show to share their stories. The show wouldn't just be about violence to women, though; it would be about facing your demons so you can live an authentic life."

"Oooooh, I like it."

"If I do decide to move forward with all this, would you write the cover story?"

"Me? Seriously?" Kate's voice rises several octaves.

"There isn't anyone I would trust more. However, I'm still figuring out the timeline of it all."

"It would be such an honor. Would you mind, though, since you're going to share your story, if I told Kai? He'd be the only one for now, and I think you know you can trust him."

"Of course."

"Olivia's very courageous, and I think she'd be doing the right thing by coming forward," says Kai as he and Kate sit on their lanai, watching the colorful show in the night's sky the following evening. "It will help others heal too."

"Olivia also told me that she feels her conversation with Grant has brought them closer."

"I'm happy for them. Grant's a good man. I'm sure he feels very protective of her."

"I know we've talked about this before, but promise me that we'll never keep any secrets between us and that we'll always share our feelings about the things that are important to us—our hopes, dreams, and fears—so that we can help each other navigate our lives."

"I promise," Kai affirms.

13

"The more I think about sharing my story, the more I realize there's another element to it that I completely forgot to address," frets Olivia. She and Kate are sitting in the comfort of Olivia's living room a week or so later. "It has to do with the media."

Kate's curiosity piques.

"Telling my story is one thing, but that will also open up another can of worms."

"How so?"

"The baby. She'd be in her late twenties now."

"Oh, I see." Kate gets it. "You're worried that someone might try to find her for an interview?"

"While it's not our way as journalists, we both know the media is relentless and that nothing is sacred or private these days."

"Agreed." Kate nods and takes a deep breath. "How do you feel about the possibility of knowing your daughter's identity?"

"Now that I'm facing my past, I would love to know who she is. I've thought about her every day since I knew I was pregnant. I've fantasized about meeting her. I would never force a meeting though. It's strange, but even though she came into the world the way she did, I've never associated negative thoughts with her. She was and always will be an innocent soul. So when I decided to give her up for adoption, it was because I truly felt stuck between a rock and a hard place."

"I think I know what you might be considering." Kate looks intently at Olivia. "And I agree that it might be wise to locate her before you share your story, so you can see what she wants to do."

"Exactly, you mind reader you. Since I've opened the door to the past, and find it so healing, I'm hopeful my daughter might feel the same. It would be important to let her be the one, though, to decide if she wants our story told. She'll also need some time to digest how it might impact her life and the lives of everyone in her circle."

Kate is impressed with how at peace Olivia seems to be with all this. "What does Grant have to say?"

Olivia smiles. "He's cool with it all."

"So what's the first step in locating her?"

"I have some ideas, but it's too much to deal with right this minute. I'm feeling the need to join with nature. Want to go for a beach walk?"

The smile on Kate's face reveals a definite yes.

"You know, after the attack …" Olivia begins to speak again as she and Kate walk barefoot along the water's edge, processing the massive revelations they have shared. "… I think I was afraid to tell my grandparents because it was such an intimate act. They were shy, church-going people who turned the TV channel if a show or movie had something too steamy going on. I was an early bloomer, coming early to puberty, so when my grandmother sat me down and talked to me about having my period, I thought I would faint, and when I got it, *I almost did faint.*"

Kate and Olivia burst out laughing.

"I was an early bloomer too," Kate admits. "I protested my new womanhood every step of the way."

"For the longest time I believed that the stork delivered babies," Olivia says with a chuckle. "My grandparents were affectionate with each other, and I know they loved each other dearly, but they were from another time where you kept intimate things private. I think that was why I held back telling them. I almost felt somehow that I had done something wrong."

"Did you ever talk to a therapist about all this?"

"I did, and it helped. My nana was also very supportive. She made me feel okay, beautiful, and helped me get back to 'myself,' if you know what I mean."

Kate nods.

"Pops was a dear soul, and he remained so sweet to me; nothing changed except he became even more protective. One memory that stays with me happened not too long after the baby was adopted. One

Sunday afternoon following church service and dinner, Pops and I were sitting in rockers on the front porch. We were swinging away in contented silence for a time, and then he reached over and took my hand and said, 'Sweetheart, I'm so proud of you. Sometimes sad things happen in this life, but God has a plan. We may not always like the plan, and we may not always understand the plan, but we must keep the faith and know He loves us. We must rise above and move beyond our trials and tribulations. Always look for the positive and give thanks and cherish the good things in our lives. But most importantly, we need to keep love in our hearts and look forward to the future with hope. You're a smart, beautiful, talented girl. You have an entire wonderful life ahead of you that you were meant to live.'"

Olivia starts to cry, and Kate embraces her.

"He smiled at me with such a light in his eyes. I could see he meant every word. He believed I would have a wonderful future, and he helped me get back to trusting it too."

"It's a beautiful memory, and so true. You do have a beautiful and amazing life."

"I give thanks for it every day." Olivia nods, taking a cleansing breath.

The friends continue to walk along the beach, reveling in the cool breeze and the warmth of the sun on their skin. Two birds fly by in the sky, squawking as they pass overhead.

"Hi, Nana and Pops." Instinctively, Olivia waves and then turns to Kate. "They must have heard me talking about them."

"I say hello to my relatives all the time." Kate chuckles. "You mentioned the other day that hardly anyone knew about your situation."

"We did file a police report, but as a minor, my name was kept out of the press."

"What about people in your neighborhood and your classmates at school?"

"After we realized I was pregnant, my grandparents and I decided to spend more time at a little place they owned—a cottage by a lake a few hours out of town. Nana homeschooled me there so I could have some privacy. Pops was an insurance agent, so he had a lot of flexibility with his work. Sometimes, he would stay at the family home when he had meetings, but otherwise, he was at the lake with us. I continued to talk to friends by phone, so I kept up that contact."

"Did you ever feel like you wanted to share what happened to you with any of your friends?"

"Not really. I wanted my privacy. My grandparents, the doctors, our minister, and my therapist were enough for me. I didn't feel the need or want to share what happened to me with anyone else. Being so young, I didn't want to be known as the girl who had this horrible thing happen to her. Then there was the fact that I chose to have the baby."

"And now?"

"I'm a mature woman who's made her way in the world. That incident and the circumstances that followed do not define me."

"Are you nervous about reaching out to your daughter … and the possibilities of what that might open up?"

"Of course," Olivia sighs. "She may not be interested in knowing who I am, or she might be angry and be holding a grudge. I worry that if and when we meet, she might not like me. Maybe, I might not like her. Then there's her family. It's all unknown right now. But on the flipside, it might be healing for both of us, give us closure. I know I can't have preconceived notions or expect any certain outcomes; I have to be open to all possibilities. I think the best way to move forward is to remain positive, pray for healing, and have faith in God's will."

"Did her adoptive parents know the circumstances of her conception?" asks Kate after a few moments of silence.

"Yes. I made sure the records reflected the true story so that my daughter's adoptive family could share the information with her when she was old enough. That way she would know that I gave her up not because of the circumstances of her birth, but because I was only a child myself, and I didn't feel I could give her what she needed. And between you and me, even though my grandparents offered and would have raised her, at the time I didn't feel that was the right thing to do. They were still raising me."

"What if she rejects knowing who her birth mother is?"

"At least I will have tried. I'll have to accept that perhaps my daughter might not feel right about opening up the past."

"From what I've read, in order to start a search, it helps to know if the adoption was arranged privately or through an agency. Do you remember?"

"It was private. My grandparents arranged it through my doctor and my attorney. That's all I remember."

"Do you know if it was open or closed?"

"I'm not sure."

"You'll need to know that in order to decide how best to proceed."

"I remember the doctor's name, so I'll have to do some research and try to locate him."

The ladies, lost in their thoughts, walk in silence for a time.

"Kate, I already told you I want you to write this story if my daughter is willing. Will you also help me with the search?"

"Of course. It's probably best if I make some discreet inquiries, rather than you. Better to stay under the radar."

"Mahalo," says Olivia appreciatively, touched by Kate's support.

Later that night back at the cottage, Kate and Kai lie sprawled out on either side of the living room sectional, reading. Kai is studying required journal articles to keep his medical license current while Kate enjoys a novel.

"When do you start the search for Olivia's daughter?" Kai asks, looking up from his papers.

"She said she'd call me back with some numbers to call. We don't want any inquiries to get traced back to her."

"So you're playing detective?"

Kate thinks about that. "Yeah, in a way, I guess I am." Before she can say more, her cell phone rings. "It's Olivia," Kate mouths to Kai.

"I have my doctor's name and what may still be his address and phone number. I'll text it to you," says Olivia.

"Okay. Love you too. Aloha." Kate hangs up the phone.

"What's the update?" asks Kai.

"She's going to text me her doctor's information, and I'll start my research tomorrow."

"It's going to be very interesting to see how it all plays out." Their conversation stops when Kai wraps his arms around Kate and she cuddles up next to him.

14

The intoxicatingly delicious smell of plumeria trees, abundant with their colorful white, yellow, and hot pink blooms, fill Kate's senses as she strolls down the meandering dirt pathway. Majestic white angel's trumpet, their pendulous umbrellas and luxurious golden chain trees showcasing masses of cascading colorful flowers, line the path. Many varieties of palm trees of different shapes and sizes intermix with yellow and orange ginger ti plants and lobster-claw heliconia.

As another wave of sweet plumeria scent swooshes by, Kate hears the playful, high-pitched chirp of I'iwi birds calling out as if talking to her. Seconds later, she's enveloped in a now-familiar energetic embrace. Catherine and Leilani appear at her side and greet her with shining smiles.

As the three women proceed down the path, Kate waves aloha to her grandmothers and grandfathers, whom she can see gathered in the distance. They telepathically communicate their mutual love and happiness at seeing one another.

It feels so good to be back. Kate walks toward a long garden table surrounded by a low wooden bench and chairs.

Once again, the beautifully decorated table showcases an abundant array of tantalizing fruits and vegetables. Moments later, Kai appears at her side and takes her hand. Encompassed in the divine fold of their ohana, they are joyous.

Just beyond the table, Kate sees Olivia in another seating area of the garden, and next to her is a beautiful young woman whom Kate immediately recognizes as Olivia's daughter. However, before she can make her way over to her friend and the young woman, she wakes from her dream.

"Fantastic dream, hon," comments Kai as he digs into his breakfast of curried scrambled eggs, multigrain toast, and sliced fresh fruit. "Love that fact, too, that we've been talking about planting a larger garden with some meandering paths."

"Maybe this dream serves as another confirmation that we're on the right path."

"There's no 'maybe' about it—we are." Kai smiles as he leans over and gives Kate a smooch on the lips. "I'll even go as far as to say that maybe you'll even find out about Olivia's daughter soon."

"If it's …"

"… God's will," they both say in unison.

"Other than telling you, I'm going to keep the dream to myself," Kate tells him. "Let's just see what unfolds."

After Kai leaves for work, Kate is glued to the desk in her home office for several hours, once again losing track of time. Finally taking a break and realizing it's still early on the East Coast, she decides to call the phone number from Olivia's text.

"I'm sorry," a woman answers after several rings. "Dr. Gates passed away not too long ago. Dr. Thomas took over the practice. I stayed on as his receptionist."

"Oh, I see," answers Kate, switching gears. "Dr. Gates had arranged a private adoption in the late eighties. I was wondering …"

"Are you a former patient?"

"No, I'm …"

"Oh, dear, I'm sorry, but I can't discuss that type of information unless you're the patient. However, even then there is a certain protocol."

"Yes, I realize that. I was just wondering if you know if the doctor worked with a particular legal firm or firms?"

"Well, as long as I've been here—and that's a long, long time—we have used the firm of Johnson and Boyers," says the helpful receptionist. "They're still in operation. However, I'm afraid I'm not at liberty to look up that information for anyone except Dr. Gate's patient."

"That's okay. I'll have my friend contact you if needed. Would you happen to have a number for the law firm you mentioned?"

"Sure. However, I'm not sure how much information that firm might be able to provide you with if you weren't their client in the case."

Kate jots down the number and thanks the receptionist then quickly dials Olivia.

"Johnson and Boyers … that rings a bell," Olivia says. After a few more seconds, she shouts, "Alistair Boyers! That was the attorney's name!"

"Wow! That's a great lead." Kate is equally excited.

"I think I better let my lawyer handle contacting Alistair. He'll be discreet and take it from here," Olivia tells Kate. "Then we'll see what's what. Woooh, I can hardly breathe."

"Please let me know the minute you hear something."

For the next several hours, Kate switches gears to work on an assignment for *Simply Aloha Living* magazine, following up with several local chefs about an article on casual, elegant outdoor entertaining and also to gather some tantalizing stories and mouth-watering recipes. On another self-imposed break, she decides to call her father in New York before it's too late.

"Hi, dear."

"Are you okay, Dad?"

"Yeah."

Kate isn't convinced. "Have plans to go out tonight? Maybe with Peggy?" As soon as Kate hears the deafening silence on the other end, she knows she's hit a wrong chord.

"She's out of town again. This time she's in Atlanta, visiting friends for the weekend."

"I'm sorry." Through the phone line, Kate tries to hug her father with the sound of her voice. "Say, Poppy, you liked visiting us in Kauai. Why don't you come back out again? Construction work on the new, improved ohana is complete."

"You two just got married and have your own lives. I don't want to intrude."

"Stop it, Dad. You could come and go as you please. Besides, I work from home. We could have lunch together, and you could keep me company when Kai works evenings. We've also been changing out our landscape, so maybe you can even help me plant in the garden. What do you say?"

"I appreciate the offer, sweetheart, and I'll think about it. Okay?"

"Sure. I love you."

"I love you too, to the moon and beyond."

Kate lets out a deep sigh as soon as she ends the call. *Even though I can't entirely accept the thought of Peggy and Dad together, I wish she were around more for him.* With that, she stands up and starts to rifle through the pantry, looking for an infusion of chocolate. While it won't stop her worrying about her dad, it will at least be a temporary distraction.

15

_____

A morning run followed by a day of casual shopping in town? Possibly. Toying in the kitchen with some new recipe ideas? That could be fun. Perhaps I should head over to one of the local nurseries to gather more information on plantings for the garden? Kate leisurely sips her tea as she takes stock of the garden progress and contemplates what to do on her Saturday off while Kai works.

Mmmm. This recipe is a keeper, Kate decides, munching on the last of her latest culinary creation, Blueberry Macadamia Nut Squares.

She makes a mental note that the lighting at this time of morning on the lanai is perfect and decides to snap a few shots of her Blueberry Squares displayed on a pretty plate for a blog post she intends to write sometime over the weekend.

Just as she finishes her impromptu photo shoot, her cell phone starts vibrating with its familiar tropical beat.

"My lawyer just told me that the adoption was open, so they're making more inquiries through legal channels," blurts out Olivia, too excited to even greet Kate properly. "Keep your fingers crossed, okay?"

"Absolutely. What great news! Say, what are you up to today?"

"Well, I have my list, but since I got that news, and technically, I'm still on hiatus, it's all out the window."

"Care to hit some local nurseries with me? I'd love to check out some plants and garden designs. I'll come your way if you're game."

"You're on, girlfriend."

The next day after church and a leisurely breakfast, Kai and Kate decide to cruise the Pacific waters near the jagged peaks of the Nā Pali

Coast in their twenty-four-foot, inflatable, motorized raft and do a little diving. The spot holds special meaning to them; it is the location of their first date.

"Our little paradise." Kate smiles as she gazes at the surrounding pristine, crystal-clear waters, varying in color from shades of teal to royal blue.

Once beneath the ocean's surface, they encounter exquisite marine life—a family of giant sea turtles and schools of black-and-white-striped fish whoosh this way and that. Cute little yellow tang flit and flutter about while spotted morays crawl in and out of the coral beds. As Kate and Kai float suspended, occasionally flipping their fins, they make sure to keep clear of red sea urchins with their prickly tentacles and stare in awe at beautiful angelfish with their impressive gold, deep purple, and blue wardrobe and green-tipped fins. Ornate and colorful butterflyfish glide by with their brilliant orange and black stripes, and parrotfish glimmer in iridescent shades of blue, red, orange, and green.

Kai gestures wildly to get Kate's attention when he spots some reef triggerfish glide through the coral, leading the way with their nose-shaped snouts. The unique colors of their bodies present as if painted by an artist's brush. Kate scoots up next to Kai for a closer look, and they marvel at the Hawaiian state fish, *humuhumunukunukuāpua'a—humuhumu* for short.

Steeped in the glorious silence, peace, and freedom from gravity that being underwater provides, Kate luxuriates in the warm sea, enjoying its caresses and delighting in how it causes her hair to fan out around her like a mermaid. As she moves smoothly through the water, flapping her fins for speed, she twists and turns like a giant fish herself. Finally, Kai tugs her hand, and they both float to the surface.

"I'm famished," he announces as the two head for their raft. Once onboard, they head swiftly to shore.

Back on land Kai removes a cooler from their car's trunk, and they roll out a large blanket on the sand under the shade of a sheltering tree.

"I'm so glad we decided to take a break today," comments Kate before chomping down on a large radish.

Kai is chewing a mouthful of veggie wrap smothered in hummus. He washes it down with several refreshing gulps of water from his thermos and points to the radish. "Hey, hand me one of those."

Kate complies and smiles when Kai gives her a thumbs-up. "Good, aren't they?"

"Let's plant some of these in our garden." Kai pulls another one of the delicious, round, red root vegetables out the reusable container.

"And herbs, too. It would be great to have all types of them at our fingertips to pick as needed."

Kai nods. "Good thinking. When we get home, let's go over the design plans and add these ideas into the mix."

"Thanks for meeting me on such short notice," Olivia remarks to Kate several days later during their weekday lunch date at The Plumeria Café. As they head toward a quiet corner table on the garden lanai, Olivia blurts out, "My lawyer located her."

"This is fantastic news!"

Olivia breathes deeply, trying to calm her adrenaline-filled rush.

"When are you going to meet her?" Kate asks.

"Well, that's the thing. I'm not sure. My lawyer has to go through the proper channels of inquiry. All I know is that neither my daughter nor I will know the other's identity unless she agrees to meet me. I'm excited and nervous at the same time." Olivia grows quiet, obviously thinking of the various scenarios.

Kate knows that while it's best to keep positive, it's also good to keep busy while playing the waiting game. "After lunch, why don't we go for a drive to Anini Beach? Leave your car here. I'll drive. You've got a lot of nervous energy to walk off."

"I can't think of anything better," Olivia agrees.

Anini Beach holds a special place in Kate's heart. It was on Kate's first trip to Kauai that Olivia suggested she visit this magical place, as it's a perfect place for relaxing, swimming, and snorkeling. Because of the picnic tables under lush foliage, Kate also found it has an ideal ambience in which to write and enjoy a picnic lunch.

Today, the beach does not disappoint. A pleasant, slight breeze rolls off the teal-colored waters that turn a deep royal blue as they progress from water's edge out to sea.

Sitting on a large blanket and wearing wide-brimmed floppy hats pulled from the trunk—a stash of "essentials" Kate keeps on hand at all times for spur-of-the-moment occasions like this—Olivia and Kate stare out to sea.

"Why don't we say a prayer for things to flow smoothly concerning your daughter and everyone's best interests?" Kate suggests.

"God's will be done," Kate and Olivia say in unison when the prayer is complete.

"I feel calm … happy, now." Olivia smiles as the friends stand up to take a walk along the shore.

"Aloha, Jessie," Kate says as she and Olivia greet their friend with hugs about an hour or so later as she approaches their table on The Plumeria Café's lanai.

"I heard through the Malie grapevine that your garden is coming along beautifully," Jessie says. "I love to garden, but where I'm staying now, I'm limited to just planting in pots. Would you mind if I came over to play in the dirt one day?"

"Are you kidding? I'd love it if you did! We can use all the help we can get."

Jessie and Kate firm up plans for a Saturday morning garden date.

"Say, can I get in on that action too?" asks Olivia.

"Absolutely! As I said, we can use all the help we can get."

Garden Healing

*The glory of gardening: hands in the dirt, head in the sun,
heart with nature. To nurture a garden is to feed
not just on the body, but the soul.*

– Alfred Austin, English critic, novelist and poet

16

Come Saturday, not only are Jessie and Olivia Kate's helpers, but several other members of Nā Pīkake drop by at various intervals with potluck fare after hearing about the impromptu gardening party. Even Malie's sister-in-law Alana drops by.

"Everything is looking so fabulous, daahling!" applauds Elaine during a break when Kate shows the ladies around the new construction and garden-in-progress. "Let me know if you need company on any future shopping expeditions for furniture and décor. I know of a magnificent hutch that would look stunning in this area." Elaine points to the outdoor dining space adjacent to the ohana. "One of my clients is planning an estate sale, and let me tell you, she has some simply amazing garden pieces, which I'm sure she'll sell to you for a song—especially if I put in a good word. If you want, I can make arrangements for you to get first peek."

"I'd love that," replies Kate enthusiastically, and then leads the women down a meandering stone path, stopping at a wooden door surrounded by an almost-magical display of tropical plants that compliments the recently constructed lava-rock entrance.

"Aloha. Please enter the Marisol Garden dining area," announces Kate dramatically as she opens the door. The name of the garden is beautifully painted with the letters interwoven between touches of white plumeria blossoms and pink hibiscus.

The ample open space behind the lava-rock entrance and tall foliage reveals yet another large garden-in-progress with various seating areas and a large fire pit. The focal point of the garden is the large, enchanting, glass-and-stone conservatory centered between the old ohana and the new suite.

The conservatory doors open to a long, rustic wooden table surrounded with comfortable and stylish rattan dining chairs. An impressive outdoor kitchen is also visible.

Just beyond one end of the conservatory is another pretty, carved wooden door, which leads to the new master suite.

"OMG! I want to live here!" Sukey cries out.

The ladies burst out laughing.

"I can't take all the credit. Kai is also responsible, and of course Olivia was my main co-conspirator in shopping."

"The pleasure has been all mine," Olivia says with a smile.

"Sukey's right to be excited. It's the perfect place for visitors and extended family to stay," comments Malie.

"Well, that was our intent. We wanted a multi-purpose area where ohana could stay and where we could entertain, hold small events and private cooking classes, and of course, provide a fabulous area to hold Nā Pīkake meetings."

"Just my two cents; this would be a great place to hold our fundraiser!" gushes Malie.

"Sure, if everyone agrees." Kate surveys the group for their reactions.

"What's Nā Pīkake?" asks Alana.

"It's a group we all recently founded to do good works in the community. We've been talking about aligning with a local charity," replies Malie.

"Can I join? I would love to be involved with a cause like that." Alana looks around at the group, who in turn look at each other.

"Of course," the ladies all concur.

"Putting a date on the calendar for our fundraiser will set activity in motion," says Sukey. "So what about it? I'm thinking at least five to six months out."

"Let's make it a spring date when the weather is at its best," suggests Kate.

"What about an evening of music and art?" asks Olivia after an event date is selected. "I have some great connections with local musicians."

"And of course I can arrange to have several local artists for sure," Sukey adds.

"We might even do a gallery-type silent auction, with some of the proceeds going to the charity we choose," suggests Jessie.

"I want to help out, so let me look into the nonprofit application process we've talked about. That way we can align ourselves with other nonprofits or work on our own," offers Alana, who gets an enthusiastic thumbs up from everyone.

"I say this calls for a toast." Elaine heads to the fridge to pull out a couple of bottles of prosecco that Kate has left over from her wedding.

"Nā Pīkake power!" the ladies cheer.

On a high, and feeling empowered after securing a date for the fundraiser, Kate decides to see if she can convince her dad to change his mind and come for a visit.

"I guess I could use a change of scenery and a new adventure," Glen's says with barely any cajoling from Kate. "I'll check into flights to Kauai and get back to you."

"Wow, that's fantastic, Dad!"

Dad's turn to hit the road—sorry, Peggy!

17

"Whatcha reading?" Kai asks Kate about a week later as she sits at the kitchen table, going through a stack of mail.

"It's a card from Jessie. 'Mahalo for letting me play in the garden,'" reads Kate. "'It was so lovely and healing. My late husband and I had a vegetable and flower garden, and last Saturday I found solace in picturing him planting alongside me. I wanted to express how much that day meant to me and how appreciative I am that you included me. I hope you'll let me come back and garden soon. Love, Jessie.'"

"Wow! That's special," comments Kai with a catch in his voice.

"Oh, hon." Kate puts the card down and walks over to comfort her husband. She loves the way he sometimes gets emotional over matters of the heart.

What a lovable softie.

Kate wraps her arms around Kai's waist and plants a series of kisses on his chest before standing on her tip-toes to reach his cheek.

"My mom used to like to help me garden at my old house," remembers Kai.

"Well, you heard what Jessie had to say."

"You think it's possible?"

"Before I even knew you, this house called to me. I truly feel God guided us to one another through this house and our family and friends. So from all the synchronistic experiences we've had since we've known one another, continue to pray for peace, solace, and see what God has in store for us. The more we pray and talk to God, the more God will speak to us."

"I love you truly." Kai pulls Kate in tightly and hugs her.

"*Aloha no au ia'oe*. I truly love you," Kate replies with a passionate kiss.

"I forgot how good it feels to dig in the dirt," Glen exclaims as he presses the earth down around a beautiful, red, flowering hibiscus bush. It's been a week since he arrived back in Kauai, and he's taken to the garden like it's his own. "Do you want me to plant all of them?" he asks as he looks at several more pots of the garnet beauties.

"Yes, all around the perimeter of the lanai." Kate makes a sweeping motion with her hand. "Space them about six feet apart."

As Kate and Glen peacefully plant in the garden, the sounds of trickling water can be heard from several of the garden's recycled water features. Now and then a hummingbird buzzes by, which thrills Glen.

"What's the book?" asks Kate, handing her father an iced lemonade as he sits on a chaise, reading in the tranquil garden later that afternoon.

"Oh …" Glen pauses thoughtfully. "It's on overcoming the loss of a loved one."

Glen's answer surprises and encourages Kate. Until now she thought he hadn't been one for too much introspection. "Are you finding it helpful?" she asks, sitting down next to her dad and sipping a tea.

Glen makes a slight sound, shrugs, and then nods, indicating to Kate that he's not that willing to open up and talk about it at the moment.

When he's ready, he'll share.

"Wheeet whew," chirps Glen after his lemonade break, conversing with a little bird.

It feels good to have Dad here, thinks Kate as she listens to the joyful, back-and-forth song between her father and the bird.

The next morning following an early rain, Kate sniffs the earthy scent that rises from the garden while her hands glide over the keys of her laptop. Almost three quarters through her novel, she is happy that her diligent efforts in keeping to her writing schedule are paying off. Meeting her page count for the day, she saves her manuscript on the hard drive and saves a copy to an external hard drive for safekeeping. Ready for another cup of coffee and a bite of breakfast, she heads toward the kitchen from her makeshift desk on the lanai and is greeted by her father, who is walking up the path from the ohana toward the main house. "You're up early today, Poppy."

"I woke up and couldn't get back to sleep. Have you had breakfast yet?"

"No. I'm going to fix some now. Kai will be up soon too. Want to join us?"

Glen nods and follows Kate into the house. She expertly whips up an omelet with hash browns made with diced scallions, sweet potato, and taro as Glen juices freshly cut slices of pineapple in a blender.

Minutes later, breakfast is served on the lanai, accompanied by Kate's Banana MacNut Bread.

"Your dad's a great guy," Glen comments to Kai as he sips his juice. "I enjoyed talking to him when he dropped by yesterday."

"He said the same about you. Why don't you give him a ring? Maybe you two can take in a movie or golf or something."

"Sure." Glen nods. "Good idea."

"I'll give you his number after breakfast. What's on your agenda today?" Kai asks.

"I think I'll walk into town, visit some of the shops."

"You can take my car if you like," offers Kate.

"It's okay. I'll walk. I like the exercise. Then this afternoon I'll probably do some more work in the garden and read a little. I'll call your dad, too, Kai. If he's not doing anything, maybe we can grab a bite for dinner tonight."

"That was a brilliant idea you had, hon," Kate praises Kai after her father excuses himself from the table and heads back to the ohana to grab his hat and sunglasses.

"It'll be good for both of them, and ..."

"I know, I know," chuckles Kate. "As a doctor, and with all the patients you've seen, you've become somewhat of an expert in homo sapiens."

"And don't you forget it," Kai teases as he leans over and plants a kiss on Kate's lips.

Today, like most Friday afternoons in recent weeks, Kate has arranged her schedule to meet at Olivia's place to work on Nā Pīkake fundraiser assignments. Olivia's primary task is to spearhead sponsorship outreach and also to use her pull to get some high-end donations for the silent auction while Kate handles program book advertising, editorials, and marketing. Malie's on task to oversee the catering, and Jessie's responsible for enlisting and supervising the volunteers. Sukey and Olivia are coordinating the entertainment and silent auction. Elaine and Alana are handling décor and spearheading overall event operations.

"Any word from the lawyers?" Kate asks Olivia, curious about the ongoing search for Olivia's daughter.

"Nothing yet," sighs Olivia.

Olivia's office is an inviting open space decorated in earthy hues and filled with abundant natural light as well as ocean and garden views. Kate and Olivia sit at dark koa-wood desks surrounded by rows of attractive dark wood shelving loaded with books, baskets, photos, island art, and beachy crafts. There's also a large comfortable sofa-and-loveseat seating arrangement adjacent to a small kitchen set up with a long wooden table surrounded by wicker chairs used for working lunches and informal conferences.

"How are you coming with your call sheet?"

"Making some headway," answers Kate as she counts the positive responses from local small-business owners. "I've got six contributors so far for a total of a thousand dollars each in program ads."

"Awesome! I've managed to wrangle up a few silent-auction items so far—an all-expenses-paid, meals-included weekend getaway at the St. Regis, a fifteen-hundred-dollar shopping spree at the shops in Hanalei, and a tour of the Kilohana Plantation and dinner at Gaylord's. Sukey and her husband have also donated a gorgeous art piece from the gallery."

"I'll donate art as well. How about two of my framed photos?"

"Perfect!"

"Once we have a complete list of silent-auction donors, I'll make sure they get included in a special thank you in the program book," adds Kate.

"You know, getting off topic for a second …" Olivia gets up to fill her iced tea glass in the office kitchen area before continuing. "Another thing about the wait to hear from my daughter … staying busy and doing something positive like working with Nā Pīkake, in between planning the magazine launch, really helps me maintain my balance. Putting my energy toward something that brings joy is giving me joy."

"I have to laugh," Kate says with a chuckle. "With you, even when you're on hiatus, you're more active than anyone else I know."

"Oh, really?" Olivia grins. "Well. I don't see you letting any grass grow under your feet either."

18

"Hon, have you seen my favorite blue T-shirt?" yells Kai one Friday morning when he's a little behind in getting out the door to work.

"Sweetheart, it's right here under all the other clean clothes that you need to put away." Kate hands Kai his shirt, which matches his dark-blue scrub bottoms.

"Thanks." Kai pulls the cotton top over his head.

"I made you a protein fruit smoothie for the road." Kate pats down a few hairs standing straight up on Kai's head.

"Mahalo," Kai replies. He heads toward the great room from the bedroom, with Kate following. "Have you seen my briefcase?"

"It's on the sofa." Kate chuckles as she grabs the smoothie, which she hands to Kai.

Kai plants a quick kiss on her lips. "I'll be home late tonight, probably around midnight. What do you think you'll do this evening?"

"My dad's going out with your father again, so I made plans to grab a bite in town with Malie and Jessie. I'll keep my cell on, so call me if you can."

The lovers kiss again, and Kai makes his hasty exit. Kate heads back toward the kitchen to freshen her cup of coffee. With mug in hand, she sits down at the lanai table and puts her feet up on the table's adjacent chair. Pausing for a minute, she looks out toward the maturing garden.

We've accomplished so much, she thinks, proud and grateful. She lifts her coffee cup to her lips, relishing the warm heat on her palms as it permeates through the ceramic mug imprinted with the photograph of the angel cloud in the sky that she took on her honeymoon.

Closing her eyes to more easily connect with the natural environment—the singing birds, the water trickling from the recycled water features, the sun's heat upon her skin—she takes several deep breaths in and out.

Hello, God. Thank you for all our blessings and for watching over Kai and me and for guiding us. Mahalo for this beautiful morning.

Kate's thoughts then turn to Kai. How they first met at a barbecue at Olivia's house, their first few dates, and how they both knew they were the "one" for each other.

Remembering these precious moments makes her feel happy and warm. While she's always heard that the first year of marriage can be a difficult adjustment, she feels blessed that she and Kai genuinely get along. Thankfully, they have similar ways of living. They both enjoy a clean and neat house, make it a point to purchase and prepare only healthy, sustainable food, have similar tastes in décor and design, love the arts and learning new things, and prefer one another's company—or the company of a small group of friends—in a quiet atmosphere, rather than partying on the town. As she examines their life thus far, she concludes they haven't had any lingering disagreements or disconcerting fights. They treat each other with love and respect and genuinely care about the other's perceptions and feelings. At the end of a long day, there is nothing better than the thought of being wrapped in Kai's arms in their little corner of the world. As Kate gets lost in her daydream, her cell phone, sitting on the table, begins to jingle.

"Aloha, girlfriend!" Cindy beams on a FaceTime call. "Vinnie checked his schedule, and we're making vacation plans for summer." She squeals with delight and promises to text Kate some workable future dates. "Say, since we're on FaceTime, want to show me around? I'm dying to see what you've done to the place."

"Let's go!" replies Kate enthusiastically.

After the FaceTime garden tour with Cindy, Kate conducts another when her sister, Carla, and brother, Derek call. Afterward, she finally manages several hours of quiet writing time.

"Sweetheart, I'm off to meet Bradford in town for a cocktail and dinner. We'll probably take in some live music afterward," Glen tells Kate when he pops his head by her garden desk as she's about to call it quits for the day.

"Make sure you keep your cell on, Dad. Sometimes you shut it off, and I want to be able to have access," instructs Kate.

"Yes, ma'am." Glen salutes Kate playfully. "Do I have a curfew?"

"No, but if you're planning to come home after eleven o'clock, please call me."

"Okay, dear," Glen chuckles, now used to the drill and amused by the role reversal. "What are your plans for the evening? Staying in and doing work again?"

"No, I also have plans tonight. Since Kai won't be home until close to midnight, I'm meeting Malie and Jessie for dinner."

"Well, then, who knows, maybe our paths will cross?"

"Who knows, they just might." Kate stands and wraps her arms around her father tightly.

"OMG, Kate! Look, it's our fathers!" exclaims Malie, wide-eyed and incredulous as Glen and Bradford make their way to a table out on Hanalei Bar and Grill's classy and comfortable lanai. The popular restaurant with spectacular views is situated in the heart of Hanalei.

Seated behind other restaurant goers, and out of Glen and Bradford's purview, Kate and Malie watch their fathers intently.

"What are you two looking at?" Jessie asks as she returns from the powder room and slips into the seat next to Malie.

"Our fathers," whispers Malie. "We're trying to keep a low profile."

Kate chuckles. "You mean we're spying on them."

"Kate and I want to see what they're up to, all dressed up in their Tommy Bahama duds and looking dapper."

"They *are* handsome," agrees Kate.

"OMG! Look at those two biddies over there giving our fathers the once over," Malie says, almost choking on her drink. "Maybe one of us should save them?"

"Why don't we invite them over to our table for a drink?" offers Kate, standing up.

"No, wait." Malie pulls at Kate's sleeve, urging her to sit. "Let's have some fun with them. Have the waitress take them both a drink and tell them that some hot women would like them to visit their table."

Jessie shakes her head at the girls' antics.

"I'll get the waitress," says Malie, flagging down a twenty-something server. Malie, Kate, and Jessie wait with bated breath as they watch the waitress deliver the invitation and the drinks.

"This is a Kodak moment," says Kate as she captures the priceless looks on Glen and Bradford's faces with her smartphone as they turn to crane their necks to see the "hot women."

Seconds later, the men laugh out loud when they eye their daughters. They make their way over to the girls' table to thank their "admirers."

"Fancy seeing you here, sweetheart," says Bradford as he leans in to kiss Malie on the cheek.

"Kate, you didn't mention you were coming here," comments Glen, planting a kiss on his daughter's forehead.

"Well, you didn't tell me you were dining here either," answers Kate. "Do you want to join us?"

Glen and Bradford pull two chairs up to the table.

"Glen, have you met Jessie? She works with me at The Plumeria Café?" Malie says by way of introduction.

"I've seen you at the café but haven't had the pleasure yet," says Glen, shaking Jessie's hand.

"Dad, I know you've met Jessie before," adds Malie.

"Aloha," Bradford and Jessie each murmur in greeting.

Bradford chuckles. "So, a drink from some 'hot women,' huh?"

"Yeah, when she said 'some gorgeous young girls,' I thought the evening was about to get very interesting indeed," Glen adds.

"*Dad!*" whines Kate, half in jest and half not liking the implications of that remark. Try though she might, and despite knowing her dad has had more than just a passing dalliance with Peggy, Kate still hasn't come to terms with the idea of her father dating—nor being such a hot commodity in his advanced years. By the look on Malie's face, she seems to share the same sentiment about her own father.

"It's hard to get used to the fact that you're single," Malie admits as she stares into her father's eyes.

Bradford shrugs. "If I had a choice, you know it wouldn't be my preference."

"Nor mine either," agrees Glen with a sigh.

"Gentlemen, have you eaten dinner yet?" Jessie interjects a few moments later to keep the evening's mood upbeat.

"We had a lovely dinner just down the road a bit. Thought we'd stop by here for an aperitif and dessert and maybe listen to some music and meet the locals," answers Bradford.

"What about you, ladies?" asks Glen.

"Our dinner was delicious, and speaking of that, here's the dessert," says Kate as a young waiter delivers a giant brownie topped with a mountain of vanilla-bean ice cream, macadamia nuts, and a decadently thick chocolate sauce.

"Shall I bring out more forks?" asks the waiter.

"Yes, and another one of those," answers Glen, pointing to the brownie plate. "This time we're treating the *'hot ladies.'*"

After the luxuriously indulgent dessert, great conversation, and a round of after-dinner drinks and cappuccino, the party bids each other aloha as they head for their respective homes.

"The night is still a little young," Glen comments to Kate on the short ride home. His watch reads 10:30 p.m.

"I forget that in New York things are just starting to get going about now."

"Are you going to wait up for Kai?"

"Absolutely. When we get home, do you want to sit out on the lanai for a bit? I can make us some of that cinnamon chai tea you like."

"Perfect."

"I like the look of the additional white lights we put up," notes Glen, perusing the gorgeous surroundings illuminated by strings of little, white sparkling lights throughout.

"Our little slice of heaven," Kate agrees as she blows on her hot tea before taking a sip.

"Jessie seems like a nice lady," Glen continues. "She told me her husband passed suddenly not too long ago."

Kate nods. "She's very nice. She likes to garden and comes over on Saturdays every so often. I invited her over again tomorrow morning since we still need all the help we can get."

Unable to hold back a yawn, Glen sighs,"Sweetheart, would you mind if I get my PJs on and turn in?"

"See you in the morning." Kate kisses her father on the cheek then watches him head back toward the ohana.

He's so lost without Mom.

"I thought I might find you reading in bed." Kai kisses Kate's cheek an hour or so later as he takes a seat next to her on the lanai.

"Dad and I were sitting out here, and I didn't feel like going inside."

"That picture you texted me of our fathers and 'the hot women' was hilarious."

"We wound up having dessert together and listening to some music for a while before heading home."

"Sounds like a nice evening."

"It was," says Kate, but it is obvious she's distracted.

"Something on your mind?"

"Oh, just thinking about my dad's vibe tonight. He had a happy smile, but looking into his eyes, I could see and feel his pain."

"It took my father quite a while before that look dissipated, and even so, it still appears from time to time." Kai takes hold of Kate's hands in his and rubs them comfortingly.

The two lovers sit in silence for a while, looking to the garden as if for answers.

"Want to go for a moonlight walk?" Kai offers, picking up a flashlight from the lanai hutch.

"You're not too tired after your day?"

"No, I want to visit with our flower friends."

Kate smiles and reaches out, taking hold of Kai's free hand. She knows he loves to peruse their garden domain, checking in on the various plants and projects. Their garden walks in the evening have become a new daily habit; it's the perfect way to wind down.

Guided by the moon's rays, the light shining from the strung lights and Kai's flashlight, they follow the stone path which leads them deep into the green. The chirping of crickets melds with the sounds of trickling water from various water features.

"The hibiscus is flowering beautifully," comments Kai.

"Dad will be happy to hear you approve. He fusses over them like a mother hen."

"As it should be," Kai says with a chuckle. "I appreciate Glen's contribution. The herb garden is coming along nicely … and the plumerias are so fragrant tonight," adds Kai as he and Kate sit on the angel bench between the two abundant beauties. Kai turns the flashlight off and sets it on the ground so he can wrap his arms around Kate.

The night is radiant, and as Kate inhales deeply, she feels warm surges of energy, seemingly emanating from the garden, surrounding and penetrating her from all angles. The overwhelming and joyous sensations bring a few tears to her eyes.

"What's this, now?"

"It's just so beautiful here." Kate wipes away some moisture from her face. "It's as if the moon, the stars, and the family of flowers and trees are enveloping us in a blanket of peace and love."

"Let's just sit here for a while." Kai says, speaking slowly and tenderly. "And take in the healing magic of the garden."

19

"I made apple spice bread," Jessie says, greeting Kate the next morning at the door of the Weke cottage with a covered wicker basket. Dressed in a straw sun hat, white sleeveless top, and loosely fitted jeans, she's ready for a day of gardening. "Maybe we can enjoy some for a mid-morning break with tea."

"Lovely." Kate sets the basket of bread on the kitchen counter before ushering Jessie out into the garden. "Kai and I put some raised beds in over here." She points and opens the gate to the fenced area. "This way it keeps away a host of critters who otherwise will eat all our harvest."

"I'll start in here then," Jessie says. She picks up a shovel and walks over to one of the beds.

"Aloha, Jessie!" Glen waves as he stands in the ohana's outdoor kitchen, scrolling through his iTunes music library on his iPad. "What type of music would you ladies like to listen to today? Classical, slack-key guitar, melodic piano and healing nature sounds, smooth jazz, pop?"

"Let's try the melodic piano first and take it from there," Jessie says, her attention already on digging in the dirt.

"You got it!" Glen makes the selection and turns up the volume.

Kate, Jessie, and Glen lose themselves in the warm caresses of the sun, the richness of the soil, and soothing sounds of the music as they tend to the earth and plants for the next several hours. Eventually, Glen prompts the trio to take a break and enjoy some lemon-ginger iced tea he prepared earlier that morning.

"This apple spice bread is delicious. It hits the spot," exclaims Glen as he cuts himself a second slice of the thick, moist treat.

"Glad you're enjoying it," Jessie replies.

"Where are you from again?" asks Glen.

"Michigan."

"And what inspired you to move here?"

"Well, I needed a change. I loved Michigan and had a beautiful home there. It was a great place to live but very cold in the winter. My husband and I used to vacation in the Hawaiian Islands during the colder months, and we always loved it here. After he passed away, I chose to make it my new home. I love the Hawaiian mana."

"Ah, the Hawaiian mana." Kate moves her arms about to emphasize the magnitude of spirit.

"I think I've been experiencing a little of that mana," offers Glen.

"Oh?" Kate's eyes widen.

"I'm enjoying being in nature, planting this garden, being so close to the ocean and the peace of it all. I can feel myself here, and I feel like I'm becoming more focused somehow and …" Glen trails off.

"And?" Kate encourages Glen to continue.

"I even thought I felt your mother next to me today as I was planting the white lilies." Glen gulps, a little emotional. "I hope I don't sound ridiculous," he adds, turning to Jessie.

"Not at all. I mentioned to Kate several weeks ago that I felt my husband here as well."

"I feel Mom here, too, Poppy," answers Kate as she rubs the top of her father's hand for support. "Just enjoy the feeling and the thought it provokes and gives thanks to God for the blessing."

"The event invitations are stunning, aren't they?" comments Sukey proudly to Nā Pīkake. The ladies have gathered around the large wooden table in the Weke garden's ohana kitchen. The colorful card showcases a photo Kate took of a lovely lei made with strands of white pīkake flowers bound together with a spray of plumeria blossoms.

"It looks like our logo," interjects Malie.

"That was the intent." Sukey hands each lady a stack of invitations with pre-addressed envelopes and some stamps. "The labels are printed. The plan is to get them in the mail tomorrow."

"Oh, this is getting exciting!" exclaims Olivia. "Kate and I locked in all the silent-auction items. Everything should be in by next Wednesday."

"Any last comments on the menu for the event?" asks Malie.

"It's perfect," answers Kate, perusing a print-out of the menu, which includes an array of tantalizing hot and cold appetizers to be served at the garden party, followed by a buffet of freshly grilled and organic fare.

"Mahalo for pulling strings to get all the wine donated for the evening, Elaine," praises Olivia.

"Of course, daaahling."

The ladies continue to touch upon every detail of the event: a valet company to park the cars, the party rental donations for the chairs, linens and decorations, a local florist who is graciously donating dinner- and buffet-table arrangements, slack key guitar music for the cocktail hour, and music and dance performances for the evening's entertainment. Through her extensive network of contacts and musician friends, Olivia has secured a group of talented artists who often play together as the evening's entertainment, and for "Night of Aloha," presented by Nā Pīkake, they'll play a selection of traditional and modern Hawaiian music.

"We're set with our volunteers," offers Jessie.

"Well, I think that about covers our agenda." Kate glances around the table. "Let's just continue to keep everyone updated on developments via email as we move forward."

"Will you look at who I ran into in town?" Glen cries out, walking up the garden path to Kate's outdoor office several weeks later.

"Aloha." Jessie waves to Kate. "Gee, I like what you've done with your outdoor workspace."

"Thanks." Kate smiles, surprised to see Jessie.

Kate is sitting at a large wooden desk under an attractive pergola with a protective roof covering. The sides of the structure are slatted, to be kept open when it's sunny and closed when it rains. She has decorated the charming niche with recycled and refurbished cabinets and a hutch, along with a wicker sofa, chair and coffee table. The welcoming area, perfect for reading and writing, sits directly outside her indoor office.

"I ran into Jessie at the bookstore," mentions Glen. "So I asked her if she might want to come over for tea."

"And scones," Jessie adds, raising a small bag.

"Can you spare a few minutes and join us?" asks Glen.

"Sure." Kate saves her document and powers down her computer. "I'll put a kettle on."

"Let me put my books away, and I'll meet you both out on the lanai," Glen replies.

"We have chai, apple cinnamon, lemon ginger, and Earl Grey." Kate reads the box labels in the kitchen cabinet with Jessie at her side.

"Earl Grey would be lovely," answers Jessie, so Kate puts on the kettle and removes three mugs from the cabinet.

"Looks like you found some books too."

"Oh, yes. I love that little bookstore in town. I think I might be one of their best customers. I'm in there at least twice a week."

"I love it too, and I like giving our local independent bookseller my business. What book did you buy?"

"Books, plural," laughs Jessie. "One is a book on gardening." She proceeds to pull the picture book out of her canvas bag.

Kate's eyes widen with delight as Jessie shows her some of the colorful pages. "I might want to borrow that one."

"I also bought Ina Garten's *Cook like a Pro*, which you'd enjoy–although you're quite a cook already–and a Mary Higgins Clark mystery."

"Good choices! Maybe, when you're finished reading them, we can do a book exchange? I swear, I could open a library with the number of books I have sitting on shelves and in boxes."

"I'd love to."

"You know, that could also be another fun project for Nā Pīkake: a book exchange club. It would give us some other fun things to talk about at our meetings."

"Great idea!" Jessie sets out a selection of miniature blueberry, chocolate chunk, and lemon-poppy seed scones on a plate before following Kate out onto the lanai.

After a refreshing break with Jessie and her father, Kate returns to her desk to finish the remainder of the tasks on her list, wrapping it up just before dinnertime.

"Bradford, Jessie, and I are going for a bite in town," Glen announces, coming into Kate's office just as she's ready to leave.

"Oh?"

"We just decided, spur of the moment. I should be home in a couple of hours," says Glen. "Want to join us?"

"Kai will be home in about an hour, so I don't think so. Just keep your cell on, Dad, in case we need to reach you."

Perusing the fridge moments later, she debates dinner. *What will it be tonight? Pasta with leftover grilled veggies and a large green salad? Maybe I'll toss a few jumbo shrimp into the mix and serve the pasta with a dash of extra virgin olive oil, some garlic salt and pepper, and an Italian seasoning blend.*

As Kate happily buzzes about the kitchen, she picks up a remote on the kitchen center island and points it to the television in the living room. The news anchor on the evening news announces that there's been another assault in town and that police are beefing up the investigation. "Are you kidding me?" Kate yells at the television.

"What's the matter, babe?" Kai calls out as he enters through the front door.

"They just reported another assault in town!"

As both Kate and Kai listen, transfixed, to the rest of the report, they are saddened to learn that the latest assault victim fell and broke her leg in the struggle with her assailant: a man who fits the description of Kate's attacker. Unfortunately, he fled the scene in a white van, license number still unknown.

Seconds later, Kate's cell phone rings. "Did you hear? ANOTHER assault! What is wrong? Why can't this creep be caught?" Olivia cries, not bothering to first say hello.

"I'm sure they'll catch him soon, but it makes me sick ..." Kate replies. "Say, since there's comfort in numbers, would you—and Grant too, if he's available—like to join us for dinner?"

"Great idea. I was thinking about what to do about supper."

It's just leftover grilled veggies I'm tossing in with some pasta and shrimp," warns Kate.

"Seriously, Kate? Your leftovers are my designer dinners. How about I bring over a salad and some cheese and crackers for appetizers?"

"Perfecto."

After the impromptu dinner with their men, Kate and Olivia prepare a fruit salad for dessert.

"Mahalo for rescuing me tonight." Olivia manages a small smile. "When I heard the news today about another attack, the memories just kept flooding back."

"Believe me, I understand."

"I know you do." Olivia smiles warmly at her friend. "When I get those kinds of thoughts, I usually acknowledge them, say a few prayers, and then work to clear them by concentrating on the positive. Sometimes, though, it just gets to my core, and I wind up in a dark place. Tonight, being with Grant and you guys, watching the gorgeous sunset, laughing and enjoying a delicious dinner in such a beautiful garden setting … it comforts me."

"Being together definitely helps. I'm sure some of your angst might be because you haven't heard anything from your attorney yet, am I right?" Kate proceeds to cut off the pineapple's leafy top and bottom before stripping the fruit's outer skin with a chef's knife.

"Yeah. I would love to know my daughter, but if she chooses not to meet me, for whatever reason, I have to find a way to live with that."

"Be easy on yourself. You know better than anyone else the importance of self-care during emotional times."

"I know, I know … rest, eat healthy, exercise, pray, do the things that bring you joy, be in nature," continues Olivia as she squirts some freshly squeezed lemon juice over the bowl of sliced fruit.

"Well, I hope you're taking some time for yourself between all the things you do," says Kate. She sprinkles cinnamon on the tops of the cappuccino and puts the brimming cups on a tray.

"I am. I'm thinking, though, for the next round of tapings, I'm going to probably do some segments on maintaining body balance and harmony when going through stress or trauma. I certainly could write a book on that."

"I think we all could be contributors," Kate says with a chuckle. "Let's take this fruit salad and the cappuccinos out before the guys wonder what happened to us."

<h1 style="text-align:center">20</h1>

Kate revels in the garden's stunning blossoms and lush greens as she follows the twisting dirt path. Each time she walks this way, there are new flowers to greet and aromatic scents to enjoy. When a family of beautifully colored, burnt-orange Gulf fritillary butterflies flies casually past, Kate takes note of one in particular that seems to be following her.

Suddenly feeling an energetic surge ripple through her body, Kate closes her eyes to feel that familiar, calming warmth.

"Aloha, Kate," her mother greets her.

"Mom." Kate opens her eyes and the women embrace.

"Come," Catherine beckons, taking Kate's hand.

As mother and daughter near a clearing, Kate hears voices—men and women talking, children laughing and playing—and the swooshing sounds of water cascading over a waterfall.

Rounding a group of tall, majestic, red, ti ginger plants, she and her mother spy her grandparents. She notes from the looks on their faces that they have been expecting her. Kate's grandfathers–the two Leos–wave aloha. There are other people she doesn't recognize at the gathering, but they all turn to her and smile. While some of those gathered are souls like her mother and grandparents and are no longer of this earth, Kate is instinctively aware that many of the others are indeed still alive.

In the distance, people sit around a garden table similar to the one in the Weke cottage garden. In another area a woman plays the guitar and sings. Children yell and laugh as they attempt to grab hold of butterflies. Adults and youngsters alike swim in a stream under a majestic waterfall.

"Aloha! You must be Kate," calls out a friendly, older Polynesian woman with large, penetrating brown eyes and wearing a warm smile.

The woman takes Kate's hands in hers and hands her a small spray of fragrant pīkake blossoms.

With this simple gesture, she makes a deep impression on Kate, who can feel the woman's overwhelming sense of gratitude.

As laughter and serenity permeate this joyous scene, Kate sees two female forms in the distance—Olivia and a young woman Kate instinctively knows is Olivia's daughter. Mesmerized, Kate watches them talk for a time. Then, as if sensing Kate is watching them, both women turn in unison to look and smile at her ...

"Ah!" Kate startles awake as the dream abruptly dissipates.

"Are you okay?" Kai asks, half-asleep.

"I dreamt I saw Olivia with her daughter in the garden again," Kate whispers as she curls up to next to Kai. "The dream had such a real quality to it. I hope it means that Olivia's daughter is going to agree to meet her."

"I hope so too," says Kai softly, spooning his wife.

"I'm still not going to say anything to her though ... just in case."

"Probably not a bad idea. Let's get a little bit more shut-eye while we can and ..." Kai's voice trails off as he and Kate fall back to sleep.

"I wish I could just go with the flow of my dreams, not need all the answers right away, or always think there's a meaning." Kate sighs before she purses her lips for Kai to kiss before he leaves for work.

"Pray on it," advises Kai. "If there's a message to get, you'll get it."

Kate dips her spoon into a bowl of creamy, Greek yogurt topped with strawberry and banana slices and plops a spoonful of the delicious mix into her mouth before scrolling her phone for messages. When nothing pops up, she turns her attention to her next task: she needs to get in some quiet time to deepen her connection to God. Maybe, after a conversation with Him, she can get to a place where she can accept rather than always question everything.

"I can be such a pain, I know," she speaks out loud to the Lord. "I'll do my best just to trust and have faith."

The Gathering

*And let us consider one another
to provoke unto love and
to do good works.*

– Hebrews 10:24

21

"The flowers are here!" announces Jessie excitedly the night of the long-anticipated fundraiser.

With the event due to start in a mere two hours, Nā Pīkake scurry about, each tending to their specific to-dos. Even their men—Kai, Trevor, Aukai, Kamal, and Alana's husband, Hani—have been given individual assignments.

"Please show the delivery men in," Kate instructs Jessie as a musician tunes his guitar and a pianist warms up his fingers, gliding them back and forth over the keys of the grand piano that has been set up on the garden stage.

Elaine helps Jessie expertly direct the delivery men in placing the exotic floral displays in the center of every round table, each set for twelve.

Decorated in pretty white linens and surrounded by high-backed, cushioned bamboo chairs, the tables sit under a large tented-roof structure strung with white lights. Festive tiki torches, strategically placed around the perimeter, and flickering white candles on either side of each table's centerpiece contribute to the ambient lighting and glamorous, festive feel.

While Malie works with staff and assigned volunteers and servers in the guesthouse kitchen area, Sukey and Alana are busy placing silent-auction items out on tables under an adjacent tent area.

On the street in front of the cottage, the men coordinate the valet parkers, bar deliveries, and other random tasks that involve heavy lifting. Even Glen and Bradford have been wrangled into helping out, and they do so with smiles on their faces, happy to be of service and take part in this joyous occasion.

Kate roams the environs with her checklist, investigating every aspect of the production with the two co-executive directors of the Aloha Helping Hands Foundation, a nonprofit that helps victims and

165

families of abuse, crime and other misfortune. Nā Pīkake teamed up with the nonprofit to host the fundraiser event, with all proceeds going to the Helping Hands organization.

In another area of the garden, Olivia, also serving as Mistress of Ceremonies for the evening's festivities, talks to some of the musicians as they perform their last-minute sound checks.

Then, with less than an hour left before guests start arriving, Kate and Kai excuse themselves and head to the quiet of their master suite to put the finishing touches on getting ready.

"As always, you take my breath away," Kai admires his wife as he fastens the last of the buttons on his colorful Hawaiian dress shirt.

"Mahalo, my love," Kate never tires of Kai's praise and appreciation of her fashion sense when they dress up for special occasions.

"I've got to hand it to Nā Pīkake. I'm impressed with how smoothly everything's come together. The atmosphere you've created for tonight is nothing short of astounding."

"I'll tell the women you said that, Dr. Stevens." Kate beams with pride as Kai lovingly kisses her lips. Following their passionate embrace, Kate chuckles. "Good thing I hadn't put on my lipstick yet."

"Lipstick or no lipstick, that's just the first of many kisses I plan to steal tonight, I can assure you of that."

"Well then," Kate flirts, "I'll have to put on one of my long-lasting, kiss-proof colors."

"The appetizers seem to be a hit," Kate tells Malie as a well-organized staff of waiters and waitresses serve cocktails and an array of hot and cold hors d'oeuvres.

"The lemon-herbed scallop skewers are delicious," Trevor says, giving Malie an enthusiastic thumbs-up.

As servers pass around trays of mini shrimp cocktails, curried-vegetable-rice cups, chicken-and-avocado rolls, and a host of other delights to appreciative guests, Malie beams. It's evident there won't be any leftovers.

"*I ola nō ke kino i ka mā'ono no ka 'ōpū,*" prays Kai and Kate's friend Haku before dinner.

Kai translates for those guests who aren't fluent in Hawaiian. "The body is nourished when the stomach is satisfied.

"*E pū pa'akai kākou me ka mahalo Ua loa'a ho'i iā kākou ka 'ai a me ke aloha.*"

"Let us share this food together with thanks that we have food and love."

"*E ho'omaika'i i ke Akua.*"

"And give thanks to God."

"What do we have here?" asks an attractive elderly woman as she scans the luxurious spread of traditional Hawaiian luau dishes. On the menu are Island favorites such as baked Mahi Mahi, Huli Huli Chicken, and Kalua Pua'a. The grilled chicken, cooked in its own juices with soy sauce, brown sugar, ginger, and garlic, and the roast pork, seasoned with salt and green onions and prepared in a Hawaiian underground steam oven called an *imu*, are two of Kate's favorite dishes.

"This dish is called Chicken Long Rice," Malie replies. "Shredded chicken is mixed with bean noodles and seasoned with garlic, onions, and ginger in a broth. Would you like some?"

"Sounds delicious." The woman replies with a nod.

Malie instructs the server to place a generous portion on the woman's plate. "Farther down the table, you'll find a selection of salads and sides," Malie adds and points in the direction of the display.

"Aloha, Kate, my name is Nani." A gentle Polynesian woman introduces herself while Kate makes her rounds through the tables after dinner.

Where have I seen her before? Kate wonders. When Nani tenderly takes Kate's hands into both of hers, Kate asks, "Have we met?"

"No, not that I recall." Nani shakes her head. "Let me introduce my granddaughter, Iolana."

"Aloha." Iolana stands to shake Kate's hand.

Kate continues to wrack her brain, wondering where she has met Nani.

"I work for Aloha Helping Hands, and this event means so much to us."

"It's our pleasure, Nani. What do you do for the organization?"

"I'm an office assistant, and my granddaughter, who's in high school now, is a volunteer."

"How did you get involved?"

"My daughter was a single parent," answers Nani, more serious now as she looks at her granddaughter with compassion and love.

Iolana, seemingly quite shy, looks away as Nani whispers, "My daughter, Iolana's mother … she had a host of mental health issues and some addictions, and well, thanks to several of the Foundation's programs, my daughter and our family finally got help. Sadly, though, my daughter passed away a few years ago."

"I'm so sorry for your loss."

"It was in an unrelated car accident, but we remain forever grateful for the peace and the healing that was brought into our lives by the Foundation before her death."

Touched, the only thing Kate can think to do is embrace the woman, and when she does, they hold one another for several long seconds before they separate.

"I don't want to monopolize your time, as there are so many other guests you probably want to greet. I have something for you, though." Nani picks up a lei made with several strands of pīkake flowers tied up with a pretty ribbon from the nearby table and places it around Kate's neck. "Iolana made leis with flowers from our garden to say thanks to each of you who are hosting this wonderful event."

"They're lovely, mahalo." The lei's delicate scent is intoxicating and Kate draws in a deep breath to enjoy the sweet air before she continues. "It was so nice to meet you. I'm sure our paths will cross again." She smiles and nods to Nani and Iolana before excusing herself to continue meeting the other guests.

Walking through the crowd, smelling the sweet pīkake lei, Kate is moved by both the conversation with Nani and the feeling that they had met before. Suddenly, it's as if time stops. The evening's sounds fade into the background. Kate remembers.

It was in my garden dream. Nani greeted me in the same fashion she did this evening—at a happy gathering around a bountiful table. She handed me a bouquet of pīkake blossoms. My dream did foretell this event.

Life is so surprising, Kate marvels as she steadies herself. *It's a beautiful, angelic web that connects us in ways we can barely imagine.*

Olivia takes center stage after the sumptuous dinner to introduce the members of Nā Pīkake, as well as the executives from Aloha Helping Hands, and to fill the audience in on all the vital work the organization does.

The evening continues with the presentation of several generous donation checks and a performance by a traditional Hawaiian dance troupe, followed by the popular group Mele, so named for the Hawaiian word meaning chants, songs or poems. The group, who play a mix of traditional and modern Hawaiian music, is well received at the gathering.

There is pure magic here.

Kate feels the joy that fills the garden. Her eye's alight on a golden flame that burns atop a white candle encased in the glass holder resting on the table in front of her. Suddenly, the glow swells and begins to dance more vigorously than any of the other candles.

Mahalo, God, Kate prays silently.

As she continues to look about the garden, Kai slips his hand into hers. Kate can't help but reflect on how, when something negative happens, more than likely something positive is waiting.

All you need is to have faith.

Kate's eyes turn to Olivia, who's talking to Grant.

If it is your will, dear Lord, and for the good of all those involved, please allow a speedy reunion for Olivia and her daughter.

22

"Seriously? We raised *how much*?" asks Kate, astonished, as she talks to Alana the following day.

"You heard me right," Alana, the group's treasurer-elect, assures her with a chuckle. "Between the donations, advertising, the silent auction, and ticket sales, we raised one hundred thousand dollars."

"Woooowie!" screams Kate, so excited that she almost knocks over the cup of coffee in front of her.

"What's going on?" Kai asks, entering the kitchen in his PJ bottoms, his hair sticking up in all angles.

"Alana's on the line. We raised a hundred thousand dollars!"

"Awesome!"

"Hear that, Alana? I'm putting Kai on speaker."

"Not bad for our first event," Alana gloats.

"I think I'm going to put Nā Pīkake on some of our hospital fundraiser details," Kai replies.

"We'll have to negotiate." Kate snuggles up to Kai, batting her eyes flirtatiously.

"Well, that's about all I have to report," Alana tells them. "Let me let you two get back to breakfast. We'll go over more details at our upcoming meeting. Aloha, you two lovebirds."

"All this excitement and success has made me very happy and very hungry!" Kate jumps up and down then playfully squeezes Kai in a bear hug. Kai responds by scooping her up in his arms and carrying her back toward the sofa. "Kai, I thought we were going to have breakfast?" Kate asks, feigning innocence.

"We will, I promise. I'll take you out this morning to a very nice, celebratory breakfast. But right now …" Kai quiets any potential for protest from Kate with a deep, soulful, passionate kiss.

An hour or so later, Kate and Kai make their way to The Plumeria Café, where patrons are lined up outside the front door. They manage to navigate through the crowd to give the hostess their name to add to the brunch waiting list, and then they bide their time sitting outside at a wooden picnic table under a straw umbrella.

"Kate, look over there." Kai points. "It's your dad. He's talking to Jessie. Did you know he was brunching here today?"

"I didn't, but I'm not surprised. My dad loves it here. Let's go sit at his table."

"Aloha, you two!" Glen greets Kai and Kate. "Look who I ran into again this morning."

Jessie smiles.

"Did you eat yet?" inquires Kate after an exchange of alohas.

"No. I was waiting for Bradford when I saw Jessie. So I put us on the list for three. What about you?"

"Not yet," answers Kate.

"Well then, let's make it a table for five," says Glen.

"I'll go tell the hostess," Kai offers.

Jessie picks up the conversation. "It was such a lovely event the other night. And I spoke to Alana this morning. Did you hear how much we raised?"

"One hundred thousand! Isn't it wonderful?"

"Makes it all worthwhile," Jessie replies, smiling.

"Aloha, folks," Bradford calls as he approaches the table. "I didn't realize we were going to make it a family affair this morning. I like it."

Bradford pats Glen on the shoulder and kisses Kate and Jessie on their cheeks.

"Malie has a table set up for us on the lanai," Kai tells the table and hugs his father.

"A prime seat without a wait? It wouldn't have anything to do with nepotism, would it?" Glen winks.

Kai laughs out loud. "Nepotism? *No, never.*"

Brunch for five winds up turning into a party of nine when Alana, Hani, Sukey, and Kamal spy their friends on the lanai. Malie manages to pop by her ohana's table every so often, bringing new muffin and scone samples for everyone to taste and weigh in on whether or not they should stay on the menu.

During breakfast, Kate notices that Bradford and her father are both seemingly vying for Jessie's attention. At one point she gently nudges Kai's leg under the table and gestures with her eyes to watch the goings-on. While she is happy her father and Bradford seem to be having a good time, she can't help but start to wonder.

Is my father interested in Jessie that way, *or is it a male competition thing? Jessie* is *an attractive widow.*

"Everything okay?" asks Sukey when Kate inadvertently lets out a deep sigh.

"Yeah, everything's fine."

Sukey gives her a pointed look that says she's not convinced.

Leave it to Sukey to notice, thinks Kate, aware that her friend is also very empathetic. At some point she'll share her feelings, but now is not the time.

"We'll talk later," whispers Kate. For the rest of the meal, she occasionally chimes in on the conversation, but the situation with her dad and Jessie has left her feeling emotional and conflicted.

"Did you see the way our fathers were flirting with Jessie?" Kate asks Kai on their walk back home from town. Unable to hold back her feelings any longer, she needs to vent and talk them out.

"They were just playing."

"Seriously? They were acting like teenage boys."

"Boys will be boys, I guess," says Kai. He laughs, trying to make light of the situation to change the mood, which only makes Kate even more upset.

"Kai!" she shouts. "Be real. They were trying to outdo one another, and to what end?"

"Okay, okay," Kai says, taking a deep breath. "I didn't mean to upset you, honey."

The silence is deafening as they continue their walk back home.

Kate picks up her pace, kicking pebbles on the road with the rim of her sandals. Finally, she speaks up. "How could my dad be flirting with another woman like that? My mother hasn't been dead that long."

"I know." Kai puts his arm around his wife's shoulders and kisses the side of her head, and when he does, Kate starts to cry. "Sweetheart, please."

"I'm sorry, but it freaked me out a little to see my father like that. I don't understand all the reasons why right now, okay? All I know is how much he loved my mother and that he's still grieving for her. So it was just a surprise, and it felt strange to see him act like that with another woman. Even though it was Jessie, and she's an awesome lady."

"If it makes you feel any better, I didn't see Jessie encouraging either one of them. She was very cool about it. She had a good marriage too, didn't she?"

Kate nods.

"Try not to worry too much." Kai offers, caressing Kate's neck.

While Kai knows that women are much more cautious about letting another man into their lives after their spouse dies, men tend to need a woman to help them organize their lives and to fill the void. However, mentioning this to Kate in the state she's currently in would go over about as well as a lead balloon.

"Time has a way of helping to heal," he says instead, knowing from personal experience and the loss of his dear mother. "I love you so much," he continues as he pulls Kate close and wraps his arms around her.

A little calmer now thanks to Kai's tender care, Kate slips her hand into her husband's as they walk down Weke Road, each silently lost in their own thoughts.

23

"You always talk about how you feel the Holy Spirit's presence in the garden—and sometimes, you feel that Mom is here. Is there something special you do to make that happen?" Glen's question comes out of the blue several days later as he and Kate putter in the garden.

Kate smiles, touched by her father's sincere interest. "You're the one who always told me when I was growing up that you can reach God anywhere, Pops, not just in the garden. Although, just being in nature is a wonderful way to connect."

"How do you do it?"

"Same way as you would. Pray an earnest prayer or talk plainly, whatever your style might be. You can even joke."

"Really?"

"Why not? God made us. So I know he must have a wicked sense of humor."

Kate and Glenn laugh out loud.

"I do talk to God, but I need to talk to him more," Glenn admits after their shared laugh.

"Share your day and what you're feeling. If you recall a loving memory, or even if you see or hear something that reminds you of Mom. Tell Him that you miss Mom and you'd like her to know, and if possible, receive a sign she has heard you or ask Him for a sign that she's okay, and then let it go. The things we inquire about must be in line with God's will and also in line with spiritual values."

"Don't worry," Glenn assures her. "I'm not going to ask for the winning lotto numbers."

They share another laugh.

"Continue to pray and see what unfolds. You might get an impression or, God willing, sometimes, Mom may come to you in your dreams. You may or may not get a sign. It's all in God's hands. I'm trying to learn to have more faith and go with the flow too."

"You mentioned signs. What kind?"

"A sign can come in a variety of ways. It might be something unusual, where you hear a song playing on the radio that was her favorite, or you may suddenly smell a fragrance that she always wore. Whenever I smell plumeria, for example, and I'm not near a tree or blossom, I feel it's my validation from God. It might also be a synchronistic event."

"How so?"

"Have you ever thought to yourself, 'What a coincidence?' For example, perhaps when you were thinking of someone you hadn't talked to in a while and you unexpectedly run into that person? Or when you overhear a random conversation that speaks to something you've been pondering? Maybe you might read or hear a particular phrase or sequence of numbers over and over in a short period. When we're aware of synchronicities, it's proof—or at least a validation— that we're on the right path. Am I making sense?"

Glen nods.

"I don't know why, but sometimes I believe I get validation when I see a bird or a butterfly."

"Tell me."

"Shortly after Mom passed … remember you and Derek drove me to JFK for my flight back to Kauai?"

Glen nods again.

"I was reading a magazine article, and it went into the history of why butterflies have long been considered a sign of renewal, a symbol of the soul, and a focus on the spiritual side of life in many cultures. Well, I silently asked God, if it was His will, to make Mom known to me as a butterfly. Ten minutes after reading the article, I was going to walk in one door of the terminal but for some reason decided to enter through another. As soon as I did, I saw a huge butterfly painting in front of me. It stopped me in my tracks. I would have bypassed it had I gone through the first door. But there, hanging right in front of me, was this ginormous orange-and-black Gulf fritillary butterfly, which also happens to be one of the most abundant butterflies in Hawaii!"

"Wow!" Glen is clearly impressed.

"There's no way we will know all the mysteries of life or Heaven, but if certain things bring us hope and do no harm …" Kate's voice trails off for a moment and then she continues. "And talk to God more. It will bring you comfort."

"Look who's the parent now." Glen chuckles and then enthusiastically starts to plant some red anthuriums. He examines the pretty, waxy blooms with their dark green leaves and remarks, "These flowers look like hearts!"

"They're called 'Hawaiian heart flowers.' They come in many colors, but I love the ruby-red ones."

"See this red anthurium." Glen holds up a pot. "Every time I gaze upon this beauty, I will thank our Father in Heaven from the bottom of my heart for the love of my sweet Catherine, and for all our blessings." Glen blows a kiss to the heavens and then turns to Kate and winks.

Kate smiles at her father. "I love you, Poppy," she says softly.

"I love you too, Katie, to the moon and beyond." Glen blows Kate a kiss.

"To the moon and beyond," Kate replies, returning the kiss.

Mahalo, Kate silently repeats over and over in her mind as she watches her father plant the red wonders with a lighter spirit. *Thank you, God.*

24

"Hey, girlfriend. What's happening?" Olivia asks on a FaceTime call with Kate.

"Just wrapping up the day at my desk. Kai's working tonight, and my dad's playing cards at Bradford's."

"That's where Grant is tonight too. Your dad's keeping busy, isn't he?"

"He's on the town a lot more than Kai and I are."

Olivia chuckles. "I love it!"

Even though Olivia sounds upbeat, Kate can hear the stress below the surface. "How are you doing?"

"I, ah …" Unexpectedly, Olivia falters. "Not so great today. Even with my positive thinking, I can't seem to shake this heavy feeling in the pit of my stomach. I keep feeling sudden waves of sadness that I can't seem to shake. It's probably about … well, you know."

Kate knows what her friend means. Olivia is feeling vulnerable, and deservedly so. She still hasn't heard any word about her daughter. When she thinks on it, Kate is amazed at how well Olivia has been handling the waiting. She's had very few "bad" days.

"Would you like to come over for dinner?" asks Olivia. "I have plenty of eats in the fridge and I could use the company."

With Kai working, and her friend in need, Kate gladly accepts Olivia's dinner invitation.

"Do you mind if Elaine and Sukey join us tonight?" Olivia's call interrupts Kate as she is driving down Kuhio Highway toward Princeville. She has been singing at the top of her lungs to an upbeat song on the radio by Hawaiian recording star Anuhea.

"After you and I hung up, Elaine and Sukey called to invite me out for a bite. It turns out Trevor and Kamal are joining Grant and your dad at Bradford's house tonight to play cards. When I told them you were coming over, they wanted to join us."

"Works for me."

"Hey, I'm having a lightbulb moment." Olivia is barely able to contain her excitement. "Let's have a girlfriend party!"

Kate chuckles at her friend's upbeat mood. "Besides dinner and a Lifetime movie marathon, what more did you have in mind?" "Well … maybe to start we can take a little swim or stroll along the shore. Then after dinner, perhaps we might do some scrapbooking while we watch movies. What do you think?"

"We better invite the whole sisterhood, or they might feel slighted if we don't let them in on it."

"I already thought of that. Malie and Alana are unavailable, and I left a message for Jessie."

"Okay, great, and maybe with the full moon, we'll even do a little moon dancing."

"I love it! Moon dancing."

When Kate arrives for the girlfriend party, she's immediately introduced to an intoxicating, sweet, woody smell permeating Olivia's great room, and she spies Elaine and Sukey, sprawled out on two large sectionals, enjoying cold beverages and appetizers.

Ylang-ylang and myrrh. Kate recognizes the welcoming scent. Olivia gifted her with a box of candles made with these same delicious essential oils a few months earlier.

The aromatic white candles burn in clear glasses juxtaposed around the room and soothing nature sounds, played through the built-in stereo system, drift through the environs following a lovely breeze as it rushes in through the open, retractable glass wall.

"Aloha," Olivia greets Kate with a broad smile and a hug. Sukey and Elaine call their greetings as well. "Welcome, my friends," Olivia announces to them all. "Tonight, we celebrate. Please follow me outside."

The ladies follow Olivia's dramatic, playful instruction and head out onto the lawn, which overlooks the ocean. The evening couldn't be more gorgeous, and the way the sun is beginning to set on the horizon promises another light show.

"Let's take hold one another's hand," instructs Olivia as the ladies form a circle. "*Ka mâlamalama o ke Akua e ho`opuni mai iâ kâkou.* The light of God surrounds us," invokes Olivia. "*Ke aloha o ke Akua e kîpuni mai iâ kâkou.* The love of God enfolds us. *Ka mana o ke Akua e ho `opakele mai iâ kâkou.* The power of God protects us. *Ke alo o ke Akua e mâlama mai iâ kâkou.* The presence of God watches over us. *Ma kahi â kâkou, e hele aku ai he Akua nô.* Wherever we are, God is."

"*Amene.* Amen," the group intones, ending the prayer.

"Since this is a girlfriend party, I thought it might be fun to start the evening by sharing and expressing our appreciation for one another and then maybe take a walk along the beach."

"I like it." Sukey gives a thumbs-up. "You start, Olivia."

"Okay." Olivia takes a few moments to look at each lady present. "I want to thank every one of you for your beautiful friendship. I can't tell you how much you all mean to me, but I'll try. Kate, I appreciate you for your tender and loyal spirit, always ready and willing to lend a hand. Elaine, I thank you for your amusing quips, joie de vivre, and compassionate spirit. And Sukey, I admire you for setting an example as a leader in business while remaining a beautiful, thoughtful soul."

"I am grateful to you, Olivia, for your generous heart and benevolent spirit, and for introducing me to my soulmate, Kai," starts Kate. "Elaine, your sense of humor and, as Olivia said, your joie de vivre, are infectious. Mahalo for making me feel immediately at home in Kauai from our first meeting. And Sukey, you're an amazing businesswoman, and your sense of style, grace, humor, and artistic spirit inspires me. I also give thanks for all you ladies for being so wonderfully supportive and caring of me after my home invasion."

"'Rare as is true love, true friendship is rarer,' to quote the seventeenth-century French poet Jean de La Fontaine," gushes Elaine. "Well, you are all my heart and my family. Mahalo, Olivia, for your limitless and loyal heart and your commitment to making this world a better place; Kate, for your loving spirit and inspiring words; and Sukey, for your spunky, down-to-earth personality and creative eye that helps foster beauty in this world."

"Olivia, mahalo for your dear friendship and ongoing support and inspiration. I am forever grateful," Sukey states with a smile. "To Elaine, my sister from another mister … for the laughter, joy, and encouragement you bring, not to mention some great customers. Kate, I'm so grateful for your sweet, loving ways and your creative spirit."

"Group hug," shouts Olivia, and the ladies comply as the soothing sounds of palm trees rustle in the wind and a swoosh of cool breeze pours in off the ocean. "I think the ocean is beckoning us to take that beach walk now."

"What a marvelous way to end the day, isn't it?" comments Elaine as the ladies sit around the lanai table, enjoying appetizers later that evening.

"Very relaxing," Sukey notes, running her carrot stick through the divinely creamy hummus.

"Mahalo for calling this impromptu get-together, Olivia. Too bad Malie and Alana couldn't make it, though," Kate adds before moving to another topic. "Did Jessie ever get back to you, Olivia?"

Kate no sooner asks the question than Olivia's cell phone dings to alert her that she's received a text.

"Ah, ha! Jessie got my message, and she's on her way."

"Kate, look at that sunset," comments Sukey when she sees the stunning rainbow of colors on the horizon. "Did you bring your camera?"

Kate digs into her bag and pulls out her digital camera. "Have camera, will travel." She moves about the grounds, capturing various flowers and greenery at the forefront of her shots that are framed with the ocean and the tangerine, hot pink, purple, and gold tones along the horizon. The day's puffy, white cotton clouds are also now transforming into a cavalcade of magnificent shapes. When Kate is finished capturing the colors and shapes of the sky, she looks down at her feet, and she gasps in awe at a large, stunning, iridescent peacock feather, a rainbow of turquoise, purple, gold, and green, lying at her feet.

As she picks up the lone feather, tears begin to form at the corners of her eyes. Kate takes the feather as a sign of comfort from God, a reminder that He knows her heart. She's never seen a peacock feather in this area before. The only other peacock feather she has ever seen close up was right after her mother passed. In biblical times, and in most religions and cultures, peacocks symbolize purity of spirit, protection, and a connection to divine guidance. Whatever tonight's meaning is, she feels the synchronicity is as beautiful as the feather itself. For tonight, she has gathered for a girlfriend party with Nā Pīkake—and "pīkake" means not only "flower" but "peacock."

How much more confirmation can I get than that?

One thing Kate knows for sure, however, is that if God wants to get her attention, He gets it.

Once, when she lived in New York, she was shopping at the hardware store, and suddenly, she heard from out of nowhere one of her Grandmother Anna Theresa's favorite songs, "Let 'Em In," by Paul McCartney and Wings. It happened to be on a day when, if anyone had asked her, she would have told them she was feeling particularly down about her old boyfriend Jason. She looked up to the store's ceiling when she heard the music. It was as if it were streaming down into the store from heaven.

Someone's knockin' at the door. Somebody's ringin' the bell. The familiar lyrics echoed in Kate's mind. *Do me a favor, open the door and let 'em in."*

Kate's grandma had such a unique way of singing and humming a song at the same time, and in the case of this particular song, Anna Theresa's humming always made Kate chuckle.

"Someone's knockin' ... *huuuummm.* Somebody's ringin' ... *huuuummm.*"

Later that same evening, in a dream, her grandmother had winked and smiled at her. That experience of hearing the song out of the blue and then having that dream made such an impact on Kate. She subsequently read that sometimes, if you have a particular dream—or experience—that you feel is significant, you should first make sure the message you receive is in line with scripture, and, if needed, pray on what to do in response, for God will always make the meaning clear.

While many of Kate's intuitive experiences and family dreams have brought her comfort from time to time, they have also conveyed specific information, which subsequently becomes validated by some real-life event. While she never seeks out this information, she is always delighted and awed when it happens.

"Kate, I think you have another winner here with this pound cake." Olivia takes another bite of the moist confection. "This would be great to serve at the café. What do you think?"

"For the right price, I think we can negotiate a deal," Kate assures her with a chuckle.

"OMG, I created a monster!"

The Plumeria Café now features several of Kate's creations on their menu; Kate, of course, gets the credit in all their marketing and advertising.

"I have an idea. After I finish my novel, what about writing a Plumeria Café cookbook?"

"That's a great idea!" enthuses Olivia.

"I'll buy it!" chimes in Jessie, who arrived while Kate was out snapping photos.

"So will I," answers Elaine. "I'll give it to the chef at our house—Trevor, naturally—and for me, well, I'll enjoy looking at the pretty pictures. Cooking is not my forte, and we're all a lot safer and healthier for it."

"Hear! Hear!" Olivia laughs. "No offense, Elaine, but remember the time you tried to make us egg salad for lunch?"

"Oh, yes. Almost burned the house down. Let the eggs boil until all the water in the pot was gone and the eggs were withered. Lunch out was my treat that day," remembers Elaine as the ladies laugh out loud.

"Speaking of books … how is your novel coming, Kate?" asks Sukey.

"According to my weekly writing schedule, I'll be done in about two months."

"Bravo, daaahling," says Elaine as she begins to tap on her glass with a fork. "To Kate, may her novel be a smashing success right out of the gate!"

After dinner cleanup, Olivia distributes a scrapbook to each lady seated around the lanai table.

"Look!" cries Sukey. "Peacocks are on the cover!"

"But of course," replies Olivia matter-of-factly as Kate places a large wicker basket of glue sticks, tape, scissors, and a stack of magazines in the center of the table.

"I've heard of scrapbooking, but I've never done it," admits Sukey.

"You cut pictures or words out of magazines to correspond with goals or things that you'd like to usher into your life," instructs Olivia. "You might have several pages of the scrapbook dedicated to your personal life, work endeavors, travel, education—whatever you desire or dream. The sky's the limit."

"It's basically allowing you to think—focus—about what you want, and sometimes, you discover you don't want what you think you want," adds Elaine.

Sukey nods, already perusing the stack of magazines. "I think I'm going to put together inspiration for our gallery remodel and for exhibits and events."

"I want to look for some inspirational rooms that I can share with my clients. It might make it easier for them to visualize what a home could look like," Elaine adds.

Kate has already selected a few images to express her objectives. "I always like to scan the magazines, because you never know what might trigger an idea for a great story."

"I'm going to see who we can hit up for sponsorships for Nā Pīkake events," enthuses Jessie.

"Hey, I like that. You go, girl!" Olivia high-fives Jessie. "I'm on a mission for some solid show-segment ideas."

The next few hours fly by as the ladies share, clip, and paste. Movie night is forgotten, and they fall into a natural rhythm of conversing and creating.

At 10:00 p.m. the doorbell rings. It's the men—Grant, Bradford, Kai, Kamal, Trevor, Aukai, Glen, and Hani.

"Kai! When did you get off work?" asks Kate, excited to see her husband.

"Oh, about an hour ago. I knew the men were playing cards, so I stopped by."

"What prompted you guys to come here?" asks Olivia.

"I knew you ladies were doing a girlfriend thing tonight, and, well, we just wanted to crash the party." Grant smiles devilishly.

"Oh, you did, did you?" Olivia, pretending to scold, playfully places her hands on her hips.

"Yeah, we wanted to get in on Nā Pīkake action," says Kamal.

The doorbell rings again. This time it's Malie and Alana, both finally off duty for the evening.

"Geez, what a group of party animals," declares Olivia.

"You've got to see this, everyone!" Elaine beckons from the lanai's open door. "There's a fabulous full moon!"

"Hey, weren't we going to do a moon dance tonight?" shouts Sukey playfully as everyone convenes on the lawn.

"A moon dance?" questions Kai.

"I may need another drink for this!" quips Trevor in his usual sarcastic fashion, which causes the group to erupt with laughter.

Elaine shakes her hips and raises her arms as she moves around Trevor like a belly dancer tempting him with her charms.

"I kind of like this dance," cackles Trevor.

Malie and Kate follow suit, moving cat-like around their men. Seconds later, Sukey works her best moves on Kamal while Jessie dances around Glen and Bradford.

Kai cocks his head and motions Kate to watch Glen and Bradford. They are obviously mesmerized by Jessie—the expressions on their faces are priceless. They look like two stunned little boys. Even Kate can't help but break out in waves of laughter.

Seconds later, Van Morrison's "Moon Dance" blasts over the audio system, prompting everyone to break out in their own crazy "moon dance," singing, hooting and howling, and enjoying the happy feeling created by the eloquent moon that shimmers and illuminates the night.

The Gift

For with God all things are possible.

– Matthew 19:26

25

As Kate looks up, she sees a bird soar high and disappear through the fluttering palms. The sun tingles warmly on her skin, and its energy encircles her in a warm embrace. Closing her eyes in sacred appreciation, she hears the birds sing and the trickling of a nearby brook. Standing still, and observing with senses other than sight, she begins to smell something sweet.

Plumeria, she notes.

"Aloha!" Kate opens her eyes to see both her mother and Leilani's smiles.

Each lady takes one of Kate's hands in theirs as they walk the garden's dirt path to a clearing.

Kate's excitement is palpable. She instinctively knows something profound is happening. In the garden's clearing, Kate sees Olivia, looking pensive and sad. Seconds later, Olivia's daughter approaches Olivia from behind. When the girl places her hand on her mother's shoulder, Olivia turns. Upon seeing the young woman's smile, Olivia's sadness dissipates. Immediately, Kate can sense an understanding between the two women. It's a healing taking place.

"Ah!" Kate catches her breath as her eyes bolt open upon waking from her dream. She looks around the darkened room, momentarily forgetting she's at home in bed until she sees Kai fast asleep beside her. Moonlight drifts into the room through slightly parted curtains, and through the open window, Kate can hear the sound of rain trickling off the roof to the ground below.

I believe Olivia will hear soon. Kate runs over every detail of her dream, now starting to trust herself and not obsess about the meaning.

Just go with the flow. Trust that what I need to know will be revealed.

The next morning, while Kai sleeps in on his day off, Kate slips out of their warm cocoon to start her work. Several hours later, after having met her creative writing quota, she continues on a roll with her magazine assignments, every so often gazing up from her computer to watch Kai and Glen work alongside each other in the garden.

The men get along exceptionally well together, and it makes Kate happy that her father has also found a friend in Kai's father, Bradford. Her father is thriving here. Kate is thankful she can witness signs of his healing, and it has helped both of them that he's been open to reading about surviving a loss.

Dad's found great solace in this garden. We all have. Why wouldn't we? It's a wonderful place to be.

"Honey …" Glen starts tentatively the next morning over coffee with Kate on the lanai. "I hope you're not going to be too upset when I tell you this."

"Tell me what?"

"Well, Peggy called me just before breakfast."

"Oh?"

"She's back in New York and asked when I'd be coming home."

"What did you tell her?"

"Well …" answers Glen. Kate knows news she doesn't want to hear is coming.

"You're not going to rush home just because she called?"

Glen shrugs. "Guilty."

"I got the impression you two weren't serious—was I wrong about that?"

Glen twitches nervously in his chair.

"Did you tell her you were enjoying your time here?"

"I did."

"Okay, then. End of story."

"I told her I'd be coming home this weekend."

"Dad, seriously? I thought you were going to stay a little longer. We like having you here."

"I appreciate that, honey. I love being with Kai and you too."

"It's okay for her to fly out of town and leave you, but now that she's back in New York, she calls, expecting you to be home at her beck and call … and you're going to jump?"

"It's not like that."

"Oh, no?"

"Sweetheart, I love it here. I've had a wonderful time. However, I've already been away from New York for a long time. I do have some home maintenance to take care of, and I *would* like to see Peggy. You understand, don't you?"

All Kate can muster is a sigh.

"Come on, hon. Don't be like that. Hey, I have an idea. Why don't I treat you to a nice breakfast? That way we won't have to dirty any dishes. We could go for a little walk afterward, if you can spare the time."

Kate thinks about it. Her heart feels heavy, and truth be told, she feels like a good cry; however, she accepts her father's offer, knowing that despite her upset, her time with him is precious.

"My lawyer just called! My daughter's name is Alia. She lives in Boston and she's agreed to meet me!" blurts out Olivia, breathlessly ecstatic as she speaks to Kate on her cell. "Pray, and then turn it over. The night of our girlfriend party, I did that. 'Thy will be done,' and I meant it, I was genuinely ready for whatever was in God's master plan. This morning when I woke up, I had such tremendous peace, even knowing I might never have all the answers. A few hours later, I got the call."

"Well, you want to know something? Last night I had a prophetic dream."

"Spill." Olivia's curiosity is piqued.

"In the dream I walked the garden path with my mother and Leilani, and they brought me to a clearing, where I saw you. At first you looked sad, but then this pretty young woman, who I instinctively knew was your daughter, joined you. She touched you on the shoulder, and I could tell by the way you both looked at one another that there might be a healing of some kind."

"And you didn't call me ASAP?"

"At three thirty in the morning?"

"Well …"

"I felt it better to wait … to see what unfolded in real life."

"I understand, I do. Still, isn't it amazing?

"A beautiful, wonderful mystery. When do you get to meet Alia?"

"This weekend. I've booked a flight for Thursday, and I'm planning to meet her Friday."

"When lightning strikes …"

"Depending upon how things go, and if the timing's right, I'll broach the concept of why we may want to take our story public," adds Olivia. "However, I think it's better to put that on the back burner right now."

"I agree. Best to meet Alia first then see what happens."

"One step at a time," affirms Olivia.

26

"Ahh!" Kate exclaims several times in quick succession to relieve her inner angst after she and Kai say their alohas to her father at Lihue Airport. Sighing deeply at random intervals has become a regular habit this past week since her father informed her of his plans to return to New York, prompted by the call from Peggy.

"Just breathe," Kai tells Kate as he drops her off at home before heading to work. "I'll call you from the hospital. Do something fun."

Okay, so what am I going to do today to keep my mood positive? Work on my novel? Maybe later. Malie's dropping by shortly to pick up some garden produce.

Instinctively, Kate heads toward the kitchen.

Muffins or bread? What shall it be? Maybe a new recipe—a bread with peaches and almonds? Kate starts to remove the necessary elements from the kitchen cabinets and fridge: organic whole wheat flour, almond meal, baking soda, pureed fruit, and a host of other ingredients.

A couple of hours later, she cuts herself a thick slice of the moist, fruity bread and sits down on the lanai with a cup of Chai Rooibos tea.

Still feeling out of sorts, she ponders all the productive things she could be doing. However, even though it's a gorgeous day outside, the idea of channel surfing has more appeal, and for the next several hours, she succumbs to numbing and mindless entertainment until her telephone rings.

"Kate, I met Alia!" Olivia screams with delight into the phone.

"Tell me, tell me," squeals Kate with matching enthusiasm.

"When she opened the door, and I saw her, it was like nothing I've ever experienced before. We have a strong resemblance, too ... she's genuine, kind, intelligent ... she's an ER doctor. How impressive is that? Oh, and she told me that for as long as she can remember, she's known of her adoption. Her parents told her when she was a young child. I shared with her everything I felt—all that I've shared with you—and that once I knew she was growing inside me, I loved her so much that I only ever wanted the best for her."

"Oh, Olivia … do think you'll meet her parents, too?"

"Yes, tomorrow night. Alia mentioned that one of the reasons she took some time responding to my request was because her mother was unsure of opening up this door and what might transpire. It's a sensitive subject, that's for sure, but her mother does want to meet."

"I'm so happy for you."

"Grant's coming in late tomorrow night, after the dinner."

"Will he meet her too?"

"We'll see … one step at a time." They both chuckle as they speak in unison.

"Please, Malie, take more zucchini. We also have lettuce and tomato." Kate points to all the fresh produce in their garden.

"I'll fill up as much as I can," says Malie, lifting up all the canvas tote bags she's holding for emphasis.

"We've also got tons of lemons, apples, avocados … just go for it," instructs Kate. "Here, give me one of those bags. I'll help you pick."

"We're going to have to figure out a reimbursement plan if we keep coming back for supplies."

"Well, this round is on us. You can talk to Kai about how he wants to handle things in the future."

Later, after Malie leaves, Kate can't stop thinking of Olivia and wondering how dinner with Alia's parents went the previous night. Then her cell rings. "How did it go?" she asks immediately.

"Oh, it went." Olivia's sigh seems to speak volumes.

"Uh-oh. What happened?

"We had dinner in the hotel suite to keep things private. Alia's parents are lovely people. Her father, Jefferson, is a pediatrician, very soft-spoken and distinguished. Her mother, Doris, is a retired elementary school teacher, and she's got quite a strong personality, and …"

"And?"

"There was tension in the air. She was very tentative, and I could tell she was trying to assess me. I felt a little like I was on trial."

"I'm sorry."

"I'm taking lots of deep breaths. Oh, and somehow, we all got to talking about telling our story before the media intercepts it. I wasn't planning to bring that up for some time, but it just happened naturally. I suggested that if we do tell our story, we could do it our way, in my new magazine, and a close personal friend would write the feature."

"And?" Kate asks, biting her lip.

"Alia's intrigued, but she's also concerned. She's got an important hospital position. Then there's her parents."

"How did they react?"

"Doris was *not* a fan of the idea. However, I brought up the fact that, under 'normal' circumstances, this issue wouldn't be on the table. But, given our story, it's just something we should all consider."

"So how did you leave it?"

"Alia's a grown woman, so her parents acknowledged that it's her decision. I was glad about that. But when they started asking me more questions, I offered them an opportunity to talk to you. If you're game, Alia and Doris would like to do a video call with you."

"That was brilliant. When do you want to do the call?"

"As soon as they give me the go-ahead. I'll do my best to give you at least some notice," Olivia promises.

"You got it. Just let me know when," confirms Kate.

"I don't want to get ahead of myself, but should they decide to do the interview, I'd want you to interview them in Boston."

"I agree. I wouldn't want to do it any other way than face-to-face."

27

Here we go, thinks Kate about a week or so later as she waits not so patiently in her home office for the video call with Olivia, Alia and Doris.

While Kate has braced herself for the unexpected, still, she feels confident about the call. Having gone over every possible issue and potential pitfall, she double checks that her cheat sheet is by her side. She takes another sip of iced tea, and then the video call comes in.

"Hi."

Kate can tell by Olivia's tone and demeanor that things are a bit tense.

"Kate, meet Alia and Doris Walker," Olivia continues. "Ladies, this is my friend and ace journalist, Kate Grace Stevens."

"Aloha." Kate waves warmly at her laptop screen. Doris is an attractive, sixty-two-year-old woman, elegantly dressed, with a subdued look on her face. Alia is fresh and beautiful and exudes positive energy.

"I'm sure Olivia has informed you why we wanted to talk to you," starts Doris. "My husband and I are very concerned about how going public will impact Alia, and frankly, all of our lives. I know my daughter is an adult and can handle her own affairs, but we'd like all our viewpoints to be represented and respected. We also don't want any three-ring circuses. We're private people who lead happy, peaceful lives, and my daughter has a wonderful career. We're concerned about unnecessary and negative disruptions. I'm sure you can understand."

"I do," Kate says warmly. "However, I believe telling the story has value on so many levels, especially when we'll have control over the presentation."

"It only needs to be told once, the way we choose," states Olivia sincerely.

"Mom, I think the focus will be mainly on Olivia and me," adds Alia. "I'm not afraid. I can handle myself."

"I know you can, dear." Doris reaches for her daughter's hand.

"Rather than live afraid or in hiding, I think it's better to get the story out. That way we're true and authentic."

"When the story breaks, what if you get harassed by journalists?" Doris frets.

"Mom, the *what ifs* are just a part of life, and it's not like any one of us has a crystal ball. However, as Kate mentioned, if we have control over how the story is made public, it will be told *our* way. Clean, to the point. We say what needs to be said. There might be some initial hoopla, but after that I think it will be okay."

"Doris, I told Alia that should she get any media calls, she can refer everything to my publicist, Connie Martin, who'll handle all inquiries," assures Olivia. "Connie's one of the best in the business, and I trust her implicitly. Working with her counsel, Alia will be able to make her own decisions on how she wants to handle any future inquiries. I want to make that same offer to you and your husband."

Doris inhales noticeably, pondering Olivia's statements.

"Once I have the article written, I'll be sure to send you a copy. I'm not opposed to editing or eliminating anything that might make you uncomfortable," offers Kate.

"Thank you, I appreciate that," replies Doris, and Alia nods in agreement.

"I want you to know, Doris, that you can also call me anytime, about anything. Your feelings matter to me," Olivia adds.

"I appreciate that." This time the smile Doris gives makes her seem a little more at ease.

"So how do you feel?" Olivia manages, turning to Alia.

Alia confirms she's in agreement with taking a proactive step, and her mother concurs.

Kate takes up the conversation. "I'll come to Boston to interview you. Just let me know what date works."

"Next weekend?" replies Alia. "Let's get it done."

After the call, both Kate and, especially, Olivia, are on a high. Olivia makes plans for her travel agent to coordinate arrangements for Kate and suggests that Kai join her if he can. "After all, there's support in numbers, and Grant's in town. After the interviews, we can all enjoy Boston."

Once Kai confirms that he's able to get a colleague to cover for him, he and Kate decide that, while they're on the East Coast, they'll squeeze in a quick trip to New York. That way Kate can check in with her *New York View Magazine* editor, Edward, in person, as well as show Kai around her old stomping grounds. There's sure to be a few family dinners thrown into the mix, and that suits them both fine.

What an incredible turn of events. I can't wait to tell Dad that I'll be seeing him again sooner than expected!

28

"We landed in Boston about an hour ago," Kate texts to Cindy. "We're on our way to the hotel now, then to dinner with Grant and Olivia. We'll see you soon. XO."

Kate inserts a funny selfie of Kai and her waiting in the baggage claim area at Logan International Airport. She immediately shoots off another round of texts to her father, brother and sister, letting them know she and Kai have arrived in the same time zone.

Respecting Olivia's wishes for everything to remain private, all her family and friends know is that she's covering a story for Olivia's new magazine and that Kai is tagging along to see everyone and do some sightseeing.

"Well, shall we celebrate?" Kate asks as they exit the airport.

"What did you have in mind?" Kai's amorous smile says it all. He walks toward Kate and encircles her in his arms. As their lips entwine, all memories and thoughts of today's events and tomorrow's deadlines luxuriously dissipate.

"Here's to Ohana!"

Grant, Olivia, Kate and Kai raise their glasses of Chianti in a toast several hours later as they dine at a quaint Italian restaurant situated in Boston's historic North End in a nineteenth-century row house.

"My bay scallop pasta looks divine. But I still want to taste some of your osso buco, Kai." Kate eyes the plate of delicious veal shanks while Olivia and Grant divide up their dishes, Lobster Fra Diavolo—succulent lobster served over a bed of pasta in a spicy tomato cream sauce—and the daily catch, haddock, prepared with an ethnic flair.

At the close of their delicious dinner, Olivia and Grant, spent from the day's emotional encounters, bid Kai and Kate adieu.

"Mmmm," moans Kai as he munches in ecstasy on one of the cannoli with chocolate-chip-ricotta filling from the North End's iconic Mike's Pastry.

"I can't believe you can eat more dessert after all the food we had at the restaurant." Kate chuckles at her husband as they stroll the narrow, historic streets. "Thank goodness we're walking!"

"Do you think we should have picked up more cannoli to take back to the hotel?" Kai asks in earnest.

Kate laughs out loud at his concern. "We bought eight. How many cannoli do you intend to eat at once?"

"It's just that we told Olivia and Grant we'd bring them some and …"

"I think we have enough. We can always go back tomorrow."

"Ooooh," Kai moans as he licks his fingers. "That was soooo good."

Sometimes, the little boy in Kai makes Kate's heart sing. So she goes with the love flow and throws her arms around him, giving him a big squeeze.

"Olivia seemed calm and grounded tonight," Kai observes. He wraps his arms around Kate as they continue the short walk back to the hotel.

"Well, she prepared herself to meet Alia and even read up on other adoptive reunions so she would know what to say and do."

"That's interesting. What did Olivia discover? I'm curious."

"Well, for one, to not have too many expectations and to operate from a position of love and understanding. Also the importance of taking things step by step once she's opened the door."

"Sound advice."

"I believe that, in these situations, the birth mother or child often 'expect' certain outcomes, and when they don't happen, they're devastated. Like any relationship, there's a give and take. Just because the other person shares your DNA doesn't mean it's going to go well … and usually, there are also other family members to consider, so it's complicated."

"Yeah, I can see there are a lot of layers." Kai is silent as he mulls over all the aspects Kate has pointed out.

"The good news is that research shows that taking it slow, with love and understanding, can be quite healing for both parties on many levels."

"Are you nervous?"

"You know, I was before I talked to Alia on the video call. But now? No. I have all my questions and notes together. For the rest I'll go with the flow tomorrow and hang loose." Kate displays the Hawaiian *shaka* "hang loose" sign, extending her thumb and pinky out and curling in her three middle fingers toward the palm of her hand.

"Do you think you'll be able to get all you need tomorrow?"

"We'll see how it goes. There's always Monday. We should be able to head for New York on Tuesday. Thanks again for taking time off; I love the fact that you're with me."

"I'm glad I can support both you and Olivia. Alia and Olivia are lucky to have you tell their story, you know."

"I'm the lucky one." Kate smiles as Kai pulls her in closer and kisses her deeply.

29

"It's so nice to meet you in person," Kate says as she and Kai shake hands with Alia on the expansive, private terrace of Olivia and Grant's suite at the elegant, waterfront Boston Harbor Hotel.

"Aloha from one fellow ER doctor to another," Kai adds, smiling. "Olivia tells me you work at Massachusetts General."

Alia nods.

"Well, I'm sure your ER is a lot busier than ours in Kauai—and definitely *not* on island time."

Kai's comment lightens the mood.

"Ladies, Kai and I have a full day, so we're going to leave you to do your thing," Grant comments before kissing Olivia on the cheek.

"I appreciate you both letting me help tell your story," begins Kate as she sets her laptop case down on the large coffee table between the comfortable arrangement of sofas and chairs. Sitting opposite Olivia and Alia, she readies her smartphone to make an audio recording of the interview. "Why don't we start with you telling me about your family and your upbringing, Alia. Do you have any siblings?"

Alia smiles broadly. "No, it's just me."

"And your parents?" inquires Kate.

"My mom's a retired elementary school teacher, so when I was growing up, she was home with me after school and was also very active in my extracurricular pursuits. She was a Brownie and Girl Scout leader and has always been my biggest supporter."

"And your father?"

"He's a retired pediatrician—a very gentle and quiet man. I'd have to say 'bookish' describes him best. He loves to read, and he's passionate about history. He also loved his job and his patients, and the children and their parents loved him too. Like my mom, his profession afforded him a flexible schedule. He and Mom always came to whatever school event I was involved in, whether it be a theatre production, a speech and debate club activity, or sports event. When I was growing up, and even today, we have always loved going to concerts and the theatre together—anything having to do with the arts—and we often share the books we're reading."

"Lovely," comments Kate.

Olivia nods in agreement then asks, "Kate, would you mind if I ask a question or two if inspiration hits? I can't help it—I have interviewer blood coursing through my veins."

"By all means. This interview is for information gathering, so whatever works."

"Alia, you mentioned to me the other day that your parents are your friends. Please tell us about that," encourages Olivia.

"I feel they are now. Growing up, Dad was always a teddy bear, while my mom was a bit of a disciplinarian, which I wasn't a big fan of at the time. But I see the wisdom in it now. And the main thing—I could always tell she was coming from a place of love."

"When did you first learn that you were adopted?" Kate inquires.

"I think I was around six or seven. It's something I just always seemed to know."

"Do you remember what your parents told you?" asks Olivia.

"They explained that my mother was a very, very young girl and that something happened to her beyond her control that resulted in my soul coming into the world. They also explained that my birth mother felt it would be best to have me grow up with parents who could care for me. My parents always say that our souls chose one another. I have never felt like I didn't belong right where I was."

"Did they share any other information?" Kate asks.

"You mean, did they tell me that my birth mother was … raped?"

Kate nods.

"Yes, when I was a little older and started asking more questions. I think I was around thirteen or fourteen or so."

"Do you remember your reaction when they told you?" asks Olivia.

"When I realized that I came to be because of a rape crime, what my parents had always shared with me took on a new dimension."

"Tell us." The look on Olivia's face reveals that she wants to know but is also afraid to hear the answer.

"To be honest, I was shocked. Then I got mad. I thought to myself, 'Why couldn't my parents be my parents? Why did I have to come into the world through such a violent act?'"

Kate proceeds gingerly. "How have you come to think about the situation today?"

"I've discovered, and accepted, that I may never know all the reasons why. While we don't necessarily know God's plan, we do have a choice of how we live our lives and how we deal with sad or unfortunate situations. We can choose to live in God's light or in darkness. I prefer the light … to look at the positive and take joy in the blessings that I do have—like my loving family."

"Olivia, what are you thinking right now?" asks Kate.

"What Alia just expressed is something my grandparents believed, and it was my grandparents who helped me through my most difficult time," reveals Olivia, honestly and plainly. "My mother had already passed, and my dad was nowhere in the picture. However, even though I was close to my grandparents, I didn't tell them I'd been raped for quite some time."

"Why not?" asks Alia.

"I'm not sure. I thought maybe somehow it was my fault. My grandparents were very reticent, church-going people. In that time and place, sex or rape wasn't talked about that openly. I guess I even tried to deny to myself what had happened. I was ashamed." Olivia starts to tear up. "I truly thought I must have somehow brought it on myself."

"Let me get some tissues." Kate turns off the recorder for a few seconds while she too tears up.

"They're in the bathroom," instructs Olivia.

"I'm sorry, Olivia …"

"It's okay, Alia. We're sharing here. It's good."

In a flash Kate is back and distributes several tissues to both Olivia and Alia, keeping a few for herself and then turning her recorder back on. "So, Olivia, when *did* you tell your grandparents?" Kate asks, continuing the interview.

"After my period didn't come for a couple of months." Olivia looks at Alia. "When I realized you were growing in my belly."

"What happened?" Alia asks.

"I told my grandmother. She took me to my doctor, and once it was confirmed, she broke the news to my grandfather. I needed her to do that. I couldn't. However, it was my grandfather who told me to always stand tall. He was my rock, and he never let me feel like I was responsible for what had happened. He was the one who helped me understand that I was a victim." Olivia gulps, remembering.

"What did you think when you learned you were going to have a baby?" asks Kate.

"I loved you from the very moment I knew," Olivia says to Alia. "Oh, I was scared, don't get me wrong, but I was also truly amazed that my body could do that. I want you to know I never felt ill will toward you, and I've thought about you every day."

"How did you decide to go the adoption route?" Kate asks Olivia.

"Due to our faith and beliefs, abortion wasn't an option. And at thirteen, I didn't think I could be a parent—I knew I was too young— and I felt my grandparents were too old to take on another child. I wanted to do what was right. I'm not going to sugarcoat it; I've thought about that decision every day of my life. Looking at you now, I know I'll have more questions, but the bottom line is that I'm so happy to see that you grew up in a loving home."

"After the adoption took place, did you ever attempt to contact Alia?"

"No. At the time I don't think I even realized what open or closed adoption was. But since it was open, I wonder if you're curious about why I never tried to contact you until now?" Olivia asks Alia.

Alia nods. "I would like to know."

"I wanted to. I thought about it many times as an adult. I just felt that I shouldn't intrude on your life. I buried my feelings ... until recently. I've discovered how detrimental secrets can be, so I decided to tell my story ... but then I realized if I did, I'd have to deal with a host of other issues. Issues that would involve you. And I wanted you to be involved in any decisions to go public."

Alia smiles showing her appreciation of Olivia's thoughtfulness.

"Alia, did you ever desire to know your birth mother?" asks Kate.

"To me, even though I knew I was adopted, 'adoption' was just a word. My parents *were my parents*. After I reconciled with the fact that my birth mother was raped, I had more questions, but I felt it better to keep that door closed."

"Did you ever try to search for your birth mother?"

"If Olivia hadn't reached out, letting me know she wanted to meet me, I don't think I would have pursued it." Alia winces, obviously not sure how Olivia will take the news.

"I understand. I do," Olivia assures her.

"What was your reaction when you heard that Olivia was reaching out to you?" asks Kate as she pours herself a glass of water from the pitcher sitting on the coffee table.

"I was very stunned. It was so out of the blue. I never expected to hear from my birth mother. I'm not sure how much you know, but the law firm that originally set up the adoption called my parents first. Mom and Dad sat me down one night over dinner at their house and told me that my birth mother wanted to contact me. They said they were reluctant at first to even tell me. However, they didn't want to keep such news from me. We don't keep secrets from each other, so we talked it over."

Kate takes a sip of water before asking, "What did you discuss?"

"Even though my parents acknowledged that the decision was entirely mine and that they would support me, they weren't so sure it was a good idea."

"For you to meet Olivia in general, or because she's a public figure?" asks Kate.

"I didn't know Olivia's name at that time, only that she was my birth mother."

"Would it have made any difference?"

"The only thing that mattered at the time was that there was an opportunity on the table to meet the woman who gave birth to me."

"Okay, so then what happened?"

"My parents and I decided to visit with a family counselor, who is also a friend, to explore our true feelings and navigate how this new information might impact our lives."

"Were you afraid that, even though your parents said they'd support you, they might be worried about you meeting your birth mother?"

"As far as I'm concerned, my parents *are* my parents, and they have nothing to fear in that regard, if that's what you mean. However, I know they had some concerns."

"Such as ...?"

"My dad's not so verbal about his feelings, so he just went with the flow, encouraging me to do what I felt was best. My mother, on the other hand ... well, you met her on that video call." Alia smiles, prompting Kate to do the same.

"She can be, how do I say this, forceful," Alia continues. "She's also fiercely protective when it comes to me … and I think it hurt her feelings a little."

"That you wanted to meet your birth mother?"

"Yes," acknowledges Alia, a little downcast. "She felt like, 'Why is it necessary? Why bring up the past?' I know she worried about having me meet my birth mother and what this information might mean for our future. However, as a doctor, I wanted to know about my lineage and family medical history. As a person—a daughter—well, I was curious. Even though I knew the circumstances of my birth, I was intrigued to find out more about my birth mother. I felt that maybe this opportunity was happening for a reason, even though the reason might not be immediately apparent. So the more I thought about it, the more I came to believe that maybe some healing needed to take place, and that's why this opportunity presented itself. I figured that I would learn something about both my birth mother and myself. It also ran through my mind that it might help another person find peace and healing, and as a doctor, those two things are significant to me. I'm still processing." Alia sighs and reaches for her coffee.

"What was your reaction when you and your parents heard your birth mother was Olivia?"

"I was shocked. I didn't know what to make of it, and then I thought, *Wow*. I'm a fan of hers, and now I'm going to get to meet the real woman."

"You know, I can see a resemblance between you," comments Kate.

"I can too." Alia looks at Olivia.

Oliva smiles. "Me three."

"I know you were reluctant to share your story, and we've all discussed the reasons why. Tell me, in your own words again, what made you agree to share your story in an article?"

"The way the media operates today, I do feel that it's probably a wise choice to tell our story right the first time out of the gate. Once the story is out, it's out, and while it may grab attention initially, the news will quickly fade for the next, best headline," answers Alia.

"You got that right," Olivia agrees with a chuckle.

"I also believe, should we tell our story, it might offer help and comfort to others."

"What are your thoughts on what happened to Olivia, including the fact that it led her to put you up for adoption?" asks Kate.

Olivia visibly gulps. Noting her birth mother's reaction, Alia reaches out and touches Olivia's hand. "You were the victim of an unfortunate event that was out of your control, Olivia. I don't take ownership of that event—it feels far removed from me. However, I mean it when I say I understand and accept why I was put up for adoption. If there's anything to forgive, then I forgive you. I do."

Olivia, touched by Alia's words, starts to cry, which prompts Alia and Kate to do the same. They all reach for the box of Kleenex.

"Would you ladies like to take a break for a bit? Anyone like more water, coffee or tea?" asks Kate.

"Or chocolate?" offers Olivia.

"Chocolate?" Alia perks up.

"Grant and I picked up some yummy dark chocolate truffles the other day in some delicious flavors. There's raspberry, peanut butter, almond coconut ..."

"Bring it on," Alia says with a laugh.

"Chocolate is always good for the soul," replies Kate, and the mood in the room immediately lifts.

After a brief, luxurious candy indulgence, they get back on track with Alia sharing more information about her childhood and education.

"One last question before we wrap—what would both of you like your futures to hold in regards to one another?" asks Kate as she looks directly at both ladies.

"I think it's important to take it one day at a time. However, I'm hoping Alia will want to be my friend." Olivia instinctively reaches her hand toward Alia and Alia grasps it without a moment's hesitation.

"I would like that too," Alia replies.

30

"Are you okay?" Kate asks Olivia after Alia leaves.

"Mahalo for being here with me." Olivia sighs deeply. "I'm so thankful that it's you writing our story and not someone else."

Kate embraces her friend in a much-needed bear hug.

"Alia is amazing, isn't she? God is good." Olivia is happy but drained.

"More chocolate?"

"I'll never say no to chocolate. But seriously, how about indulging in something a little stronger than water and iced tea to wash it down with?"

Kate chuckles at her friend's suggestion. "Works for me."

"I'm a little hungry, too, and we still have a bit of time to decompress before the guys get back. I'll order up some appetizers to tide us over until dinner."

"You handled everything so beautifully today, Olivia. You should be proud."

"I just spoke from the heart."

"Yeah, well, speaking from a place of love was what was needed, but not many people dare to speak their truth."

After a celebration dinner with Olivia and Grant later that evening, Kate and Kai are spent, and with an early flight to JFK Airport in New York the following day, they are sound asleep by nine o'clock.

"Do you think you'll have to do any further interviews with Olivia and Alia for your story?" asks Kai the next morning while they wait for their plane to board for the quick flight to New York.

"Possibly, although I already have a lot of information from our interviews. Once I sit down to write it, I may have to make another inquiry or two. We'll see. I feel terrific about it though."

"I'm looking forward to visiting *New York View* today." Kai is anxious to see Kate's former workspace and meet the rest of her friends and coworkers that didn't make it to the wedding.

"Uh-oh," responds Kate seconds later as she checks her smartphone for messages.

"What is it?"

"A text from my ex, Jason. He says he's heard I'm on the East Coast and he'd like to chat. Says he's sorry for so many things, and that he wishes us well, but he'd like to get some closure. He asked if I would be open to at least talking to him on the phone.

"And ...?"

"I'm okay with it if you are," answers Kate.

"Well, I don't love the idea, but then again, understanding and closure are positive steps. I trust you, and I think it could be healing for you both," says Kai.

"Thank you," says Kate and her reply is heartfelt. She hugs Kai, grateful for his wisdom and understanding.

Kai is a smashing hit at the *New York View* offices. After Kate proudly introduces him to her magazine cohorts, he takes in some of the city sights while Kate tends to a tight schedule of editorial meetings. Once finished, she texts Jason to let him know she is ready to speak to him.

"Hi, Kate," Jason starts when, a few minutes later, he calls Kate.
He sounds nervous.
"Thank you for agreeing to talk to me."
Kate remains silent, just listening, wondering what he has to say.

"I'm very sorry for how I treated you, Kate," Jason continues. "I should have appreciated you more and taken the whole marriage thing a lot more seriously."

"Thanks for acknowledging that. I did let you know how important it was to me—and why—on many occasions. I trusted you, and I was very patient with you ... for a long time."

"I know. I don't even really know why I acted as I did, but now that there's some distance, I realize it was wrong."

"Life is a journey, and I think timing plays a big part," Kate finally says, compelled to fill the void. "Even when you love someone, not every relationship is meant for marriage. Sometimes, people are brought into our lives so that we can learn and discover things we need to know. Have you talked to a counselor?"

"I did, um, not in a professional sense, but I became friendly with a therapist I met at the gym. We got to talking, and he put things into perspective."

"About our relationship?"

"Well, I told him my history … it was after a relationship I was having that went south."

"Oh," says Kate, wondering if it was that "Heather" person.

"Do you think you can forgive me?"

"Yes," Kate responds after a few moments of soul searching.

"Well, as I said in my text, I wish you and Kai the best, and thanks again for taking my call today."

"Take care of yourself, Jason."

As the call ends, Kate's mind drifts to all the heartache and complete devastation she faced when it was clear to her that her relationship with Jason was over.

To think that, at one time, I would have sworn he was the one for me. I learned, and I survived—no more pain or remorse. Kate sighs, relieved. *Mahalo, God, for my life now.*

Knowing that the will of the Divine is sometimes not always apparent, her next thoughts go to her father.

Will Poppy, in time, find love again?

Although it's not something she has wanted to face, she certainly knows now that time does have a way of helping to lessen the pain of loss, even though that feeling of loss never completely dissipates. That's where prayer, hope, and faith play essential roles. Kate has also come to understand that loving one person doesn't mean you can't or never will love another. She had certainly loved Jason, and one point in time she couldn't have imagined being with anyone else. Finding Kai was a revelation; she now understands that the possibility to love again is a reality for her father too—whether it's romantic or even just a close friend and companion.

I hope Dad finds peace and joy, whatever form that takes. Kate wishes she could hold her father in her arms at this very moment.

New Horizons

*Take the first step in faith. You don't have to see
the whole staircase, just take the first step.*

– Dr. Martin Luther King, Jr.

31

"Hey, you two." Glen waves when he spots Kate and Kai at the Greenport station on Long Island's North Fork about a half hour or so before dusk. "I thought you two were going to arrive a little earlier this afternoon."

Kai and Kate climb into Glen's silver Lexus for the drive to the family home in Cutchogue, less than twenty minutes away.

"No problem, though," adds Glen. "Our dinner reservation is at eight o'clock."

Minutes later, they drive up the long circular driveway at the Grace residence. The family home, a sprawling custom ranch with a classic exterior, sits on several lush green acres with spectacular views of West Creek all the way to Peconic Bay. The home exudes a warm, inviting feel. It's country elegance at its best.

"Beautiful," remarks Kai as he steps into the great room, decorated in a sophisticated, casual country style with the still waters of Peconic Bay visible through the wall of French doors at the back of the room.

"It does have a good *mana*." Glen smiles, proud of his use of the Hawaiian word. "We've made many wonderful memories in this house. However, I don't know how much longer it will be in the family." After dropping that bombshell, Glen heads toward the kitchen, which sits adjacent to the great room, half of which is visible from Kate and Kai's purview.

"You've been rethinking selling the house?" Kate is incredulous.

"Yes, Katie, dear, I'm seriously thinking about it … especially, now that Peggy and I have called it quits."

"You did? When did that happen?"

"What can I get you two to drink?" Glen asks, evading Kate's question. "Kate, I know you like iced tea. I have some freshly brewed."

"Make that two," comments Kai.

"It's really over, Dad?"

"It's really over, dear," states Glen. "Why don't you put your suitcases in the guest bedroom, and then, Kate, show Kai around. Make yourselves at home."

"I can't believe Dad didn't tell me he and Peggy ended it," Kate bursts out as they unpack their suitcases in the privacy of their room.

"Maybe it just happened."

"I guess. I hope Dad will give us more info."

"My parents built this house and moved here when they became empty nesters," Kate mentions as she nostalgically escorts Kai around the charming and spacious ranch house, proudly pointing out the soaring cathedral ceilings and pristine hardwood floors.

As the pair makes their way around the house, Kate takes pictures with her smartphone to document what may be her final visit. "It feels strange to be here without my mom."

"I felt the same way after my mother passed. You know, after she died, my father wanted to move out of the cottage almost immediately. If it weren't for Malie and me insisting he keep the house, he would have sold it."

"I'm glad he didn't. Otherwise, we wouldn't be enjoying living there now."

"This is a beautiful home with a lot of memories, but it must be cold in the winter."

"My parents always used to rent a townhome in Florida for the winter for just that reason."

"Do you think he'll come and stay with us for the winter, instead?"

"I hope he does. We'll see."

When Kate and Kai make their way back to the guest bedroom, she pulls Kai close. "I love you so much."

"To the moon and beyond." Kai doesn't miss a beat as he looks down into her adoring eyes.

"Oops, sorry. Didn't mean to interrupt," Glen says from the open doorway, a tray laden with glasses of ice tea in his hands.

Kai and Kate quickly end their lovers' embrace.

"Don't worry," Glen assures them. "You two aren't doing anything I haven't seen or done before. Are you hungry?"

"Famished," answers Kate.

"So am I," Kai agrees.

"Good. The restaurant we're going to tonight is just superb. Then maybe, afterward, we'll come back here and watch a movie. Just like old times, Katie, remember?"

"Of course, Pops, and I can't think of anything I'd like better. Dinner and a movie with my two best men."

The next morning Kate, Kai and Glen enjoy a leisurely breakfast outside on the large deck. The sun sparkles over the bay's calm waters. On the agenda for the day is a tour of the historic North Fork, Suffolk County's thirty-mile-long peninsula that runs parallel to the South Fork, home of the well-known, high-profile Hamptons.

After hours spent soaking up the local history and exploring the Hampton's eclectic shops, they decide to dine at a historical restaurant in a clapboard-fronted inn, dating back to the 1600s, located in East Hampton Village.

"I'm completely and utterly stuffed." Kai rubs his stomach as he finishes the last spoonful of dessert: iron-skillet apple crisp with a maple-honey gelato. "This has been a great day. I've enjoyed taking in the history and the views."

"It's something else, isn't it?" Glen agrees. "Very different from Kauai, but beautiful and unique in its own special way."

Seconds later, Kate notices her father's smile dim and his eyes glaze over as he sips his espresso.

Dad's mind is somewhere else. He's probably thinking of Mom.

Kate gently nudges Kai's arm with her elbow and Kai quickly reads her silent message.

"We know how harsh the winters are back East," starts Kai. "So again, if and when you sell your home, or even if you decide not to, our ohana is your ohana."

"I appreciate it, and I'll think about it, I will."

For the next hour or so, to digest their meal, the trio walks the picturesque streets, enjoying the sights and sounds of the town until, finally, they head for home. Exhausted from their event-filled day, they all head straight for bed.

In her dream Kate soars in the sky as she views lush landscapes, expansive crystal waters, and inviting colonials dotting the New England coast beneath her. As she flies higher and higher, delighting in every aspect of her adventure, she turns to her right. A stunning, bright-orange butterfly with dark black spots appears next to her. Kate knows this butterfly—it's a Gulf fritillary. It does flips and turns to get her attention and make her smile. Kate thinks of her mother in her mind's eye and calls out with joy, "Aloha, Mommydoo, I love you!"

Suddenly, to Kate's amazement, the butterfly *becomes* her mother. The two women smile at one another, so joyous to be together, their love overflowing as they soar across the beautiful landscapes and vistas.

"It was such a good life," says Catherine, nostalgically.

"It was the best," agrees Kate. "If the good Lord allows, please visit Dad and let him know you're still around."

Catherine smiles warmly at Kate.

Kate and her mother continue to chat about many things as they visit different landscapes and vistas. Every so often her mother tells her how much she loves her, and when she does, Kate can *feel* the power in that love.

"I love you too, Mom." Kate's last words to her mother before waking are, "To the moon and beyond."

What an amazing dream!

For the next twenty minutes or so, before Kai wakes, Kate takes the opportunity for one of her daily chats with God, thanking Him for another day and sharing what's on her mind and heart.

"Morning, sweet," yawns Kai shortly after that and plants a kiss on her cheek. "How'd you sleep?"

"Like a babe, and I had an awesome dream about Mom. We had an in-depth conversation, and she made some funny remarks about Dad and his cleaning—'definitely not his forte,' she said—and she mentioned how she felt some of the old ladies in the neighborhood are acting like kids around him."

Kai laughs. "Well, your dad *is* prime meat, Kate."

"Kai," shrills Kate as she swats Kai with a pillow, which results in an all-out tussle.

"A glass of wine with your lasagna, Pops?" Carla inquires as she serves everyone at the dinner table at a family gathering in her home later that evening.

"No, thank you," replies Glen, who typically enjoys a glass of red wine with his pasta. "We toured several of the North Fork's finest vineyards this afternoon, and those little sips multiply. I think I've had my fill today."

The ohana that has gathered includes Kate's brother, Derek, and his wife, Julie, with their daughters, Ashley and Dawn; Carla's husband, Frank, and son, Lucas; and Cindy and Vinnie.

"Kai and Kate have offered me their ohana to stay in, just for fun and especially during winter," announces Glen after he leads the family in grace for the dinner Carla and Kate lovingly prepared.

"We might want to visit Kauai in the winter too," Carla pipes up.

"Hey, as long as you guys don't stay in our suite," cracks Cindy.

Kate laughs at Cindy's protest. "Don't worry, we have plenty of room inside the cottage, and the ohana now has two master suites."

"Julie," Glen says, changing the topic. "I think I may have a real estate listing for you."

All eyes are suddenly on Glen.

"You do?" Julie's eyes widen.

"You're going to sell the Cutchogue house, Dad?" asks Carla.

Glen nods. "As you all know, I've been giving it a lot of thought. I think I might like to buy a condo or find a rental here. I don't need all that house anymore."

"Dad, you're welcome to stay in our new bedroom suite when you're not in Hawaii," offers Derek. "Julie and I have already talked about that."

"Since we added that extra room and bath to the downstairs, you could also use here as a base," offers Carla.

"And when you're in Manhattan, you know who to call," Cindy blurts out before taking another bite of chocolate mousse.

"Well, I'm a lucky man, aren't I?" Glen says proudly, touched by this show of support and willingness to share. "It's nice to know I have so many places stay. Until I figure out whether to buy or rent a place here, we'll rotate—how about that?"

"Sounds like a good plan," Derek agrees with a smile. "Let's toast to that. And to family."

32

On the six-hour flight from New York to California, Kate doesn't waste any time writing the first draft of her cover story for *Olivia!,* and since Kate is immersed in her writing, Kai alternates between reading his medical journals and watching free movies.

"Aloha, house!" sings Kate when they finally enter the cottage and set their suitcases down.

"It feels so good to be home!" Kai says with feeling. "I'm just going to take care of a few things and then get into my PJs and unwind. I've got an early day at the hospital tomorrow."

"Why don't you run the bath and add in some essential oils, light some candles and let the flight roll off?"

"Now, that, my lovely, is a fantastic idea." Kai kisses the top of Kate's head as he heads toward the master bath.

"I love it, Kate!" declares Olivia, holding the final draft of Kate's interview about a week later. The two women sit on the Weke cottage lanai. "It's perfect. The article has heart, and it's compelling. I couldn't ask for a better piece. Alia and my publicist, Connie, also think you did a great job."

"Mahalo. I was a little nervous at first. It's such an important story. It means a lot to me that it represents what you intended."

"That and more," confirms Olivia. "Our photographer aced it, as well. I especially like the shot of Alia and me on the deck." Olivia points to a lovely photo taken on the hotel veranda, surrounded by greenery and with the Boston skyline behind them.

"So, the magazine hits the stands next month?"

"I can hardly believe it. It's been quite a journey."

"Are you ready for the onslaught of attention?"

"I am. I don't want to rehash what I already said in your article. Let your article represent Alia's and my story. However, I've been talking with my producers about doing a series for my show where people can glean more information on the adoption process," Olivia takes a sip of tea, deep in thought, and then changes the subject. "Say, shall we take our lunch plates inside and then pursue some gardening therapy?"

For the next few hours, Olivia and Kate chat while they plant a host of flowering, native seedlings and cuttings in various garden locations.

"I'm looking forward to enjoying more of the fruits of our labors. Nothing beats that farm-to-table taste." Olivia chuckles as she plunges a hand shovel into the dirt.

"Remind me to give you some romaine, tomatoes, and some other veggies before you leave. The quantity of our produce is off the charts."

"You know, since we have such an abundance of fruit, I've also started to puree apples, bananas, and other fruits to use in smoothies and to use as a replacement when my recipes—especially, baked goods—call for granulated sugar. It's not as sweet tasting, but it's healthier, and it works for Kai and me. Although I'm not so sure some of my friends will be so keen on the idea." Kate laughs as an image of Cindy springs to mind.

"Who wouldn't appreciate healthier food?"

"I was thinking of Cindy and how much she loves sweet things. When she visits, I'm going to have to devise some extra-sweet, natural creations specifically for her so she doesn't go into withdrawal."

"Hey, do me a favor. Make sure you give me those recipes. Or better yet, call me up, and I'll come on over to help you sample," Olivia tells her.

"Say, Olivia, when will you share your story with Nā Pīkake?" asks Kate a bit later after they plant the last of the herb seedlings.

"I've been thinking about the timing of that. You know, I wanted to share my news that night at the girlfriend party. But I didn't want to involve the others until I knew what was what. Now that we've done the interview and the story's about to come out, I think I'll tell everyone at our next our group meeting. I'll have some advance copies of the magazine by then."

"Perfect."

"It's a good thing you took a lot of photos of the house on your last trip," Glen tells Kate, talking to her on the phone a few weeks later. "Only two weeks on the market and I received several offers. I still can't believe the house sold so fast."

"It's a gorgeous home, right on the Peconic. The new owners should be thrilled."

"They are."

"Feeling nostalgic at all?"

"No. I said my goodbyes to the house, and I have your mother in my heart. I'm not ready to make any quick, permanent moves, so coming to Kauai will give me time to think."

"I'm glad," says Kate.

"Say, how's your book coming?"

"I'm just about done with my final draft. My boss, Edward, at *New York View* offered to read it. Fingers crossed."

"Crossing them right now, sweetheart."

Speaking with Edward a few weeks later by phone, Kate is thrilled to learn her boss thinks her novel is "a great read" and that he intends, with Kate's approval, to send it to the magazine's proofreading department for a spelling and grammar check.

"Then, when you're ready, I'll send it off to my literary agent friend, Michael Gabriel.

"You will?" Kate just about falls off her office chair when she hears the top literary agent's name.

"I told him about your novel, and he said he'd be happy to read it."

"That is *so* awesome. Thank you, thank you, thank you!"

"He's enjoyed your work for the magazine, and while he can't commit to represent it until he's read it, let me tell you, it's quite an honor to have Michael take the time to personally review it. Usually, he lets one of his staff do the first pass."

"I owe you one for this, Edward," gushes Kate.

"Later, alligator."

Kate ends the video call and launches into a happy dance around her home office.

A few weeks later, after Kate picks her father up from Lihue Airport, they make a stop at The Plumeria Café. Glen's arrival is met with enthusiasm from the staff, who came to know him as a "regular" during his last trip.

"Aloha, pretty lady." Glen smiles at Jessie when she comes to greet him.

"So, the Garden Isle called you back?"

"That and my daughter's determination," Glen says with a laugh.

"Ha, ha," Kate mocks.

"Here you go." Malie hands Glen a well-stocked doggy bag.

Kate grins at her father. "I thought you said a *few* scones?"

"Well, there *are* a few other things in there that I know you like."

On the way home to the Weke cottage, Kate can't help but notice her father's demeanor. He seems genuinely happy to be back in Kauai, and for the first time in a long time, she can't help but notice a little spark in her father's eye.

"Jessie's a nice lady," he mentions trying to sound nonchalant.

Is it possible he ...? No. Why read something into it when there's nothing there.

"You look handsome, Dad. Why are you all spiffed up?" asks Kate one evening the following week.

"This?" Glen tries to act nonchalant. "It's just one of my old Hawaiian dress shirts."

"You're also wearing your nice khaki pants." Kate sniffs the air. "And you smell good, too. Meeting Bradford for a drink and some dinner?"

Glen shrugs.

"Dad?"

"Maybe."

"Maybe?"

"I'm just going out."

"Dad, I'm not the Hanalei police." Kate chuckles at her father's avoidance in answering her forthrightly. "I'm just curious."

"Bradford called Jessie, and we're meeting up with her and a friend. It's nothing, just a bunch of people getting together," says Glen, shuffling his feet.

"A friend? Okay ..." Kate feels there's more to the story but doesn't want to pry.

"You're not upset?"

"Why would I be upset?"

"Well, because I'm going out to dinner with some friends ... some of which happen to be women."

"I think it's nice you have some friends to hang with."

Poppy is so darn cute.

"You do?"

"Yes. It is 'just' friends, right?"

Glen nods.

"Well, have fun."

"I will, thank you, dear. And I'll keep my cell on in case you need to reach me."

"Love you, Pop," Kate says as he kisses her forehead before heading out.

"To the moon and beyond," Glen finishes after embracing Kate.

"It's good they're both getting out," says Kai as he and Kate take their usual nightly garden walk. "Before your father arrived, mine found every excuse to stay home."

"I know," Kate sighs audibly. "It just feels strange, having to think about my dad and what he's doing. I worry and wonder if Dad's healed enough, if he's going to meet someone to date and if she'll be good for him. The list goes on."

Kai chuckles. "Now we know what our parents went through when we first started dating as teenagers."

Switching gears, Kate pipes up, "When you've loved so deeply, do you think it's possible to move on?"

"I don't think it's always a matter of moving on. Sometimes, it's just moving that helps with the healing. If you're worried about your father, keep the lines of communication open. I know this is a bit hard for you to accept, but it's healthy that he's interested in female companionship. For now, just breathe. It'll be okay."

Kate gives up a tiny smile.

"If it's any help, it's weird for me too. My folks were soulmates, and even though it's been a long time since my mom's passing, I'm still not used to the idea that my dad could end up with someone else." Kai reaches for Kate, and together, their arms around each other, the pair sits quietly, absorbing the healing energy of the garden.

33

Olivia and Kate, wearing comfortable stretch pants and tops, find a secluded garden spot not too far from the Weke cottage's lanai. It's particularly lush and colorful and home to various cherub and angel figurines. They lay out beach towels on the soft green ground and sit in the sublime space.

"I have to admit, I'm a little nervous about sharing with Nā Pīkake tonight," Olivia confesses. "I have butterflies. Can you believe it?"

"You're going to share something very personal. So, sure, it's understandable. Just remember how much your circle of friends love you. We have a little window before the ladies arrive. Let's just chill."

After a peaceful few minutes, the other ladies arrive and join them in the garden. Kate gathers more towels for the group to sit on and they all form a circle.

Olivia leads. "I thought it might be nice to start the evening sharing our day or something that's on our mind. Does anyone wish to start? Elaine?"

"I had a rude client today," moans Elaine. "It wound me up. I wanted to give him a piece of my mind, but I also didn't want to sour the deal, which is about to close. So I bit my tongue."

"And kept the anger and frustration bottled up?" Sukey correctly guesses.

"Precisely." Elaine expunges the residual anger in a long exhale.

"I was feeling a little sad this morning," Jessie admits. "I had a wonderful dream about my husband last night. We were walking hand in hand and laughing, and then I woke up knowing we'll never do that in waking hours again." She takes several audible deep breaths before adding, "Later, after praying, I felt such peace for the rest of the day."

Malie touches Jessie's arm to comfort her.

"I've had dreams like that where I talk to my mother," comments

Kate.

"Me, too, with my grandparents," acknowledges Olivia.

"We've all had loved ones pass over," empathizes Elaine. "Praying to God and staying surrounded by supportive ohana, that's the secret to healing."

"Does anyone else have something to share?" Olivia looks around the circle, landing on Kate.

"I've finished the first draft of my novel, and the *New York View Magazine* team is proofing it. After that, it'll be sent off to a high-profile agent. I'm a little nervous, to say the least."

"I have every confidence in you. It's all going to work in your favor. You'll see." Olivia looks around for another speaker. "Anyone else?"

"Kamal and I have decided to expand the gallery space," Sukey tells everyone.

"You are? Good for you!" Malie's cheer is followed by more encouragement from the group.

"We're trying to work out the details right now," Sukey adds. "Originally, the idea was just to remodel our existing space. But the next-door tenants will be leaving in two months, so we've decided to expand into that space and remodel it, too. We want to have room to accommodate larger exhibits and events. It's a big step; it's given me a bit of an acid stomach and has Kamal a little on edge."

"Okay, let's pray for a smooth unfolding of events for Sukey and Kamal," instructs Olivia. "I know I intend to have a blast at the ribbon-cutting reception in their new, extended space."

"Here, here!" pipes up Alana. "The only thing I have to share is that my mind has been on finding the perp who's been going after women in Hanalei. I'm hoping we'll be able to make an arrest soon."

"And that justice is served!" exclaims Elaine.

"I'd like to share something too, something from my childhood." Olivia clears her throat, sensing this is the perfect moment. "I value our friendship, and before the media gets ahold of this news, I want you to hear it from me." She scans her friend's faces. There is no easy way to share this news. "I was raped as a young teen."

"Oh, Olivia," gasps Elaine in unison with the other women.

"There's more," inserts Olivia quickly before she loses her nerve. "I had a child, a baby girl."

More gasps rise from the group, then utter silence.

"It's a secret I kept for years. I tried to push it aside, out of my mind, and I was good with that for a long time, never realizing how my silence was damaging me. When the attacks started to take place around town, and when I heard about Kate, and how the man came through her screen door at night, well, my memories came back with a vengeance. I realized I didn't want to hold onto the secret any longer, and when I let go and told Grant, I started to feel tremendous healing." Olivia says it all with hardly a pause. It's as if, once she's opened up, she can't stop until it's all been said. "I want you all to know how much I value you, how you give me strength, how your love and friendship is so nourishing. Mahalo for listening to my story."

She dabs tears from her eyes after her friends express their support. "I'm so overwhelmed … but I do have some good news share, too. My attorney was able to locate my daughter."

"He did?" several women blurt out.

"Yes. Her name is Alia, and we recently met."

"I know this is exciting news, but let's let Olivia speak." Kate tries to subdue the commotion and barrage of questions.

"I hope you can appreciate that I had to keep my news under wraps until I could speak to and meet with my daughter. After much conversation and debate, we decided that, before any media got ahold of our story, we wanted to go public with it first. So with Alia's blessing and participation, I brought Kate into the mix to write my story as the cover story for the first edition of my new magazine, *Olivia!*"

"When will the magazine come out?" asks Sukey.

"Kate has an advance copy of the magazine for each one of you on the lanai." Olivia beams with obvious pride. "It'll be on the newsstands and available in an online edition tomorrow. I wish I could have told you all sooner, but I wasn't exactly sure how the story would play out, and then, I also wanted to do it in a way that Alia was on board with."

"We understand, daaahling," Elaine hugs Olivia.

"We're here for you, Olivia," pipes up Malie and each of the women take turns embracing Olivia.

Later that evening, during the potluck buffet, the ladies agree to host their next event, an art exhibit, at Sukey and Kamal's art gallery once construction is complete.

"I'd love to see your new space." Kate says when she joins Alana and Sukey at the dessert table.

"I'll give you a call, and we can look at our calendars and pick a date," replies Sukey, munching on a chocolate-covered macaroon.

"Olivia mentioned you had a few dreams about an attack on a teenage girl," Alana admits to Kate.

"I also had a dream that gave me the impression Olivia would meet her daughter."

"Uncanny. Do these dreams happen often?"

"I can't control them, nor do I try. Looking back on it, though, my dreams have always provided me information, especially, as it relates to happenings to myself and my ohana, both immediate and extended. I've always been amazed and appreciated the information."

"It's a blessing," states Sukey unequivocally.

Elaine winces. "Gives me the heebie-jeebies."

"Well, I've heard stories like this before, and I know some things defy explanation," replies Alana. "Still, I'd classify myself as more as a meat-and-potatoes, show-me-the-facts kind of woman. But do me a favor. If you have any dreams or intuitions about this perp, let me know, will you? I might have to investigate."

"Well, scripture says we're not meant to pursue or predict, but one thing I've learned for sure of late, if it's God desire for me to know something, I'll get the message."

34

It's a bright sunny day with a slight breeze as Kate window shops the stores of Princeville Shopping Center. As she glances into a store window featuring lots of collectible items, she is captivated by a pretty angel holding a butterfly, and she zooms inside for a closer look at the beautiful sculpture.

How lovely.

Kate feels a warm bolt of energy course through her body and smells the sweet scent of plumeria. Immediately, she becomes aware of a loving presence beside her. When she turns her head slightly, she can see it's her mother, smiling broadly.

"Aloha, sweetheart," her mother says as the pair embrace.

Instinctively, Kate knows her mother wants to go for a walk. As they head toward Sukey and Kamal's gallery, Kate realizes that she and her mother are wearing dresses befitting a cocktail party, and the setting, once daylight, is now dusk. Kate peers into a nearby window and is mesmerized by the numbers on a wall clock. Her eyes focus on number 7. When she turns her head, she notices that her mother is gone. Kate looks around and glances at the license plate of a parked car: 7 is the first digit. Suddenly, it strikes her that there is something significant about that 7. But before the revelation can unfold, she is abruptly pulled from the dream.

Oh, no. Just when it was getting really interesting!

Upset she's been awakened, Kate gets up from the sofa where she has spent the majority of this lazy, rainy Saturday afternoon, waiting for Kai to finish work. As she heads toward the kitchen to make herself a cup of tea, her mind wanders.

Okay, so I saw the angel; I saw Mom. We were at the Princeville Center, dressed in cocktail dresses then I saw the number seven in two different places. Hey, this is easy. Just let these dreams and thoughts drift through my mind. Don't read too much into it. If it's meant to be, I'll get the message and know what to do.

Moments later, as Kate pours more hot water into her cup, and nowhere near her phone, a song from her iTunes app pops up, "It's a Crime" from Sade's "Promise" album.

Okay, chuckles Kate as she looks at the phone incredulously.

It's been a while since she's had a specific song pop up on her phone like that without the app being open. She thinks back on the first time it happened, just after her mother passed. She had turned on the radio, looking for some music to soothe the family, and "I'll Take You Home Again, Kathleen" played. And it wasn't just the lyrics of the old song, which had been recorded by many artists, including Elvis, it was also the significance of the title itself and the fact that Kate's father often sang that song to their mother in a funny Irish accent—which always made Catherine smile.

Now, moments later, sipping a soothing cup of cinnamon chai tea, nibbling on a sliced banana, and watching the rain pour down from the sky, Kate suddenly feels energized. *Go with the flow,* is the message that pops into her head.

"Okay, I will," confirms Kate out loud, amazed how easy it is to be in the moment and let go.

Later that evening, Kai treats Kate and her father to a celebratory dinner at a fun, atmospheric Hawaiian grill in the Princeville Marketplace.

"Aloha!" Alana and Hani, coincidentally dining at the same restaurant, stop to greet their friends as they follow a pretty hostess to their table.

"You all look like you're in a festive mood ... what are you celebrating?" asks Alana.

"Kate's publisher arranged for his literary agent friend to read her novel," exclaims Glen before anyone else has a chance to answer.

"It's not an actual deal yet, but any good cause for celebration ... Kate chuckles, leaving the sentence unfinished.

"Why don't you and Hani join us for dinner?" offers Kai. "We've only just ordered."

Alana and Hani pull up two chairs, and after a delicious dinner, the group decides to head over to the Princeville Gallery to check out the progress of Sukey and Kamal's remodel. The men walk ahead, talking, leaving Kate and Alana trailing behind. Kate stops to gaze into a window featuring a host of beachy gift items, while Alana drifts over to another storefront to check out a sales rack of sleeveless dresses.

Beautiful handmade ornaments and quaint gifts have Kate's undivided attention, and then she notices a charming little angel holding a butterfly that's exactly like the angel in her dream. As she turns around, she sees the number 7 on a parked car's license plate. Suddenly, it dawns on her that it's the seventh day of the seventh month and that the hostess at the restaurant referred to their dinner table as number seven.

The angel from my dream, the license plate, and today's date and time. Synchronicity?

As Kate looks around, she sees the men chatting in the distance, and Alana still looking at the sales rack. The back of Kate's neck tingles—something is happening, she can feel it.

Although it's dark, the marketplace is lit from both the stores and the exterior lighting and portions of the parking lot are clearly illuminated.

Suddenly, Kate hears a commotion and swiftly notices that there's a scuffle partway down the parking lot between a young woman and a tall, stringy-haired man wearing jeans and a white T-shirt.

It's him! It's my attacker.

"Come on, baby! It'll be fun!" slurs the intoxicated man as the young woman screams.

"Alana!" Kate yells at the top of her lungs as she points to the nearby struggle.

Alana runs toward the man and, over her shoulder, yells, "Hani, call the station and let them know I need backup!"

In a flash Alana tackles the stringy-haired man and swiftly restrains him. Although he struggles, he's no match for Alana.

A quick minute later, a patrol car pulls up, and the officers join Alana in reading the man his rights, cuffing him, and putting him in the car to go to the Hanalei police station.

"Wow, you've got some moves, Alana," Kai says admiringly,

clearly in awe, after the commotion has died down.

"That's why she's the boss at home." Hani chuckles, despite the seriousness of the scene.

"Hani, I need to head over to the station with Kate," Alana instructs.

"I'd like to come to the station to give Kate some moral support," pipes up Kai.

"Me, too," offers Glen.

"Okay, why don't you all follow Hani and me. We'll meet you there," says Alana.

"I'm relieved," Kate whispers as she wraps her arms around Kai in the comfort of their master bedroom a few hours later. "I hadn't realized how much tension I was still holding on to."

Kai kisses the top of her head. "I feel you," he says softly.

"It's amazing, isn't it?"

"What?"

"How life works, how God works."

"It is a wonderful, awesome mystery," agrees Kai, holding Kate tightly.

35

"Kate, this turmeric rice is divine," exclaims Olivia, sneaking a sample from the dish Kate has prepared for the evening's casual soiree in the Marisol Garden with all the usual suspects. "How do you make it?"

"I sauté onions and garlic, then add in peanuts, diced celery and carrots, and toss them into jasmine rice with some peas, dried cranberries, and some ground turmeric, and other Indian spices."

"I love the way you say it, so matter-of-factly."

"It's super easy."

"Yeah, for you."

"No, seriously. I'll show you. We'll make it together one day. Okay?"

"It's a deal," Olivia agrees with a nod.

Kate finishes tossing a large green salad and places it on the buffet island next to a large bowl of her turmeric rice while Olivia arranges a selection of cheeses and crackers on a koa-wood serving tray shaped like a surfboard. Both sway to the melodic, slack-key guitar music that plays over the sound system.

Outside at the grill, Grant, Kai and Glen chat as they keep an eye on the ono while Trevor and Aukai chat with Elaine and Malie, who are sipping their drinks and enjoying crudités and a trio of hummus in various flavors. Only Alana and Hani are missing, but they wind up arriving seconds later.

"We got our guy, thanks to your help, Kate," Alana jubilantly declares. "He admitted to everything."

"Oh, what a relief!" exclaims Olivia.

Elaine lifts her glass of chardonnay. "I say this news calls for a toast."

"I second that," Trevor shouts.

"*Huli Pau!*" the group toasts in unison.

"While we're toasting, Olivia, shall I—or would you—like to do the honors?" asks Grant.

"Go ahead," Olivia encourages.

"You all know how much Olivia and I love poetry and prose, so I call your attention to an exquisite sonnet by Shakespeare. Number one sixteen, to be exact. 'Let me not to the marriage of true minds admit impediments. Love is not love which alters when it alteration finds, or bends with the remover to remove: O, no! It is an ever-fixed mark …' I could go on, but what I'm trying to say is that it's my pleasure to share our news with you, our ohana: Olivia and I are engaged to be married!"

The garden erupts with cheers and well-wishes.

"Kate, it was your prompting and patience that helped me deal with my past," Olivia says after the congratulations die down. "I want you to know that I'll be forever grateful." She sobs with tears of joy as the two ladies embrace.

"Does anyone have tissues?" Alana cries out.

"Here, you can use mine," comments Elaine, handing Alana a wet, crumpled tissue, which causes both ladies to burst out laughing.

"Here," Malie chuckles as she pulls a small Kleenex pack out of her purse to pass around.

"Oh, we are a sad sort," says Trevor, sniffing. "I say, this calls for another toast."

"Of course, *you* say it calls for a toast," Aukai playfully teases.

"Hey, Aukai, that's my line!" Elaine protests with a laugh.

"Well, here's a line for you; I don't know who first said it. 'Marriage is a relationship in which one person is always right, and the other is the husband,'" Trevor yells out.

"Oh, no, here we go," Malie says, shaking her head.

"Olivia, daaahling, you'll be on the right track as long as you remember that 'Husbands are like wine. They take a long time to mature,'" professes Elaine dramatically.

Trevor clutches at his heart and mocks pain. "Touché!"

"Hey, what about that Chinese proverb, 'Man is the head of the family; woman, the neck that turns the head'?" blurts out Kai.

"Enough joking around," Kate tells the group. "Let's make a toast. *Ka mau ki aha!*" She raises her glass in a traditional Hawaiian wedding toast, translating, "May you never thirst again!"

"Here's to love, laughter, and happily ever after!" Kai follows.

As the crowd toasts, Kate sees her father has made his way to Jessie's side. Kate instantly knows this 'friendship' has started to blossom into perhaps something more.

"Kate," Glen acknowledges when she opens the door to the ohana. "I thought you and Kai were going to bed."

"He's inside. I just wanted to give you a goodnight kiss."

"Oh? Sure, dear." Glen and Kate kiss one another on the cheek. "The kettle's on. Would you like a quick cup of tea?" asks Glen, sensing Kate may want to talk. He has a good idea what might be on her mind.

Kate nods and follows Glen's lead into the ohana kitchen.

"Chamomile? Apple cinnamon? Sleepytime?"

"Sleepytime sounds good," answers Kate.

Glen takes two mugs out of the kitchen cabinets and places a tea bag in each. "Kate, I've got something to ask you," he says, turning back toward his daughter.

Oh, no, Kate thinks. Her stomach instinctively flutters, nervous over what her father will say next.

"You know, no one can ever take your mother's place, don't you? I love her and will always love her. She was my soulmate."

Kate nods, blowing on her tea as she waits for her father to continue.

"Jessie is … a nice woman. Don't you think?"

"I do."

"We have a lot in common, and I like her company. Would you mind if I ask her out?"

Kate stares at the endearing look on her father's face.

"You like her … *that* way?" Kate thinks she understands, but she wants to be sure.

"I like her. That's all I know. I want to spend some time with her, but I don't have any expectations. I'm sure you've probably noticed Bradford and me vying for her attention from time to time. I think that's made me realize I'd like to ask her out."

It takes Kate a few moments to gather her thoughts and navigate her emotions. "You deserve to be happy, and I know how sad and lonely you've been since Mom died," Kate says slowly. "Jessie's a wonderful lady whose company I know you enjoy, and you're both adults …" She smiles to let her father know she's okay with it. "What do you think Bradford will say?"

"I'm not sure, but then again, he's been around when I'm not, and he hasn't asked her yet. So …" Glen reaches for Kate and enfolds her in his arms.

Time and prayer help to heal, even though the depth of feeling we have for our deceased loved ones never diminishes.

36

In the weeks that follow Olivia and Grant's announcement, good news seems to be on a roll. The public outpouring of love and support for Olivia and Alia in response to Kate's article is overwhelming. Riding the tide of her success, Kate gets more good news from Edward: his agent friend Michael is interested in signing her as a client with the intent of securing her a publishing deal.

To add more excitement into the mix, the latest gathering of Nā Pīkake has transformed into a surprise bridal shower for Olivia. The only clouds on the horizon—and they are relatively small ones in the scheme of things—is Kate's continuing discomfort with the idea of her father dating her friend Jessie.

"Kate," Jessie says, beckoning her to a private area where they can talk. "I haven't seen you around the café much in the last week or so."

"I know," sighs Kate. Accepting the idea that her father is going to start dating is one thing; facing the reality of it is another.

Jessie, aware of Kate's sensitivity to the issue of her father starting to date, speaks softly. "Your dad asked me out."

"He told me he was going to."

"I wanted to talk to you about it because I value our friendship."

Kate is all ears.

"I know it might be a difficult concept to embrace—your father going out with someone who's not your mom. We've had conversations about our losses and healing, and I want to make sure you're okay with this."

Kate wants to respond; she tries, but her words won't come. Her mind is racing, and she is feeling so many emotions. There's a noticeable pressure in her chest, in her heart; even so, she reaches for Jessie and embraces her, still speechless.

The moment feels surreal.

As they stand with their arms around each other, neither Jessie nor Kate can seem to let go. Since Kate can't seem to find the right words, she hopes that by their embrace, Jessie knows that she approves. Finally, they part. When they do, Jessie lovingly touches Kate's cheek.

"Shush!" Sukey suddenly yells. "Olivia and Malie are here!"

"Olivia is going to be so surprised when she sees you both." Elaine smiles at Alia and her mother, Doris, who have flown to Hawaii to surprise Olivia.

The ladies immediately take their positions, hiding in strategic areas throughout the garden, which is decorated beautifully in pastel colors and glorious, blooming flowers for the elegant tea party and bridal shower.

As part of the plan to keep Olivia off track, Kate meets her friend and shows her in.

"The garden looks amazing … like you're going to have a party. Why is it so done up?" asks Olivia as she enters through an intricately decorated floral archway.

"Weelll …" starts Kate …

… and the ladies converge. "SURPRISE!" they yell at the top of their lungs, crowding around Olivia.

"Happy Bridal Shower!" screams Malie.

"What? Oh, my …" Olivia tears up. Alia comes up behind her, taps her on the shoulder, and then quickly grabs her birth mother in a firm embrace.

"I can't believe this!" cries Olivia joyfully.

"Congratulations, Olivia." Doris says, making her presence known by laying a hand on Olivia's shoulder.

"Doris!" Olivia wraps her arms around her in a bear hug. Everyone is a mass of laughter and tears.

"Mahalo, mahalo. I'm overwhelmed," is all Olivia can muster. "And very underdressed."

The crowd laughs along with Olivia.

"Don't worry, I snuck one of your favorite outfits into the car today, so you can change whenever you're ready," Kate says.

"Unbelievable. Just unbelievable!" Olivia shakes her head, still taking in the celebratory atmosphere. "You guys are great secret-keepers, is all I can say! I can't believe this. I am so honored and so touched. I love you all so much, you know?"

"We love you too, Olivia … to the moon and beyond!" exclaims

Kate.

"To the moon and beyond!"

~~ The End ~~

Photo of Maryann Ridini Spencer by Maria Gregorio-Oviedo

Maryann Ridini Spencer

Writing Aloha

"I feel most at home when I'm among trees, plants, and mountains, by the ocean, or in wide-open spaces," says Spencer. "I feel so connected when I'm in the natural world that I can literally 'feel' the energy. I find it inspiring, empowering, and the perfect place where I can allow my mind to be quiet to entertain the creative thoughts that pop into my head."

"My feelings about being in nature, as well as my interest in sustainable living practices (eating fresh, organic, and farm-to-table foods), and protecting the Earth's environment for future generations is in line with what the Hawaiians' believe in living 'The Way of Aloha' or in the 'Spirit of Aloha.'"

"I knew I wanted to incorporate the Aloha philosophy in *Lady in the Window* as a means for Kate to help heal herself and find her center. Her journey continues in *The Paradise Table,* as it will in future Kate Grace Mysteries."

"I'm committed to writing themes that promote faith, hope, healing, forgiveness, understanding, humanity, love, compassion, and living the life God has intended for each one of us to live," continues Spencer. "Whether it be a novel, movie or television screenplay, or in my work as a food and lifestyle journalist, radio and TV host, or on my Simply Delicious Living blog."

"Both my characters, Kate and Olivia, believe that love never dies and that, with God's grace, we get divine inspirations validating that we are not alone."

"As humans, I believe we're all connected and as we live and navigate life, we're constantly learning, changing, and healing as we grow," says Spencer. "A vital part of our journey on Earth is to learn to love and help one another. If we incorporate God's teachings in our hearts, our thoughts, and our actions, we can all make a valuable difference in this world."

Maryann Ridini Spencer writes themes of *Aloha* … penning award-winning novels and writing and producing critically-acclaimed projects for film and television. She began her career as a producer/writer for Cable News Network. Later, she was appointed Director of Publicity for Miss Universe, Inc., and also served as Senior Vice President of Stephen J. Cannell Productions/The Cannell Studios before founding Ridini Entertainment Corporation. As company president of the award-winning PR, marketing, multimedia-content-creation, and TV-and-film-production company, she is committed to creating, writing, producing, and promoting content that entertains, inspires, educates, and uplifts.

A member of the Writers Guild of America West and Producers Guild of America, Maryann has produced numerous movies and series for television. Her projects have appeared on Showtime, SyFy, TMC, USA Networks, CBS-TV, Time Warner Cable, and in the foreign theatrical market. She is celebrated for co-producing/writing the teleplay for the Hallmark Hall of Fame movie *The Lost Valentine*. Based on the James Michael Pratt novel, the movie stars Betty White and Jennifer Love Hewitt. Over fifteen million viewers tuned in to watch the film, which won CBS-TV the night in ratings. The film, winner of the Faith and Freedom Movieguide® Award, has since become part of Hallmark's Gold Crown (DVD) Collector's Edition and the film can also be live-streamed on Hallmark's movie channels.

Maryann is also the creator, writer, producer, and host of the Telly award-winning healthy living cooking series, cookbooks, and blog, *Simply Delicious Living with Maryann*®. The series is broadcast on PBS-TV station KVCR in Southern California, DirecTV, DishTV, and to a global audience on Roku (*Simply Delicious Living* Channel), YouTube, and Maryann's blog at *SimplyDeliciousLiving.com.*

Throughout her career, Maryann has worked as a freelance writer and contributing editor for such publications as *Palm Springs Life Magazine*, *Desert Magazine*, *Ventura County Star* (part of the *USA Today* Network), *Ventura Breeze*, and *Los Angeles Magazine*.

Author of the *Simply Delicious Living with Maryann*®– *Entrées* cookbook (Santa Rosa Press, 2019), and two Kate Grace Mysteries, *Lady in the Window* (SelectBooks, 2017, Santa Rosa Press, 2019) and *The Paradise Table* (Santa Rosa Press, October 2019), Maryann is currently working on the third novel in the series.

Visit *MaryannRidiniSpencer.com* or *AlohaWriter.com.*

The Paradise Table

Q&A with Novelist Maryann Ridini Spencer

What gave you the idea for *The Paradise Table*?

As I was writing *Lady in the Window*, the first book in the Kate Grace Mystery Series, the title and general concept for *The Paradise Table* just came to me. I wanted to write about friends helping friends, the necessity of living one's authentic life and truth, how something positive can come out of a negative, how we can learn to have more joy in our lives by being connected to God and following his Word, and "doing unto others …"

Incidentally, as I wrote *The Paradise Table*, the title and concept for the third book, *Secrets of Grace Manor,* came to me. I hope I continue to get ideas for future books as I'm writing in the present.

Why did you decide to set *The Paradise Table* in Hawaii?

I've been traveling to the Hawaiian Islands for many years now, and we have a family home on the Big Island. My first visit took place in Maui, and when I boarded the plane for home, I wept. I resonate with living aloha, and the stunning, magical, and abundant beauty of the Islands fills my soul. In Hawaii, I am at home.

Is the Kate Grace Mystery series somewhat autobiographical?

I believe that a writer draws from his or her life experiences and perceptions, so yes, bits and pieces are my story, but not entirely. In particular I drew from my experiences when it came to Kate's relationship and experiences with her parents, her career, and much of the "mystical" elements experienced by Kate.

You share similar hobbies to Kate—cooking and photography—and you chose to incorporate them into the Kate Grace Mystery novels. Explain why.

As I said, I believe that a writer draws from his or her life experiences and perceptions, so yes, some of Kate's hobbies are mine because they work for the character and the types of stories I'm writing. For example, cooking for family and friendly gatherings has always been important in my life, and I believe that tremendous joy and a feeling of "connectedness" ensues when you bring people together in this fashion. Of course, these events always include a meal—at least in my family!

I grew up watching my mother and grandmothers cook and enjoyed helping them in the kitchen. Today, I still find cooking and creating my recipes very relaxing and creative—and a break from writing—and I felt these hobbies would translate well into Kate's life.

Photography is also another activity that gives me great pleasure and satisfaction. When I capture an image that inspires me, I love sharing that beauty with others. Because Hawaii is "my heart and my soul" place, and so amazingly beautiful, I felt that Kate's enthusiasm and desire to capture what she was seeing would emphasize her complete enthrallment with the land.

There are many mystical elements in *The Paradise Table*. Do you believe in life after death?

A definite "YES." I believe in God and the Bible and have always known in my soul that we live on after death. I also believe that under God's direction and by His will—and without us seeking it out!—that we are sometimes blessed with divine messages and inspiration. When I was a young girl, I even wrote about these themes—and I used that fact in my novel. I've also had many experiences, which I won't go into here, but which served as research and content for both *Lady in the Window* and *The Paradise Table*.

When did you know you wanted to become a writer?

I've known for as long as I can remember. However, although I always knew I wanted to write novels, it wasn't until recently that I began to pursue writing fiction. In 2014 I opened a box filled with my childhood memorabilia. Reading through those stories, which I had long forgotten, inspired me to "get my show on the road" and start writing novels. I used this incident in *Lady in the Window* when Catherine gives Kate her box.

In fact, like Kate, I put myself on a schedule to write. Previously, I had been writing for newspapers and magazines, as well as producing and writing projects for television. However, around 2002, as a TV/film producer, I began to feel the need to write movie screenplays as a way to tell the stories I felt were meaningful. In fact, at the time, I made a conscious decision to concentrate exclusively on writing and producing my own projects. Then, as soon as I began to write screenplays based on an outline, I realized that I could also plot out a novel in a similar fashion. That was a breakthrough moment for me because I finally had a roadmap of how to start. The rest was discipline and hard work, but realizing I could break it down was what made something I always said I wanted to do become a reality.

Describe your typical workday?

I work out at the gym the first thing in the morning. Exercising makes me feel great and gets my engine going. I'm usually in front of my computer by 7:30 or 8:00 a.m. and remain there until about 6:30 p.m. I take short breaks to grab a tea or to fix lunch—which I then eat in front of my computer as I work.

For the first few hours at my desk, I either work on the novel or script that I'm writing. My schedule is usually pre-planned, and I always know how many pages a week I need to deliver to keep on track. The rest of the day is spent working on other projects or client assignments with immediate delivery dates.

What inspires your stories?

Art, nature, music—everything I see, hear, watch and read. I also get my best ideas when I'm driving, relaxing, on vacation, or doing activities other than writing!

What types of stories are you attracted to and feel you need to write?

When I read I enjoy mysteries, romances, historical novels, and contemporary fiction, so I'm compelled to write the same. I'm also committed to writing stories that exalt family values, uplift and offer hope, healing, understanding, and faith.

What is your process?

I always craft a detailed, chapter-by-chapter and then a scene-by-scene outline. I work on this process for quite some time until I feel it's how I want the story to unfold. At the same time, I'll develop my characters. Then, when I start to write, other ideas may come to me—little nuances and actions—but I very rarely deviate from my outline. I also always commit to a schedule that I'll mark on my calendar as to how many pages a week I'll write. That's how I stay on track.

You've written original screenplays, adaptations, and novels. How different is writing a book vs. a screenplay?

First, as mentioned above, I always have a detailed outline, so I know exactly how the plot and scenes or chapters will unfold. I also visualize everything I write as I'm writing—whether it is a novel or screenplay. However, there is so much more freedom, exposition, and examination on the part of the characters when writing a novel. When writing screenplays, the scene must unfold in a way that tells the story in a very concise, visual style: in approximately 126 pages, while novels often have hundreds of pages.

When you begin writing a novel, do you know the ending?

Yes. Because I follow a detailed outline, I always know how my story will end. Sometimes, I change or add to elements of the story as I write, but not so significantly that the ending changes. I guess the best way to put it is that, even though I know what will transpire, I sometimes get a thrill out of what suddenly pops into my consciousness. All I can tell you is that I thoroughly enjoy the process. It's like going on a journey that transports me into another world.

What types of stories do you plan to write in the future?

I plan to write more Kate Grace Mysteries, as well as other novels. As mentioned previously, I gravitate to a bit of mystery, themes having to do with family relationships, romance, and stories that inspire and give hope for the human condition. What determines my immediate focus and pursuit is how much a particular plot, theme, or character pulls at me.

In addition to screenplay and novel writing, you are a journalist and television host. Describe how you blend these careers.

After college graduation, I landed a job in commercial production in New York City. I worked at that job for a year before I got up my nerve to move to California. My first job in Los Angeles was working as a writer/producer for entertainment news at Cable News Network (CNN). During that time, I also began working as a freelance newspaper and magazine journalist. After my stint at CNN, I wrote and produced for other networks, and when I got burnt out working 24/7 in production, I was eventually offered a lucrative job in publicity. As a PR and marketing executive, I helmed campaigns for most of the major networks and Hollywood studios, as well as serving as senior vice president of Stephen J. Cannell Productions/The Cannell Studios during its heyday. Eventually, I founded Ridini Entertainment Corporation, a PR/marketing, content creation and TV/film-production company, to continue to pursue my writing and producing passions.

What can tips you impart to new writers?

Once you have a theme, plot out how your story unfolds to use as a guideline when writing. Knowing where you're going is invaluable and will save you time when it comes to reviewing and editing the book. Another bit of advice: write every day, even if just for an hour. If you're working on a project, give yourself a certain number of pages a week. Then, if you finish your count in four or five days, you get two free days. If you feel like it, you can always write more, but I like to know that I've achieved my goal and only then will I allow myself a present of a leisurely day.

***The Paradise Table* – ISBN Numbers:** Hardcover: ISBN 978-0-9890405-1-8, Paperback: ISBN 978-0-9890405-6-3, eBook: ISBN 978-0-9890405-7-0

Find out more about Maryann, her books and film and television projects at *maryannridinispencer.com*.

For media inquiries, interviews and speaking engagements: Call Ridini Entertainment Corporation (818) 884-0104 or email: recprinfo@gmail.com. Indicate your request in the email subject line.

Reader Discussion Guide

- In *The Paradise Table*, Kate, Glen, Olivia, at various points in the book, are "healing" from events or experiences. Discuss these events and the importance of facing your feelings as part of the healing process.

- The Hawaiian culture revolves around ohana (family)—whether they be blood relatives, adopted or intentional—and the natural world, and the care, protection, and support of both. Discuss these Hawaiian beliefs and what we can all learn from them. What role does ohana—friends, family, community—play in *The Paradise Table*?

- Kate loves to cook, and in *The Paradise Table* there are many scenes where friends and family gather to share a meal. Why is this type of togetherness "food for the soul"?

- Discuss the significance of gardens and tables in *The Paradise Table*.

- Kate's relationship with God is significant to her in *The Paradise Table*. Discuss this and why this relationship is vital in her life.

- In *The Paradise Table,* the concept that our loved ones live on even after death is at the forefront. Take a moment to talk about this concept. Do you believe in life after death? Share your thoughts and experiences.

- In *The Paradise Table*, Kate's dreams are often prophetic. Have you ever had a dream or intuition that has transpired in real life?

- Not too long after the death of her mother, Kate learns that her father, Glen, is starting to date. What are your thoughts on that subject if you were in Kate's position? What about Glen's? Do you think it's possible to love another after the death of a beloved spouse?

- Synchronicity is defined as a series of events occurring with no causal relationship yet which seem to be meaningfully related. One way to ascertain if you are having a synchronistic event is if you find yourself saying, "What a coincidence." You might also overhear a conversation or see something that speaks to a situation in your life, giving you insight or perspective. In *The Paradise Table*, Kate shares several "synchronistic" events that have special meaning for her. Share and discuss these events from the book, as well as examples from your own life.

- In *The Paradise Table*, one of the main characters keeps a decades-old secret that hinders her from finding peace. Why can keeping secrets sometimes be detrimental to ourselves?

- *The Paradise Table* addresses the topic of unwanted pregnancy. Discuss your views on pregnancy and abortion. When do you believe life starts and why? What are your feelings about adoption?

- In *The Paradise Table*, Kate has a close relationship with her father. Some experts say that while children may sometimes become distant as teens, as they mature, they become closer to their parents. Do you believe this? If so, why do you think this is so? Discuss your experiences.

- Kate is a successful journalist. Her mother, Catherine, also had a successful career, as well as being a wife and mother. Discuss the importance of pursuing one's passion and talk about the "balance" necessary to achieve such multi-tasking.

- Through Kate's eyes, her photography, and experiences in Kauai, the reader can glimpse a taste of Hawaii. What scenes or images resonate with you most?

- Which scenes/chapters in *The Paradise Table* moved you the most and why?